I'm happy that I'm back with Todd, Diary. But I'm not so sure that all's well. I'm not even sure that the mess between us has ended. Even as Todd held me close this afternoon, I couldn't help thinking of Jeffrey. And as we discussed our plans to go to the Pi Beta Alpha costume party next Friday, I couldn't help wishing I were going with Jeffrey.

Am I a terrible person, Diary? Is it awful of me to want to have two terrific guys? I know, after the last few weeks, that I can't live without Todd. But I also know that I can't stop thinking about Jeffrey. I love them both. And I have no idea what to do about it.

ELIZABETH'S SECRET DIARY

VOLUME II

**Written by
Kate William**

**Created by
FRANCINE PASCAL**

BANTAM BOOKS
NEW YORK · TORONTO · LONDON · SYDNEY · AUCKLAND

RL 6, age 12 and up

ELIZABETH'S SECRET DIARY VOLUME II

A Bantam Book / August 1996

Sweet Valley High® is a registered trademark of Francine Pascal
Conceived by Francine Pascal
Produced by Daniel Weiss Associates, Inc.
33 West 17th Street
New York, NY 10011
Cover art by Bruce Emmett

ISBN: 0-553-57005-6

Published simultaneously in the United States and Canada

Bantam Books are published by Bantam Books, a division of Bantam
Doubleday Dell Publishing Group, Inc. Its trademark, consisting of the
words "Bantam Books" and the portrayal of a rooster, is Registered in
U.S. Patent and Trademark Office and in other countries. Marca
Registrada. Bantam Books, 1540 Broadway, New York, New York 10036.

PRINTED IN THE UNITED STATES OF AMERICA

OPM   0 9 8 7 6 5 4 3 2 1

To Megan Walsh

Prologue

The restaurant smelled delicious—spicy tomato sauce and cocoa-dusted cappuccino. My boyfriend, Todd Wilkins, sat across the table from me with candlelight gleaming in his sexy brown eyes. And a strolling violinist was just finishing "Santa Lucia" near our table.

In other words, all the ingredients were there for an incredibly romantic Friday evening. Except for Todd. Oh, he was there in body—and what a body, I might add—but his mind was somewhere far away.

"Earth to Todd!" I called, waving my hand in front of his face. "Have you heard anything I've said in the last ten minutes?"

"Oh, sure," Todd said. He blinked as if he'd just woken up from a trance. "You were talking about the school newspaper, right?"

I sighed. The least he could do was pay attention. "That was ten minutes ago, Todd. You know, if I'm keeping you awake—"

"No, no," Todd interrupted, reaching across the table to hold my hand. As usual, my annoyance melted away at the touch of his fingers. I know, it's corny. But Todd is tall and lean, with a basketball player's body and a movie star's face. He's also funny and smart and thoughtful—well, most of the time.

Todd enveloped my hand in his warm, strong ones. "I'm sorry, Elizabeth," he said. "It's not you. I'm just kind of spacey tonight. I can't keep my mind on anything. Look, there's something I need to tell you. It's good news, really. But I—" He stopped as a waitress materialized in front of us and set our dessert on the table: cannoli for me and chocolate cake for Todd.

Todd shrugged. "I guess it can wait until after dessert," he said, his eyes glued to that chocolate cake. I couldn't help noticing the relief in his voice. For a moment I was annoyed again. Whatever the big secret was, I wished Todd would just spill it.

I examined his face. He was focusing on a forkful of cake as if he expected to be quizzed on it. But instead of flashing a chocolate-induced grin as he tasted the cake, he bit his lip as if he were wor-

2

ried. He had sounded so serious about whatever he wanted to tell me. Could it be something awful?

No, I decided. Todd had said it was good news. He wouldn't lie about something like that. But what could the good news be? And why was he so nervous about telling me? The anniversary of our first date was coming up the next weekend. Could he be setting up some fantastic outing?

Yes, that's it, I decided. And I instantly knew why he was hesitating. *He's probably planning something expensive, and he doesn't want me to feel funny about his spending too much money on me—especially after I let him shell out so much for dinner tonight at Venezia.*

Spending money like a rich person always makes Todd a little nervous, despite the fact that by most people's standards Todd *is* a rich person. OK, so he's not as rich as my sister Jessica's best friend, Lila Fowler, who's known as the wealthiest, snobbiest girl in Sweet Valley, California. Todd used to be no richer than anyone else. But the Wilkinses had moved away, to Vermont. When they moved back here a few months later, Todd's father had a big promotion and a whole new lifestyle.

To Todd's credit, he's had trouble getting used to having money. In that way—in every way, really—he's a far cry from Lila, who makes sure

3

that everybody knows she spends more on clothes in a year than my Jeep is worth.

In the middle of all this musing, I took a bite of my dessert. Suddenly I couldn't blame Todd for putting off his news. The cannoli was delicious—even more delicious than the fantastic dinner we'd just eaten.

I have to admit it: There are advantages to dating a guy whose family is loaded. A year ago, Todd and I would have felt incredibly guilty about blowing so much cash on dinner. Todd is still a down-to-earth guy. But now he's a down-to-earth guy who drives a BMW. And who takes me to restaurants like Venezia a lot more than he used to, even if he's embarrassed about living in a mansion and belonging to the country club. He's still friends with Winston Egbert and Ken Matthews and the other regular guys at Sweet Valley High—not with the rich snobs like Bruce Patman and Lila.

Of course, money doesn't matter. Being together and talking to each other and loving each other are more important than laying out sixty dollars on dinner.

I guess I'm always saying things like that (lecturing, my sister would say) to anyone who will listen. But I looked at the pretty restaurant and Todd's expensive new tie and the scrumptious desserts, and I told myself I had to face facts: As much as I try to hide it, Elizabeth Wakefield is as materialistic as anyone else. And I *like* the fringe benefits of dating the son of the president of Varitronics.

I could never tell that to anyone—not even my best friend, Enid Rollins. I wouldn't even say it to my identical twin sister. And Jessica knows everything about me. Well, almost everything.

Does that make me a hypocrite? Everyone says I'm selfless and generous and thoughtful. It's Jessica who's supposed to be hung up on superficial things like money and clothes and looks. But maybe I'm no better than she is. Maybe I'm worse, since I pretend to be different. *With Jessica,* I thought, *what you see is what you get.*

That was a strange choice of words. Because, of course, what you see when you look at Jessica is exactly what you see when you look at me. We're both five foot six, with long blond hair and blue-green eyes. We both have trim, athletic figures and deep tans. In fact, strangers can tell us apart only by our clothes. Jessica is into the wildest colors, the shortest hemlines, and the latest fashions. I go for more of a classic, no-fuss look—khakis, oxford shirts, and comfortable shoes.

As long as I'm doing the true-confessions thing, I'll admit something else that nobody realizes: I'm a lot more vain about my looks than I let on. I know that I'm attractive; I just don't broadcast to

5

the world that I'm devastatingly gorgeous, the way Jessica does. I pretend to be annoyed when guys scope me out on the beach or in the halls at Sweet Valley High. I think women should be judged by their brains, not their builds. But sometimes it kind of gives me a rush when guys stare at me. Is that pathetic or what?

Jessica thinks I don't care about my looks. But sometimes I do try hard to make myself look prettier. I just do it in subtle ways. I hate wearing tons of goopy makeup and clothes that make me feel self-conscious.

Jessica is about as subtle as her leopard-spotted miniskirt. She's the twin in purple lipstick, coordinating fingernail polish, and Technicolor eye shadow—or a cheerleading uniform, complete with pom-poms and megaphone.

Jessica is in-your-face in other ways as well. She never hesitates to say exactly what she's feeling. I tell her she's too blunt. And it's true. She's about the least sensitive person on earth—except for Lila, I guess. But deep down, I wish I could be more like Jessica. Well, just a little bit. I mean, I'm too uptight, and I think too much. What amazing freedom there would be in saying and doing exactly as you please, without stopping to analyze the consequences or to consider another person's point of view!

"But I could never do that," I said under my breath.

Then I froze, embarrassed. I hadn't meant to speak, even if my words had been covered by a sigh. But Todd wasn't paying the least bit of attention to me. Heck, I could have stuck straws in my ears and sang the school fight song, and he wouldn't have noticed.

I stared at him expectantly, my jaw clenched. I'm not obsessed with being the center of attention, like my sister is. But when I'm on a date, I do expect my boyfriend to look at me now and then.

No such luck. Todd was avoiding my eyes as if I were Medusa from my mythology unit in English class, able to turn men to stone with a single glance. I wished he would just spill his big news and get back to being his usual self again.

Then I had to laugh at myself. I'd been fuming about his being too preoccupied to carry on a conversation. But all along I'd been psychoanalyzing myself instead of trying to talk to him! Besides, how could I be mad at someone who was about to divulge some exciting plans for celebrating our anniversary?

Todd and I finished our dessert at exactly the same moment, and we set down our forks with twin clinks. I looked up at him. "So, what did you want to tell me?" I asked, smiling in anticipation. "Don't keep me in suspense."

7

Todd took a deep breath. Suddenly I felt nervous. He didn't look like a person who was about to reveal a wonderful surprise. "Maybe I'm making too much of this," he said in an apologetic tone. "It's just that a friend of mine from Vermont is coming to visit this week. I was hoping you two could get to know each other."

I was a little disappointed that he didn't have special plans for our anniversary. At the same time I felt relieved that the news wasn't bad. Mostly I was pleased. I always enjoy making new friends.

I squeezed his hand. "That's great!" I gushed. "I don't know why you were so afraid to tell me. You know that any friend of yours is a friend of mine!"

"Liz, we'll have to change our plans for Monday," he began. Then his face turned hopeful. "Unless you wouldn't mind having a third person along . . ."

So that was it. Todd hated having to cancel commitments. And we'd both been looking forward to a quiet, romantic afternoon at Secca Lake. Monday was a teacher conference day, so there would be no school.

"Of course I wouldn't mind!" I assured him. "In fact, I insist that we bring your friend with us. Let's ask Enid too. We haven't been on a double date in ages!"

Todd cleared his throat and stared into the candle flame. "Uh, Elizabeth . . . ," he began. "I don't think that's going to work. My friend's name is Michelle Thomas."

My stomach plummeted to my feet. "Not the same Michelle Thomas we almost broke up over?"

Hot tears were building behind my eyes, and I was angry at myself for being so upset. But I was even more angry at Todd for being insensitive enough to expect me to like the idea of Michelle's traveling thousands of miles to be with him.

"That's ancient history!" Todd reminded me. "I thought we were over all that. You know that Michelle is just a friend—she doesn't mean any more to me than Ken or Winston."

"Really?" I demanded. "When was the last time Ken or Winston wrote you a letter on perfumed stationery and called you 'cute-buns'?"

Todd had just moved back to California when I'd found that darn letter from Michelle. In addition to the cutesy nickname, she'd sent him "lots of love and a hundred kisses." And she used way too many exclamation marks.

The thought of Michelle Thomas made me want to run my fingers through Todd's wavy brown hair—and yank it out by the roots.

I controlled that impulse and kept my voice low and steady. "I can't believe you had the nerve to invite that girl to California to see you."

9

"I didn't invite her!" Todd insisted. "Her aunt has to go on a business trip to Los Angeles, and Michelle decided to come along for a visit. Please, Liz. You're the one I'm in love with. And I'd really like it if you and Michelle could be friends."

I folded my arms and glared at him. "Maybe we can be," I said, "when southern California freezes over."

Todd and I had gone through some hairy times after I read that letter. But he'd convinced me that he wasn't in love with Michelle and never had been. And I'd assured him that I loved and trusted him, and that I believed him when he said there was nothing going on between him and Michelle.

But a girl doesn't travel three thousand miles to be with someone she calls "cute-buns" unless there's something going on—or unless she *wants* something to be going on.

"You know Michelle was manager of the boys' basketball team at my school in Vermont," Todd reminded me. "She was just like one of the guys. We kidded around a lot and had a good time. That's all! I think you'll like her."

I felt like I might throw up. Instead, I stared into his eyes for a long minute. I let the acid seep into my voice: "Don't hold your breath."

"Oh, Liz," Todd pleaded, reaching across the

10

table to grasp my hand. I yanked it away. A sharp edge crept into his voice. "Be reasonable about this!"

"Reasonable?" I fumed. "Your East Coast *girlfriend* is traveling thousands of miles to see you, and I'm supposed to be *reasonable?* Tell me the truth: Have you two been writing letters to each other all along?"

"Calm down," he said. His voice was quiet, but I could see that he was angry. "It's not like you to be so paranoid. Look, Michelle arrives Sunday evening. Give her a chance. Once you see me and her together, you'll know we're only friends."

"For your information, I don't plan on seeing you and Michelle together!" I told him. "In fact, I don't want to see *you*—or even talk to you—until Michelle is on a plane back to Vermont!"

Todd reeled as if I'd slapped him. "That's ridiculous!"

"What's so ridiculous about not wanting to share my boyfriend?" I jumped to my feet and collected my purse.

"You don't have to—" he began.

"Don't bother to get up," I interrupted. "I'll take a cab home."

My parents went to dinner at the Egberts' house Sunday night. Jessica was at Lila's place,

11

cramming for an algebra test she should have studied for days earlier. That left me alone at home—
except for Prince Albert, our golden labrador.

I was sitting at my computer, trying to edit an
article for the *Oracle,* which is Sweet Valley High's
student newspaper. But the article was about the
basketball team, and it mentioned Todd's name at
least a dozen times. I hadn't talked to Todd since
Friday night—though he'd left me a bunch of mes-
sages. But not talking to him didn't mean I wasn't
thinking about him. Every time I came to my
boyfriend's name, I imagined him fidgeting at the
airport, wearing his new tie. His eyes would light
up when the flight from Boston was announced.
Then Michelle would step through the gate, and
they'd run toward each other, arms outstretched—

"No!" I barked, slamming my fingers down on
the keyboard. A line of gibberish jumped onto the
screen.

Of course, I didn't even know if Todd was
meeting Michelle at the airport. And her aunt
would be with her when she arrived. But I couldn't
keep the images from crowding my mind. We writers have overactive imaginations.

I finally admitted to myself that I was in no
condition to edit articles. So I saved the file to my
hard drive and flicked the computer off. The telephone rang, and I stared at the extension in my

room. Todd might be calling again, and I was in no mood to talk to him. I hate myself when I act so childish. Most of the time I'd rather just be honest with people. But I was still too angry to be reasonable. I decided to let the answering machine pick up the call.

"This is driving me crazy!" I yelled to the empty house. In response, Prince Albert barked once from Jessica's room and then was silent. I clenched my fists and blinked away tears of frustration. I needed a diversion. Desperately. The phone clicked, and I knew the caller had finished leaving a message. I grabbed the receiver, dialed Enid's number, and invited her over.

"Chocolate chip cookies!" I decided as I hung up the phone. Enid and I would make a huge batch of our favorite cookies and eat every one. That would get my mind off Todd and Michelle's reunion. At least it had better.

In the meantime, I reached for my diary and scribbled the first words that popped into my head:

> *There once was a girl named Michelle*
> *whose motto was "I kiss and tell."*
> *She took her best shot—*
> *My boyfriend she caught.*
> *She's the Basketball Groupie from Hell.*

OK, so it wasn't Wordsworth. It was even kind of mean. But I didn't care. I really didn't! Michelle knew about my relationship with Todd. What kind of a girl would plot to steal somebody's boyfriend from three thousand miles away?

Luckily, Enid showed up before I got really nasty. I had already filled her in on Todd's visit from Michelle, and she was as sweet and as understanding as she always is. She led me to the kitchen and promised to help me drown my troubles in cookie batter. A few minutes later we were standing at the counter, measuring flour and baking powder, and getting goofy.

Then the doorbell rang. I popped a handful of chocolate chips into my mouth and headed to the front door, wiping my flour-dusted hands on my jeans.

"Yes?" I began as I pulled open the door. Then I froze. Todd stood on my doorstep, dressed neatly in a crisp white shirt and navy chinos. My good mood evaporated.

"Hi, Liz," Todd said. He flashed me his usual grin, but his eyes looked nervous.

"You could have called first," I said sharply.

"I tried," he said. "But your answering machine was on. I saw the Jeep in the driveway, so I thought I'd stop by. Can I come in?" Behind me, I heard Enid step into the foyer from the kitchen.

14

I took a deep breath and nodded. I was hoping Todd would apologize. I willed him to say he'd changed his mind and had told Michelle he couldn't see her because he had some rare, communicable disease.

No such luck. When I stepped aside to lead Todd into the living room, I saw that he wasn't alone. The girl who walked in behind him was tall and trim—graceful and athletic-looking—with raven hair and eyes so dark they were almost black. She smiled, and I felt my face freeze into a scowl. This could only be Michelle.

"You must be Elizabeth," she said, reaching out her hand.

"That's right," I said, challenging her with my eyes.

"You have no idea how much I've wanted to meet you," Michelle continued, sounding entirely too cheerful. "Todd never stops talking about you."

"Oh, really?" I asked. "That's funny; he hasn't said much at all about you." For instance, he'd never bothered to mention that she was drop-dead gorgeous.

Michelle seemed confused at the expression on my face. Frankly, I didn't care if I looked hostile. I didn't care what she thought of me. I just wanted her to get out of my living room—and away from my boyfriend. I glared at Todd, and he blushed.

"Uh, Michelle," he said, gesturing toward Enid,

"this is Enid Rollins, another good friend of mine. This is Michelle Thomas."

"Hi," Enid said, an uncomfortable smile on her face. "Welcome to California."

I was totally aware of the flour smudges on my jeans and face. Next to tall, graceful Michelle, I felt like a six-year-old. I glared at Todd, blaming him for my discomfort.

"Michelle just flew in from New England," Todd said unnecessarily.

"How was your flight?" Enid asked.

"Long," Michelle said with a smile. "I couldn't wait to get here and see Todd again." She reached over and squeezed my boyfriend's hand. "It's been a long time."

I pressed my lips together tightly. *How dare she!*

"Uh, Liz, I was telling Michelle about your work on the *Oracle*," Todd said. "She just signed up for the school paper back in Burlington. We thought maybe you could give her a few tips."

I could give her a few tips, all right, I thought. *Like tips on how to get out of my side of the country.*

"I'll be covering sports, mostly," Michelle said. "Todd says you're a whiz at any kind of writing. I'm not very good at it, but I'm hoping I can learn fast."

"Don't sell yourself short," I said in the coldest voice I could muster. I thought of her "hey cute-buns" letter, with all its exclamation marks and its hundred kisses. "I bet your writing is really . . . memorable. And I'm sure you're right about being *fast.*"

Part of me was mortified that such a catty statement had come out of my mouth. It was the kind of thing Lila would say to someone who'd slighted her. But I wanted to hurt Michelle the way she was hurting me.

She looked uncertain, as if she wasn't quite sure my words meant what she thought they meant. Let's face it—Michelle was not headed for a brilliant career in brain surgery.

"Elizabeth—" Todd began in a shocked voice.

Enid cut him off. "I guess sports is a natural subject area for you," she said to Michelle in an overly bright voice. She took the taller girl's arm and led her to the couch. I wished Enid weren't so polite. There was a reason why I hadn't invited Michelle to sit down. I didn't want her to feel comfortable enough to want to stick around. "I hear you're the manager of your school's basketball team," Enid said to her. "What does that involve, exactly?"

Michelle smiled gratefully and began talking about basketball statistics and organizing bus trips to other schools for away games.

I glared at Todd. He stared back at me, his eyes wide with surprise. "What are you doing?" he mouthed. I shook my head and turned away. How could he even ask? I had made it clear that I didn't want to see Michelle. He had no right bringing her to my house. No right at all!

"We need to get back to the kitchen, Enid," I reminded her, taking a few steps toward the couch.

Michelle stood up quickly and reached for Todd's arm. "Sorry," she said, smiling uncertainly at me. "We've been keeping you from whatever you were doing."

"That's OK—" Enid began. I threw her a meaningful glance, and she stopped. I was sure she'd been ready to invite them to stay a while longer. But I couldn't put up with another minute of having Michelle in my house, hanging all over my boyfriend.

"We really only dropped by to see if you were free tomorrow, Liz," Michelle said. "In fact, Todd and I were hoping that both of you would join us for a picnic in the afternoon."

That did it. I don't know if it was the way she said "Todd and I," as if it was the most natural thing in the world, or if it was the way she'd stolen *my* Monday afternoon picnic with Todd. But I lost it. I mean, I completely and totally lost it.

"You hoped we would join you at the lake?" I

screeched like some sort of predatory bird. "I would rather have my teeth drilled!"

Todd gasped. "Elizabeth!"

"What did you expect?" I demanded of him. "I told you how I felt!"

"I think we'd better go," Todd said, ushering a shocked Michelle out of my house.

As soon as Todd slammed the door, Enid whirled to face me, hands on her hips. "Elizabeth Wakefield!" she exclaimed. "If I hadn't seen it with my own eyes, I would never have believed it!"

"I know," I said. "Instead of letting Todd make a fool of me, I decided to stand up for myself for a change. What's wrong with that?"

"Liz, there's a difference between standing up for yourself and being outright rude!" Enid said, leading me back to the kitchen. "In all the time we've been friends, I've never known you to be intentionally mean and hurtful! What is this all about?"

I couldn't stop the tears that gushed out of my eyes. "How could he do this to me?" I asked. "He knows how upset I am about Michelle! Why would he bring her here?"

"Because he cares about you both, and he wants the two of you to like each other," Enid said in a sympathetic but reasonable voice.

"How can I like her when she's trying to steal

19

my boyfriend?" I sobbed, collapsing into a chair.

Enid put her hand on my back. "You know you can trust Todd," she reminded me.

I shook my head. "How can I?" I asked. "He's supposed to be *my* boyfriend! He was supposed to take *me* for a picnic by the lake tomorrow!" By now, tears were running down my cheeks like Niagara Falls, and my eyes felt like boiled onions. "Oh, Enid," I choked out, "I'm so afraid of losing him!"

"Todd likes Michelle," Enid said gently. "But he *loves* you. You always say your relationship with him is based on trust. Have some faith in him!"

I nodded. "I do have faith in Todd. It's Michelle I don't trust!"

"Your argument isn't with Michelle," she said.

"Michelle stole—"

"You don't even know Michelle!" Enid interrupted. "And she doesn't owe you anything. Todd's the one you're mad at. But you love Todd, so it's easier to be mean to Michelle."

"You're right," I said, wiping my eyes with a paper towel. "But if he loved me, he wouldn't have brought her here! He wouldn't be seeing her at all this week!"

"And if you loved him, you wouldn't be choosing his friends for him," she reminded me. "Elizabeth, Todd made a mistake in bringing Michelle here. He should have known it would

20

upset you. But it's not wrong for him to be friends with her. And it's you he loves."

"Not anymore," I acknowledged, sniffing. "Not after the way I just acted."

"He'll forgive you," Enid assured me. "He knows you're only jealous because you love him."

"So what can I do?" I asked in a small voice. "I don't think I can act as if she's my best friend."

"You don't have to like Michelle," Enid said, "although you might *try,* for Todd's sake. But the important thing is to trust him. Unless you have some real proof that there's something going on between Todd and Michelle, I think you have to accept that they're just friends, whether you like it or not."

"You're right," I admitted. "How can you be so reasonable when I'm such a basket case?"

Enid grinned. "It's my turn," she said. "You've been reasonable for me enough times when I was a basket case."

I ran my finger along the inside of the mixing bowl, scooping up a dollop of cookie batter. I licked it off my finger, thinking hard. "All right," I concluded, choking back a fresh round of sobs. "It'll be hard, but tomorrow I'm going to show Todd that I trust him and that I'm sorry for being rude."

Enid raised her eyebrows. "You're going to join them for that picnic at Secca Lake?"

"No," I said, shaking my head. "I don't think I

21

can manage that. But I *will* stop by his house tomorrow with a dozen of these cookies."

"A peace offering?" Enid asked.

"Exactly."

"Then we'd better make a double batch," she suggested, reaching for a second bag of chocolate chips. "We wouldn't want to deprive ourselves!"

I balanced the plate of cookies on the palm of one hand as I rang the doorbell at Todd's house the next morning. I waited for what seemed like ages, but there was no answer. Todd's BMW was in the driveway. Maybe he was having brunch on the patio in the back.

I followed the flagstone path around the side of the brick mansion. There on the patio was Todd . . . and Michelle. His arms were around her, and he was kissing her—not a quick, casual, just-friends kiss, but a real kiss. A long, slow kiss that had both of them so occupied that they didn't hear me approaching.

The world tilted beneath me. For a moment I couldn't breathe. I couldn't even move. Then I lost control. The plate of cookies slipped from my hands and smashed on the slate patio, shards of pottery flying. Todd and Michelle's horrified faces turned toward me.

"How can you do this to me?" I demanded, sobbing. "I . . . loved . . . you!"

Todd pulled away from Michelle as if she were on fire. "Elizabeth, it isn't what it looks like—"

"I'm not an idiot!" I screamed. "I know what I saw. And I never want to see you again!" I turned on my heel and fled down the flagstone path.

Twenty minutes later I stood by the answering machine in the kitchen, staring at it as the phone rang. I knew exactly who it was, and I wasn't about to pick it up.

"I'll get it!" Jessica yelled, running in from the dining room wearing her pink bathrobe. It was eleven in the morning on a school holiday—the crack of dawn, by Jessica's standards.

"Don't touch that phone!" I screamed.

"Why not?" Jessica asked. "It's probably for me!"

"Elizabeth!" crackled Todd's voice through the answering machine. *"I know you're there! Please pick up the phone."*

Jessica's eyebrows shot up, and I gave her a warning glance. Naturally, she ignored it. "Ooh, trouble in paradise!" she said happily. "Did you and lover boy have a fight?"

"Go away," I told her. "My love life is not a spectator sport."

Jessica yawned. "You can say that again. Most of the time it's even more boring than watching golf on television."

"*Elizabeth!*" repeated Todd. "*It wasn't what it looked like. Michelle and I both know it was a mistake. It didn't mean anything!*"

Jessica's mouth dropped open. She pulled up a chair and sat down, her eyes glued to the answering machine as if she were watching a soap opera.

"*Michelle told me the real reason for her visit,*" Todd explained. "*Her parents are getting a divorce, and she's upset. She was crying this morning. I only wanted to comfort her. And I was so frustrated about the way you were acting—*"

The machine clicked off. I stood for a minute, staring wordlessly at the tape as it rewound.

"What's going on?" Jessica asked, her eyes wide with a combination of sympathy and excitement. Leave it to Jessica to be amused by my entire life crumbling. But she never has approved of my relationship with Todd—she says I'm too young to limit myself to one boy.

"Don't ask, Jessica!" I said. She opened her mouth to ask again, and I cut her off.

"*I mean it!*" I screamed. I raced upstairs to my bedroom and slammed the door behind me. Then I threw myself down on the bed and wished I were in Tunisia.

"Liz!" came Jessica's voice from behind the door a few minutes later. "I'm sorry I made fun of your fight with Todd," she said, sounding genuinely contrite. "Do you want to talk about it?"

"Maybe later, Jessica," I said. I suddenly felt completely drained. "I think I need to be alone right now."

As her footsteps moved away, I stood and stepped slowly across the room to the window. Outside, the sky was blue, the grass was green, and the surface of our backyard swimming pool sparkled in the California sunlight. It was a normal, beautiful Sweet Valley day. But Todd was in love with somebody else, and nothing would ever feel normal again. I sighed and turned away from the sunlight.

I tried to remember what my life had been like without Todd. When he moved to Vermont, I'd been devastated. But I'd gradually gotten used to living without him. I'd even fallen in love with Jeffrey French. At the same time, I realized now, Todd had been in Burlington—falling in love with Michelle Thomas.

On an impulse, I scanned the books that were lined up on the top shelf of my bookcase. My feelings about Todd and Jeffrey—about everything— were neatly recorded in a row of clothbound volumes. My journals contained all my private thoughts, the things I could never tell anyone. I reached for one volume, settled myself on my velvet-covered chaise longue, and began to read. . . .

Part 1

Friday evening

Dear Diary,

    I think I'd better stick with writing, because I'm not showing great talent as an artist. We just finished the first week of our two-week arts and vocations workshops at school. Enid and I are taking painting. It's loads of fun, but I never could draw anything but stick people. The "masterpiece" I'm working on could have been painted by Prince Albert!

    The real surprise in class is Olivia Davidson. I always knew Olivia was artsy. I mean, she is the arts editor for the Oracle. *But I never knew how truly talented she is. She's by far the most artistic person in the class. Stuart—the teacher, Stuart Bachman, insists that we use his first name—says she shows tremendous promise.*

Stuart is talented, a great teacher, and very laid-back. I also have to say that he's quite cute, with curly dark hair and artsy-looking glasses. Everyone likes him. But Olivia is taking things too far—she's obsessed! Frankly, Enid and I are worried about her. Yesterday Olivia practically admitted to me that she's in love with our art teacher. . . .

I confronted Olivia in study hall Friday afternoon about the *Oracle* page proofs she was supposed to have checked. Her big hazel eyes got bigger, and she clapped her hand to her mouth. "Liz, I can't believe it!" she said. "I totally forgot!"

That wasn't at all like Olivia. She was usually so conscientious. "Do you have them with you?" I asked. "Maybe we can check them during study hall."

Olivia had left the page proofs at home, but she promised to go over them that night. And she swore that it would never happen again. "To tell you the truth," she explained, "I've just been so caught up in our painting workshop. I've never in my whole life met a man like Stuart before. I think it's just knocked me off my feet a little."

I think Olivia's headed for trouble, Diary. Nothing good can come out of having a crush on a teacher. I guess Stuart came along at just the right time for Olivia. Or the wrong time, depending on your perspective. She was just complaining to me about not having a boyfriend. I think Olivia envies my relationship with Jeffrey French. And I can't blame her. He is wonderful. After Todd left town, I thought I would never love anybody else again. But then Jeffrey moved here from Oregon, and we've been blissfully happy ever since. I am so lucky to have Jeffrey. In fact, he's picking me up any second.

Jeffrey and I had dinner at the Dairi Burger and then went to a movie. But the best part of the evening came later, when we walked on the beach, his arm around my waist. My feet were bare against the warm, damp sand, and my sandals dangled from my hand.

"How's the electronics workshop going?" I asked him.

"It's harder than I expected," he said. "But I'm finding it interesting."

I laughed. "That's not exactly the way my sister feels about it," I said. "It serves her right! Next time she should choose a class based on the subject matter—not the male-female ratio!"

"Ooh," Jeffrey joked. "You get me all excited when you say things like 'male-female ratio.'"

"It doesn't take much," I said, stopping to look at his gorgeous features—his warm green eyes, his soft blond hair, and his perfect profile.

"Not when you're around," he said, so low that I could barely hear him over the pounding of the surf. I realized that I was holding my breath. I forced myself to breathe deeply of the salty air as I gazed up at him. Then Jeffrey took my face in his hands and kissed me on the lips—first gently, and then more passionately. After a moment my heart was pounding as hard as the waves.

The whole scene was like something out of the old romance movie we'd just seen. The sky was a velvety midnight blue, dotted with pin-pricks of stars. The ocean waves rolled toward us, moonlight dancing on their swells. In the distance, light and music spilled from the open-air dance floor of the Beach Disco. But Jeffrey and I were alone with our own little corner of the Pacific Ocean. And I was sure I would never love anyone as much as I loved Jeffrey at that moment.

✿   ✿   ✿

Late Friday,
one week later

Dear Diary,

Oh, no! Diary, I am in shock. My hands are trembling, and I can't catch my breath. I can't believe it.

Todd Wilkins is coming back to Sweet Valley! Todd, my first love. What am I going to do?

Saturday, 9:30 A.M.

Diary, now that I've had a few hours of sleep, I'll try to put the events of last night onto paper. I found out about Todd at Olivia's surprise birthday party. . . .

By the time I jumped out of the Davidsons' hall closet, yelling "Surprise!" along with everyone else, the day had already been full of enough surprises to last a month.

Jessica's success in electronics—no doubt due to the brains of her study partner, Randy Mason—had thrown everyone for a loop that afternoon. She'd put together a lie detector machine that was the hit of the project displays. Personally, I'd have taken an ax to the thing at the time if I'd known how much grief it would bring me at the party that evening.

30

Everyone was talking about how Stuart had managed to get Olivia's painting displayed in a gallery beside an exhibition of his own works! Luckily, Olivia learned about more than just art at the exhibition opening. She finally realized that Stuart's interest in her was purely professional—and artistic, I guess—and she decided that she could live with that. From the way her eyes lit up when Rod Sullivan asked her about her painting at the surprise party, I'd say that Olivia doesn't need to worry about being lonely anymore.

But then came the news that blew me away.

Jessica had brought that contraption of hers to the party, and someone got the bright idea of hooking me up to it.

"I have a question for Liz," said Lila, of all people. I couldn't imagine what she would want to ask me. But hey, I figured I had nothing to hide. So I shrugged and let them turn on the silly machine.

Lila waited until every person in the house was watching us. Then she placed her hands on her hips, gave a sly—almost nasty—smile, and dropped her bombshell: "I happen to know for a fact that Todd Wilkins is moving back to Sweet Valley!" she announced. My heart plummeted to my feet and continued through the floor. "Now, tell the truth, Liz," Lila continued smugly. "Are you the slightest bit concerned about the reappearance of your old boyfriend? Or are things going to stay the same between you and Jeffrey?"

I gasped, and dead silence fell over the room. Todd? Moving back to Sweet Valley? Joy, panic, and indecision flooded through my body. I honestly thought I would faint. Thank goodness Jeffrey wasn't at the party.

I kept my voice low and even as I slid my finger from the machine. "I don't think I need this thing," I said calmly. Then I stood up and left the room without saying another word. I jumped into the old red Fiat that Jessica and I shared, and I gunned the engine. But before I headed for Calico Drive and home, I made a couple of detours.

First I drove to Jeffrey's neighborhood. I didn't want to see Jeffrey. In fact, I knew nobody was home; he and his family were visiting his grandparents for the weekend. I slowed the car to a stop in front of the neat one-story, Spanish-style house and sat there for several minutes, my eyes fixed on the window of Jeffrey's room.

"I love you, Jeffrey French," I said aloud, thinking of our walk on the moonlit beach exactly one week earlier.

I thought of Jeffrey's silky blond hair and dark green eyes. I could see him running easily across the soccer field, strong and athletic, to score the winning goal in the recent state championship match. I remembered the sound of his deep, warm voice in school just that day as he asked me to pose near my painting; he'd been photographing the arts and vocations assembly for the *Oracle* and insisted that I was the star of the event.

Jeffrey's car sat in the driveway, and I gazed at it, sighing. After our walk on the beach, we'd driven to Miller's Point, the most romantic spot in town, and we'd kissed in the front seat, overlooking the lights of the valley. He'd told me he loved me, and I said I loved him too.

But if I loved Jeffrey, then why was Todd's homecoming such a big deal for me? I had moved on. I had a new boyfriend. I should have been able to accept my relationship with Todd as a happy memory—a part of my past.

"What Todd and I had together is over!" I said aloud.

To prove it, I revved the engine and sped to Todd's old house, surprised at how natural it still felt to drive that route—even after so many months. I slowed the car to a crawl and glided slowly by the ordinary, comfortable split-level home that looked so much like my own. I almost expected to see Todd's beat-up blue Datsun in the driveway. I'd been to Miller's Point in that Datsun plenty of times too.

For just a moment I longed to see Todd

sauntering down the front walk, his curly brown hair disheveled by the breeze. He would have that special smile on his face, the one he reserved only for me. And he'd take me in his arms and—

No. I clicked my imagination off. I had no business thinking like that. I was in love with Jeffrey.

So why did the sight of Todd's old house bring tears to my eyes?

Now you know, Diary. Todd is coming back, and part of me is so excited about seeing him that I can't think straight. And another part of me wishes he would just stay in Vermont, now that I've finally gotten over him.

How will I stand having him here, so close? What will it do to my relationship with Jeffrey?

I wish I had a crystal ball and could see a few weeks into the future. I have an awful feeling that my entire life is about to be turned upside down.

Monday evening

Dear Diary,

Before homeroom this morning I told Jeffrey that Todd was moving back to Sweet Valley.

Jeffrey didn't move to town until after Todd and his family had left. So my current boyfriend has never met my ex. And I suspect that arrangement suited Jeffrey just fine. I can't believe how nervous I was about telling Jeffrey about Todd. He seemed unsure, but he accepted the news with grace. . . .

"Say something!" I begged, wishing we weren't surrounded by dozens of students scurrying to homeroom.

Jeffrey closed his locker door slowly and turned to look at me. I wrung my hands and waited, my tension growing. I had expected him to be surprised but not speechless.

I tried to imagine what Jeffrey must be feeling. Todd was practically a legend at Sweet Valley High. He'd been the star center on the basketball team, he was totally gorgeous, and he was just about the sweetest guy anyone could ever hope to meet. Not to mention the fact that Todd and I had once been one of the hottest couples around.

Finally Jeffrey gave me a weak grin. "Well, um, I guess I'm looking forward to meeting Todd," he said. "I know his old friends think a lot of him. He must be quite a guy."

Part of me wanted to throw my arms around

him right there in the middle of the hall. Despite his brave, polite words, I could see that his eyes were troubled. That was the moment to tell him, *"Don't worry, honey. Not even Todd can come between you and me. You're the one I'm in love with now."*

I wanted to say it. I swear I did. But I couldn't choke the words out. Because deep down, I knew a part of me was still in love with Todd. The thing I didn't know was whether it was bigger than the part that wanted to pledge my undying affection for Jeffrey.

Oh gosh, Diary! What if I have to choose between them? I don't know how strong my feelings are for Todd anymore. I guess I won't know until I see him again. What if his return to Sweet Valley changes everything between me and Jeffrey?

I just got this ridiculous mental image about something Jessica said this morning. Imagine Jeffrey and Todd fighting over me—dueling it out with french fries at the Dairi Burger!

Despite the silly image, it's a romantic thought, in a way. Imagine having to choose between two guys who are both madly in love with me! Like Ingrid

Bergman in Casablanca, *torn between remaining with her husband and reuniting with her first love, Humphrey Bogart. That has got to be the world's most romantic movie.*

I can't believe I'm letting myself think this way. Maybe I'm making too much of this whole thing. I mean, who am I kidding? What makes me believe Todd still wants to go out with me? He hasn't even written to me in more than a month. He told Winston about his upcoming move weeks ago. If he was still in love with me, I'd have received a letter or a phone call from him by now. Right?

On the one hand, it would be simpler if Todd has decided we should only be friends. I could breathe a sigh of relief and keep my life—and my relationship with Jeffrey—pretty much intact. It would be easy. No muss, no fuss.

Right. If it's so easy that way, then why am I crying all over this page?

Wednesday night
Dear Diary,
You're not going to believe the news I heard about Todd today. . . .

We were all there at the Dairi Burger this afternoon—me and Enid, Jessica and Lila, and Ken Matthews and Aaron Dallas. And Jeffrey.

Jeffrey looked gorgeous. His hair was still wet from his shower after soccer practice. And he was wearing shorts that made his legs look extremely sexy and a green T-shirt in the same shade as his eyes. He gave me a big smile and put his arm around my shoulders when Enid and I joined the others at the table. I crossed my fingers under the table and hoped nobody would mention Todd. For a change.

No such luck. As soon as I was settled, Lila tossed her hair over her shoulders, opened her big mouth, and said "Liz, you'll be interested in *this*."

Of course, I knew exactly what *this* was. I mean, consider the source. With me and Jeffrey together like that, and with other people around to see us squirm, there was only one topic that somebody like Lila would bother to bring up. Lila thrives on making people uncomfortable. After shopping, it's her favorite hobby.

Then she dropped her second bombshell in less than a week: "Mr. Wilkins has been named the new president of Varitronics!"

Six months earlier Lila had been treating Todd like the butler. Now I could practically see dollar signs flashing in her cool brown eyes as she blabbed on about the Fortune 500. Enid caught my eye, and I tried not to laugh out loud. Lila Fowler is the world's biggest snob!

A minute later I didn't feel like laughing.

"Guess what?" Lila announced. "The Wilkinses have bought a *mansion*, right down the street from Fowler Crest! Todd and I are going to be neighbors!" I couldn't picture it. Todd was an everyday kind of guy who was always bored to death by Lila, Bruce Patman, and the rest of the country club set.

Well, it seemed as though Todd would be seeing a lot more of their kind, like it or not. The next news flash came from Ken Matthews a minute later, and it floored me.

"Well, I got a letter from Todd yesterday," said Ken, who's the quarterback for Sweet Valley High's football team. My heart sank. Along with Winston, that made two of Todd's friends who had heard from him lately. "And get this," Ken continued. "His folks signed him up to go to that really snobby private school, Lovett Academy. So Todd won't be sinking baskets for the Sweet Valley High Gladiators anymore."

I was stunned. I mean it. I sat there like a complete fool, my mouth hanging open, just staring at him. It was bad enough that Todd seemed to have written to everyone in town except me. But now he wouldn't even be going to our school anymore. I wasn't sure exactly how I felt about it. It was just too weird.

Friday, before school

Dear Diary,
Last night I dreamed of Todd and Jeffrey. . . .

I was sitting with Jeffrey at a corner booth at the Dairi Burger, with piano music playing in the background. Our eyes met over our french fries, and he took my hand in his. Then we were on the beach, and Jeffrey handed me a long-stemmed red rose. He held me tightly in his arms and kissed me—deeply and passionately—under the velvety sky as moonlight spilled over the rolling waves. Somewhere in the distance, a piano played "As Time Goes By."

Suddenly Jeffrey was gone, and I stood alone on the beach, clutching Jeffrey's red rose in my fingers.

Then I saw him, walking straight out of the waves, silhouetted dark against the moonlit sky, like some sort of ocean god. He was tall and muscular, and his hair glistened in the moonlight. But his hair was dark, not blond. And I realized it was not Jeffrey but Todd.

Todd grasped my shoulders and gazed deep into my eyes until I thought I would melt into the sand and sea. Our lips met, and I felt as if the strength of the ocean was roaring through me. His hand played along my shoulder, dancing there as lightly as moonlight but as warm as the sun. As we kissed, his fingers glided slowly down my arm and rested on my hand. Suddenly he pulled away. I followed his gaze and saw Jeffrey's rose, still grasped between my fingers.

He stared at me with shock in his eyes. Then he walked off down the beach and vanished into the darkness. I was alone.

"Todd!" I screamed. "Jeffrey!" The music had stopped.

Now it's Friday night, Diary. Friday the thirteenth, I might add. I'm feeling mostly good about today—although I'm confused too.

I still can't get that dream out of my mind. But something else happened today: I received a letter from Todd! I didn't know whether to laugh or cry when I saw his messy handwriting on that creased, smudged-up envelope. It was originally postmarked more than three weeks ago, Diary! The scribbled address was almost impossible to read; I guess the post office had trouble getting it here. . . .

I couldn't believe how hard my hands were shaking as I tore open the envelope and pulled out Todd's letter. I even started to cry, though I managed to stop myself before I turned into a soggy mess.

Todd's letter said all the things I'd heard from Winston and Lila and Ken—about his father's promotion, the family's impending move, and Lovett Academy. He seemed excited about the news. *Vermont's not home,* he'd written. *Not like California.*

He also said that he wanted *me* to be the first to know about all of it. I felt a huge thrill of relief and happiness, just knowing that he hadn't blown me off. Not by a long shot.

I've never stopped caring for you, Todd's letter said. *No girl has ever meant as much to me as you did—as you still do. I'm only wondering: Where do I stand with you?*

I couldn't believe it. He still cared! He still wanted me! I wanted to sing and dance and shout for joy.

I also wanted to beat my head against the wall. I couldn't still be in love with Todd. I was in love with Jeffrey!

❖   ❖   ❖

42

Dear Diary,

I saw him! Obviously, by "him" I mean Todd. The Wilkins family arrived in town this morning. And Todd came over to see me as soon as he could get away from the new house. I watched through the window as he pulled up in his new car—a shiny black BMW!

When I saw the car, I told myself that Todd and I had nothing in common anymore. But then he stood in front of me in the doorway, so close that I could see the familiar way the corners of his eyes crinkle up when he smiles. And it was like he'd never been gone. . . .

Todd hesitated a moment before wrapping his arms around me in a big bear hug. It literally took my breath away. I mean, his arms felt so comfortable and warm, like they belonged there, around me. Against my cheek, I could feel his heart pounding in his chest.

"Liz, I've missed you so much!" he said, his chin grazing my hair.

"Todd," I whispered, wanting to stay locked in his embrace forever.

Then we pulled away, suddenly awkward. I

wasn't sure what he was expecting. I wasn't even sure what I wanted him to be expecting.

"Did you have a nice trip?" I asked lamely. I sat on the couch, twisting my hands in my lap like somebody on a first date. He sat about a foot from me and replied with something equally as lame about his flight. I buried my fingers in a throw pillow in a pointless attempt to hide my fidgeting.

Then we both started talking at once. We both stopped immediately and laughed.

Todd cleared his throat. "You're as beautiful as ever, Elizabeth," he said. I know, it's just one of those polite things people say when they haven't seen each other in a long time. But it gave me a warm, tingly feeling all over.

"Oh. Thanks. You look great yourself," I replied. Then I said something so inane I can't believe I heard it come out of my own mouth. "You're still—tall!"

I blushed, and we both laughed. He must have thought I'd had a lobotomy in his absence.

The conversation improved from there, thank goodness. And Todd made it clear that he wants to date me again but that we can move slowly. He wants me to take my time to decide for sure.

Oh, Diary, there are so many emotions

*whirling around inside me right now. I
don't know how I feel. And I don't know
what to do. Is it possible to be in love with
two boys at the same time?*

Wednesday, midnight
*Todd came over tonight for a family
dinner. I've talked to him on the phone a
few times, but this was the first time we'd
seen each other since Sunday morning. It's
hard scheduling time together, with him
going to a different school. And I have to
admit that I was relieved to see him over
dinner, with my family around. At least it
was safe.*

*It was a typical Wakefield dinner. And
it felt good having Todd here—just like old
times. Dad made a corny welcome-back
toast. And Jessica started pumping Todd
for information about the rich kids at
Lovett Academy. Well, that explains why
Jess has been urging me to dump Jeffrey
and start seeing Todd again. Todd is her
ticket to dates at the country club and boys
who own Jaguars!*

*I wonder how Todd fits in with a glam-
orous crowd like that. He seems to like
them just fine. But what about me? If Todd*

45

and I get back together, will I fit into his new world? And do I even want to?

After dinner, Todd told me that Lovett was his parents' idea, not his. And then he actually asked me out. Nothing major—just for an ice cream on Saturday night before Winston's big party. But I'd already told Jeffrey I'd go to the party with *him*. So I had to say no. Todd was wonderful about it. He said he understood and that we would go out for ice cream some other time.

Then I walked him to his car. "There will be another time, won't there, Liz?" he asked.

I couldn't help it. I nodded. "Yes, there will," I told him. And I meant it too. It seemed unnatural to let him climb into the car without kissing him good night. But I managed to summon up enough loyalty to Jeffrey to ignore the temptation.

After Todd left, I was so racked with guilt that I ran inside and called Jeffrey from the extension in my room.

"How was dinner?" he asked as soon as he recognized my voice on the phone. I'd wanted to be completely up-front with him, so I'd told him at lunch that Todd was coming over to my house that evening. Of course, I had assured him that he had no reason to feel threatened, but Jeffrey knew me too well to be fooled. Now he asked me

46

point-blank if he, Jeffrey, was still my boyfriend.

"Of course you are," I said. But in all honesty, I wasn't sure if things would stay that way.

*Saturday night, so late
that it's Sunday morning*

Dear Diary,

   I need to escape everything that's running through my head. But sleep eludes me. My mind is too filled with images of both Todd and Jeffrey. I've never felt as confused as I did tonight at Winston's party. . . .

Jeffrey and I were standing near the sliding glass doors in Winston's living room. We were just hanging out, talking with Enid, her boyfriend, Hugh Grayson, and a few other kids—Olivia Davidson, Rod Sullivan, Terri Adams, and Patty Gilbert.

When I'd first arrived at the party, I was so much in love with Jeffrey that I was sure I'd be immune to Todd. I mean, Jeffrey had taken me to the Valley Inn for dinner the night before. He'd bought me roses, and he'd been extra super nice for the last few days. By early that evening, I thought I'd come to my senses and realized that Jeffrey was my true love.

Then I saw Todd across the room, and I

freaked. Well, I didn't make a spectacle of myself or anything. But no matter what else was going on for the rest of the night, I was completely and totally aware that he was there. I'm sure Jeffrey and Enid noticed how distracted I was. And they probably both guessed why. Apparently Jessica knew it, too—she had the gall to drag Todd over and introduce him to Jeffrey. I wanted to murder her on the spot. How dare she put the three of us in such an awkward situation!

Jeffrey stuck out his right hand, moving about as naturally as a department store mannequin. "Heard a lot about you, Todd," he choked out. "Welcome back."

Todd held out his hand just as stiffly. "Thanks. Nice to meet you," he said in a formal voice.

I looked at Todd's curly hair and warm brown eyes. I looked at Jeffrey's perfect profile and strong chin. I looked at my sister and my friends, all glancing awkwardly from me to the two guys. I knew what Jessica was doing. She wanted me to get a good look at Todd and Jeffrey together, side by side, so I could make my choice. She wanted me to choose the guy behind door number one—the door to a ritzy private school full of guys Jessica hadn't yet dated.

I can't do it, Diary! I can't act as though Jeffrey and Todd were two dresses at

Lisette's. I can't try Jeffrey and Todd on for size and discard one like an old rag. It's not fair to either of them.

Here I am, talking about what's fair and right. But deep down, part of me actually likes having two wonderful boys in love with me. Am I a hypocrite? One thing's for sure: I'm heading for trouble, no matter what happens.

The Choice
How to choose between sun and moon?
Which is happier: May or June?
You make me dream. He makes me smile.
But triangle love is not my style.
Two in love is what should be.
I never meant to be
one of three.

Maybe I need some advice from a better poet than me. What would Shakespeare say about my situation?

He would probably tell me, "This above all, to thine own self be true." A fat lot of help that is. How can I be true to myself if I don't even know what I want? Maybe he'd say, "The course of true love never did run smooth." No kidding. It took a bard to figure that out?

Dear Diary,

Jessica and I just got back from a tour of Lovett Academy. Todd has been trying to tell me that the students at Lovett are just like kids at any other high school. Personally, I had trouble seeing the resemblance. . . .

The first thing that struck me as different about the students at the ritzy private school was their clothes.

Jessica and I had just left our ordinary, comfortable public school, where our friends wore T-shirts and jeans or other casual styles. OK, so we do have the occasional Lila Fowler, whose father brings her the latest fashions from Paris, and Bruce Patman, who probably sleeps in a button-down shirt. But people like Lila and Bruce are the exceptions at Sweet Valley High. At Lovett Academy, they seemed to be the rule. A lot of the guys wore jackets and ties. And most of the girls had wardrobes to rival Lila's.

The common room at Wolfe Hall looked like the ballroom at the Patman mansion. My scuffed loafers sank into an exquisite Persian carpet. Crystal chandeliers tinkled gently in the breeze from the tall French doors that opened onto a palm-filled courtyard.

"Todd, I see you brought Elizabeth," said a deep male voice. "Whoa!" it added. "Two Elizabeths!"

Todd wrapped an arm around my waist, and I relaxed against his side. It was nice knowing that Todd had told at least one of his new friends about me. Todd introduced Jessica and me to the boy, whose name was Sheffield Eastman.

Jessica nudged me in the ribs. Sheffield was tall and well-built, with a dazzling smile, a chiseled chin, and the world's brightest blue eyes. Out of the corner of my eye, I noticed Jessica checking out his expensive sports jacket and tanned face. We all exchanged greetings, and I was surprised that Sheffield sounded natural and unaffected— not snobby. I began feeling better about Lovett Academy.

"Why, hello, Todd!" said another voice. I looked up, and my optimism plummeted to the Persian carpet. The speaker was a tall, sexy girl with rich mahogany hair falling in a sleek curtain against one bronzed cheek. Clusters of wine-red gemstones gleamed at her ears. This was the infamous Courtney Kane, daughter of the chairman of Varitronics. I hadn't paid much attention when Lila said that Todd had been playing a lot of tennis at the country club with Courtney. I had chalked up those stories to Lila's usual name-dropping. Now, eyeing Courtney's body-hugging suede dress, I was having trouble ignoring Lila's claims.

Courtney looked me up and down without saying a word. Then she spoke with Todd for a few minutes about some reception they'd attended. For all the attention she paid me, I might as well have been a lamppost.

When she strolled away, the suede dress moved with her body like paint. "She seems . . . nice," I said casually. But secretly I was wondering what would happen to suede if someone were to, say, upset the contents of an entire punch bowl over it.

"She's nice enough," Todd said with a shrug. "What she was talking about—last night—"

"You don't have to explain anything to me," I interrupted. Every instinct in my body was screaming out: *How dare she go out with my boyfriend!* But my brain was arguing right back: *Jeffrey is my boyfriend. Todd can go to the country club with anyone he pleases—even if it is a superficial snob with more curves than the Pacific Coast Highway.*

"It wasn't like a date or anything," Todd said. "There was this reception for Varitronics VIP types and their families."

I hoped that meant he had just happened to attend the same reception as Courtney, but then he told me the truth.

"I kind of escorted her," he admitted. "Now

that my dad's president of Varitronics, well, there are certain social obligations that he has to fulfill—that *we* have to fulfill as a family."

I felt my face go white, and I realized I was clenching my fists. That had sounded like something Lila would say. "It's all pretty dull, Liz," Todd said a minute later. "This school, and that reception last night. Believe me, I'd much rather be hanging out at the Dairi Burger."

Sure, I thought. *It's combat duty, having to escort a babe like Courtney to fancy receptions and the tennis courts.* And what a drag, having to attend one of the best private schools in California, with its own ballroom and state-of-the-art everything. I felt sorry for him. Really.

> *I might as well face it, Diary. Todd belongs to an exclusive social circle now, and I don't. Things will never be the same between us again. I admit it: I was jealous when Courtney flirted with Todd today. So jealous I was trembling all over. But why? Jeffrey is my boyfriend, not Todd.*
>
> *Jeffrey is my boyfriend! Why is that so hard to remember whenever Todd is around?*
>
> *Saturday noon*
> *I look at the last words I wrote two days*

53

ago. And it seems appropriate to repeat them here, to remind myself:

Jeffrey is my boyfriend.

So why do I feel like my heart is being run through a shredder every time I think about the party Todd is having next week—the party where Courtney will be his date? At least that's what Lila says. I shouldn't care who Todd's date is. I shouldn't! But I do. I must remind myself again of how much I love Jeffrey. Jeffrey is my boyfriend!

In fact, I think I'll remind Jeffrey of it, too. Tonight. We're not doing anything special. He's renting a movie—it's his turn to choose—and we're going to curl up on the couch at his house and watch it. I'm bringing the popcorn. . . .

Saturday night, late

Oh, boy. I blew it tonight. Jeffrey rented Casablanca, *of all things. I'd have thought he would have more sense than that! Maybe he did it on purpose. Maybe he remembered that Ingrid Bergman ends up staying with her husband instead of going back to her first love, Humphrey Bogart. . . . Nah. Guys don't think that way. Jeffrey knows that* Casablanca *is one of my*

*favorite movies of all time. I guess he was
just trying to please me.*

For a while it was working. . . .

The popcorn bowl sat forgotten on the coffee table.
The side of my face rested against Jeffrey's strong
shoulder, and his arm was around me, warm and pro-
tective. On the television screen, Ingrid Bergman was
telling Bogie that she couldn't think anymore, that he
would have to think for both of them.

Suddenly Jeffrey's lips found mine, and I responded with a passion that surprised me. I felt
totally at peace and totally excited at the same
time, and I couldn't get enough of the sensation.
His hands kneaded my back. Then his lips, as soft
as raspberries, traced a line of kisses down the
side of my cheek, to the place where my pulse was
pounding at my throat. A delicious warmth spread
within me, like honey. I ran my fingers through his
dark hair.

"Todd," I whispered in a voice as gentle as cob-
webs.

Geez. Make that blond hair. Make that Jeffrey,
not Todd. *Jeffrey is my boyfriend, not Todd!* my
mind screamed out at me. *Jeffrey is my boyfriend!*

*The weird thing is that I'm not sure if
Jeffrey heard it. The movie was a little loud*

just then. Or maybe he did and was too angry or embarrassed to say anything. It's impossible to know.

Sometime during the week
(who cares what day it is?)

A glitzy invitation arrived in the mail today. It came in a cream-colored envelope, with my name in calligraphy: Ms. Elizabeth Wakefield and Friend. "And friend?" I said out loud when I saw it. What the heck is that supposed to mean? I guess it means exactly what Lila said—that Todd's date at the party will be Ms. Courtney Kane. Todd said he would wait for me to make up my mind. But obviously he's made up his. I guess Todd is too high on the social chain (why do I want to say food chain?) to be in love with Ms. Elizabeth Wakefield. I have to be strong. . . .

Something about that invitation made me shiver. And I don't mean the part about "and friend." I mean, since when does a party at Todd's house require an engraved invitation?

Jessica says I should be happy. Before, I was confused. Now, if Todd's decided he likes Courtney better, I no longer have a *dilemma. I didn't want to break up with Jeffrey, she reminded me. Now I won't have to. I guess now that she and Sheffield Eastman are an item, she no longer needs my connection to Lovett.*

I'm being unfair. Jessica, being Jessica, will always find a way to make the most of a situation. But she also wants me to be happy. She began extolling Jeffrey's virtues in an obvious effort to cheer me up, but I wasn't listening very carefully. I think she was saying something about how Jeffrey has better legs than Todd does when I suddenly remembered something my mother said to me last weekend: Listen to your heart.

And for the first time, I started to. Only it's telling me something I've been trying not to admit. It's telling me that Todd is the one I love the most. Unfortunately, I've just lost Todd—for the second time in my life.

I still have Jeffrey. I love him, and he loves me. Jeffrey is the most wonderful, most understanding guy in the world.

Jeffrey is my boyfriend.

I think I'll hurry back to school before soccer practice ends. I want to invite Jeffrey to Todd's party on Saturday. It's time to stop mooning over the past and get on with my life.

Saturday afternoon

Dear Diary,
    Tonight is The Party. I'll be friendly and poised. No one will know that inside I'm screaming and crying. OK, so maybe Jessica will know. And probably Enid. But nobody else. Especially not Jeffrey. He's my boyfriend now, and he doesn't deserve to feel like a consolation prize. He's worthy of all the love I have to give.

My dress for tonight is hanging on my closet door. It's royal blue, with a swingy skirt and spaghetti straps. Jeffrey always says he likes me in blue. So, here goes nothing. . . .

It was weird, walking up to the front door of Todd's new house. The stately, brick-fronted mansion with its big white pillars reminded me of the engraved invitation—so formal and elegant. So unlike Todd.

As much as I'd resolved to put on a good face, I knew that Jeffrey could tell I was uncomfortable about this party. But when I'd told him a few days earlier that I wanted him to be my date, I'd seen relief in his eyes. We both knew what it meant—that he had won, even if only by default. Now he was doing his best to be patient with me. He offered me his arm and we walked to the entrance. (Houses like that don't have mere *doors!*) We strolled into the grand foyer.

Todd stood inside, as handsome as always. But he looked even taller than I remembered, and very un-Todd-like in a crisp white dinner jacket with a red carnation in the lapel. For a moment I longed to see him in his sweaty old basketball uniform, with *SVH* on the front in red letters.

But it didn't matter what Todd was wearing, I reminded myself. I wasn't Todd's date.

Unfortunately, Courtney was. She stood beside him with a smug, triumphant smile on her face, wearing a low-cut, mermaid-shaped gown of emerald satin. Strapless. Of course. Her glossy hair was piled loosely on top of her head and held in place with glittering barrettes. She raised an eyebrow as I entered, as if she was surprised that someone had invited riffraff like me.

Todd and Courtney were greeting guests and making small talk, like a bride and groom in a receiving line after a wedding. I gulped. *I can't do it,* I thought. *I'd rather die than face the two of them standing together like that.*

Jeffrey is a saint. He squeezed my hand as if he could pump encouragement into me, and he led me forward. We all greeted each other with artificial smiles. I wanted to flee to somewhere quiet and dark and private, so I could cry in big, sloppy, wrenching sobs until I had cried every last tear.

The party wore on, and it was even harder than I anticipated. I knew it would be agony watching Todd dance with Courtney, so I tried to look anywhere else in the big, fancy ballroom. But my eyes were constantly drawn back to the tall, attractive couple. My stomach lurched every time I saw Todd's arms brush against Courtney's bare shoulders as they danced, every time I glimpsed his hands on her back, on the green silk of her gown.

Several times I saw Jeffrey follow my gaze. He had to know what was going on in my head. But he only held me tighter and forgave me for having loved Todd first.

As we danced, I came to a realization that I'd been trying hard to ignore: Until I was over Todd, I was being unfair to Jeffrey. I had said I wouldn't make him feel like a consolation prize. But that's exactly what he was; in my heart, he was the second choice. And somebody as sweet and loving as Jeffrey deserved to come first. *I can't go on treating him this way,* I admitted to myself.

I hated what I was thinking, but I knew I was right. I had to break up with Jeffrey. Of course, that would hurt him, but for only a little while. Then he'd be free to find a girl who would treat him the way he deserved to be treated.

I had a vision of myself in fifty years, living alone in a cramped apartment with only my books and a half-dozen long-haired cats for company. I sighed. Maybe Jessica would stop by to visit me once a year, on our birthday—if she could tear herself away from Sheffield Eastman's yacht. She'd told me that when Sheffield had asked her out, she'd been the happiest girl in the world.

As for myself, I couldn't imagine ever feeling happy again.

Sunday, over breakfast

Dear Diary,

I am the happiest girl in the world! You will never in a million years believe what happened at Todd's party last night. It all started when I ducked into the powder room to fix my hair. . . .

When I reached into my jacket pocket for my comb, I found a slip of paper I had never seen before. It was a note from Todd, asking me to meet him outside, in the gazebo.

My breath started coming in quick, uncomfortable puffs. Had Todd had a change of heart? Maybe he'd realized he didn't want to be with Courtney. Maybe things weren't over between us!

I hurried toward the orange grove, my heels sinking into the grass as I followed the directions in the note. The moon shone across the wide lawn, turning it to silver. A pretty little gazebo gleamed white against the dark trees, as if it were posing for an Impressionist painting. The scent of orange blossoms hung heavy in the air, and the gazebo seemed suspended in a cloud of the pale, delicate blooms.

A shadow moved within the dark gazebo. My heart began to race. It was Todd! But he wasn't alone. Todd and Courtney stood together in the gazebo. And they were locked in a passionate embrace.

"How can you do this to me?" I whispered. It was bad enough that he would rather be with Courtney than with me. But he was the one who had asked me to meet him out there! I knew I'd been right about the change in Todd—the old Todd would never have chosen such a hurtful way of telling me he'd picked Courtney over me.

I let the note fall from my trembling hand. My face was wet with tears as I backed up through the line of trees. I couldn't force myself to walk back into that ballroom, so I raced across the grounds to my car.

I didn't realize where I was going until I was almost there. Secca Lake, 1.5 Miles, said the sign, blurry through my tears. Once upon a time Secca Lake had been a special, romantic retreat for me and Todd. I pulled into our old spot—a lakeside clearing near an old boathouse—and cut the engine. Then I leaned my head on the steering wheel and cried for everything I had lost.

After ten minutes I had myself under control. I unhooked my seat belt, pulled off my shoes, and stepped out of the car. A broad, flat rock jutted out over the bank of the lake. It had always been one of my favorite places for sitting and dreaming. I picked my way across the pebbly shore and sat on "my" rock, hugging my knees with my arms.

The surface of the lake was as smooth and still as glass, ornamented by a shimmering trail of moonlight. The air smelled of pine needles, and the silence was as thick and heavy as mist. After a few minutes, my tense shoulders began to relax, and the tight feeling in my chest began to dissipate. It seemed as if the night had been the longest one of my life. But the morning would come, and for the first time I knew for certain that I would find a way to go on. Without Todd. And without Jeffrey.

Suddenly I heard the roar of an engine, startlingly loud in the still of the night. In a moment Todd's BMW pulled into the clearing.

"Todd!" I cried, stunned. His white dinner jacket practically glowed in the moonlight as he ran toward me.

"I knew I'd find you here!" Todd exclaimed, his voice hoarse. "Oh, Elizabeth . . ."

Before I could respond, he pulled me to his chest and held me tightly, in the warmest, most comfortable embrace I could imagine.

"Jeffrey told me everything," he explained. "I drove past your house, but your car wasn't there. I just had a feeling you might be at our spot by the lake. Instinct, I guess."

"Jeffrey?" I asked. "What did Jeffrey tell you?"

Todd put an arm around my shoulders and led me back to the large, flat rock. When he sat beside me, that rock felt like home. He held my hand as he told me the whole story. Todd hadn't written that note to me at all. Courtney had written it, to set me up. Then she'd pretended she needed some air and asked Todd to help her out to the gazebo.

"I know how it looked, Liz," Todd said softly, squeezing my hand. "Courtney kissed me, and, well, I guess I let her. I wasn't thinking. I mean, I *was* thinking. But not about her. I was thinking about you and how miserable I was without you."

I looked into his dark eyes. "You mean you're not in love with Courtney?"

"Not even close!" he exclaimed.

I'd never been so glad to hear Todd's laughter as I was at that moment.

"I couldn't wait until tomorrow to straighten this out," Todd said. "I couldn't leave you thinking I didn't care. Because I do care, Liz. I never stopped caring."

I told him that I wasn't mixed up anymore. "I think I know myself and my heart better now than I ever have," I said.

"And what does your heart think about us?"

My heart wasn't feeling very articulate at that moment. So instead of talking, I put my hands on Todd's shoulders and kissed him slowly and gently.

There you have it, Diary. The awesome thing in all of this is Jeffrey's role. He saw Courtney slip something into my jacket pocket. He followed me to the orange grove and witnessed my reaction to Courtney and Todd's kiss. And he told Todd the whole story—knowing that he would be sending me straight back into my old boyfriend's arms. He loved me enough to want me to be happy, and he realized that

I can't be happy without Todd. We both owe him so much.

So now Todd and I are together again. And starting last night by the lake, we began making up for all of those months apart, when he was in Vermont. Todd says he feels as if he's truly come home.

Welcome home, Todd.

Sunday night
I just saw Jeffrey. He stopped by to make sure everything had worked out between me and Todd—and to say good-bye. I could tell how hard he was trying to be happy for me, but his eyes were so sad that I felt my heart break into a million pieces. I hope I made the right decision. . . .

We sat in the living room, a foot apart on the couch, and tried to think of something to say. My hands felt about as big as boxing gloves. I kept twisting them in my lap, wishing I knew how to knit or something. I suddenly remembered being in that same awkward spot with Todd the day he'd returned from Vermont. I couldn't believe it had been only a week earlier. So much had happened since then. So much had changed.

I looked up at Jeffrey, who stole a glance at me

at the same time. His eyes were a darker shade of green than usual and were rimmed with red.

"Are you happy, Elizabeth?" he asked in a small, pained voice. "Is this really what you want?"

I nodded slowly. I loved Todd more than anything. I was sure of that now. But at the same time, another part of me longed to throw myself into Jeffrey's arms and beg him to give me another chance. "Thank you for telling Todd what you knew Saturday night," I said, gazing at my hands again. "I know how hard that must have been—"

"No, you don't," Jeffrey interrupted, bitterness creeping into his voice.

Two burning teardrops spilled from my eyes as I looked back into his face. "Please don't be mad at me, Jeffrey," I begged. "I can't help the way I feel about Todd."

Jeffrey nodded and took my hands in his. "I know," he said. "You can't help loving him any more than I can help loving you. But what about the way you feel about me?"

I gazed at him for a full minute before telling him the truth. "I still love you too," I admitted. "I guess I always will."

"But you love him more," he said simply.

I nodded and reached out for one last bittersweet embrace. I felt his warm, familiar back beneath my hands. And I smelled the woodsy aroma of his aftershave for what I was sure would be the last time.

Then we kissed, Diary. And that long, tender kiss was somehow filled with the memories of every moment and every kiss Jeffrey and I had shared in our months together. Then he pulled away abruptly, tears shining in his eyes. I watched his back as he left the room. I heard the front door shut behind him, and its echo seemed to reverberate through my body. It had a hollow, final sound to it.

I wish I didn't have to hurt Jeffrey so badly. I wish that I didn't have to hurt so much too.

But most of all, I wish him all the love in the world.

Tuesday lunchtime
I'm sitting at my favorite bench in the courtyard at school. Todd and I used to sit here to eat lunch at least once a week. It's strange, being together again but not being able to talk with him during the day. I miss helping him with his English papers in the library before homeroom and running into him unexpectedly in the hallways between

classes. Sometimes it feels as if he's still in Vermont.

Don't get me wrong. I love being back together with Todd. It's just that our relationship takes a lot more work now than it used to.

For instance, I went over to Todd's house last night. We had a wonderful time snuggling together and watching a movie in—get this, Diary—his family's private screening room. But because I was with Todd, I neglected my math homework and got reprimanded in class this morning. I was so embarrassed, I wanted to hide under my desk. After school today I'm going to Secca Lake with him. But I'll have to leave an Oracle meeting early in order to do it. And I know I've been neglecting Enid terribly. Luckily, she's being supportive about the whole thing—I guess she understands better than anyone, since her own boyfriend, Hugh, goes to Big Mesa.

It's amazing how much I think about Todd when we're apart. Everyone in English class noticed what a daze I was in yesterday while Mr. Collins was explaining Wordsworth. I couldn't help it. We were studying a love poem, and something about

*it reminded me of Todd, and suddenly I
was a million miles away—or at least forty
miles away, at Lovett Academy in Cedar
Springs. Was I this giddy the first time I
fell in love with Todd? I guess my distrac-
tion proves that I made the right choice.
I've never been so madly in love. And I
can't get enough of it!*

Penny Ayala, the editor in chief of the *Oracle*,
threw me a dirty look when I left the newspaper
staff meeting at four o'clock. I knew she was disappointed in me, but I couldn't help it. Todd was
waiting.

Besides, I told myself, I had been the most de-
pendable person on the staff for a long, long time.
Everyone else was allowed to screw up occasion-
ally. Even Olivia had missed some deadlines a few
weeks earlier, when she fell for Stuart. *Why don't I
get a turn?* I wondered. I was getting sick and tired
of trying to live up to my "perfect twin" reputation.

*Tuesday, 7:30 P.M.
Jessica doesn't know how good she's got
it. Nobody expects much of her. She can be
late, or get a D on a test, or not know the
answers in class, or stick me with making
dinner when it's really her turn, and people*

shake their heads, roll their eyes, and say, "Oh, that's just Jessica, being irresponsible again." And if Jessica lucks out and gets an A, people act as if she just discovered the cure for acne. Not me. If I get a B, people ask me if I'm having an off day. If I skip out early on a newspaper staff meeting, they look at me as if I had planted a bomb.

Todd, it turns out, had to cut basketball practice to meet me this afternoon. But it was worth it for both of us. The lake was wonderful. We hung out at our favorite spot and kissed and talked and kissed a little more. On the way there, Todd told me more about Lovett Academy. . . .

"Some of the kids are nice," Todd said, "but some of them are hard to be around. I really miss Sweet Valley High."

Then come back! I wanted to scream. It sure would have solved the problem of trying to find time for each other. But I held my tongue. Todd had made his decision, and it wasn't my place to tell him what to do.

Apparently it *was* his father's place.

"It's important to my father that I go to Lovett," he explained. "All the other Varitronics execs send their kids there."

"Why should that matter?" I ventured. "I can't believe they sit around the office all day discussing high-school sports."

Todd shrugged. "Every time we go some-where—like to something at the Sweet Valley Country Club—everyone talks about Lovett. I think Dad would be really upset if I asked to go back to Sweet Valley High."

That seemed a little weird to me. I mean, it's one thing to want to please your parents. But Mr. Wilkins wasn't a control freak. I couldn't believe he would want Todd to stay at Lovett if he knew his son would be happier at SVH. And I didn't like to think that Todd would allow his parents' wishes to dictate such an important decision without even trying to change their minds.

Saturday morning
Sheffield Eastman turned out to be a major disappointment to my materialistic sister. It seems that rich, handsome Shef was more into donating money than spending it—more into making the world a better place than making it his own. For his senior project, he's going to spend time living and working at a homeless shelter. As soon as Jessica heard that one, she ran screaming into the night!

72

Despite her disillusionment with Shef Eastman, she's decided, for some bizarre reason, that she wants to transfer to Lovett Academy. She says it's to "expand her intellectual horizons," which sounds like she swallowed the Lovett admissions brochure. I think she wants to expand her dating horizons to include a different class of guys . . . a wealthier class.

I simply can't see Jessica trading in her miniskirts for kilts and blazers. I guess this is just the latest installment in Jess's Kooky-Scheme-of-the-Month Club. She's even studying overtime—yes, Jessica's studying!—to pass the Lovett entrance exam. It'll probably all blow over in a couple of weeks, and then she'll move on to scuba diving or macrobiotic foods.

The other thing that's happened, Diary, is that Todd and I both realized we're going to have to sacrifice some of our time together. Todd could get kicked off the basketball team if he keeps cutting practices to see me. And I can't go on neglecting school and the newspaper and my other commitments. But it's murder trying to schedule time together around all those things! We even got into a fight about it at the Box Tree Cafe the other night. . . .

We had been trying to come up with a time when we would both be free to get together. After vetoing several other suggestions of Todd's, I said I couldn't make it Monday evening.

"You know, Liz," he said, "if you really don't want to see me—"

I clenched my fists at my side. I couldn't believe I was hearing this from him. "Who says I don't want to see you?"

"You've got time for everything else in the world except me," he said.

"Don't act like it's just *my* schedule keeping us apart!" I retorted, struggling to keep my voice low. "What about the basketball team?"

"That's one lousy activity!" Todd said. "But you've got your dance committee and the newspaper and your mother's job and even the stupid car as excuses."

"Excuses?" I exploded. "Well, it's not my fault I can't see you during school! When I was dating Jeffrey, we had lunch together almost every day!"

Todd slumped back against the window as though he'd been punched, and I knew I'd gone too far.

"I'm sorry," I said. "I shouldn't have brought

74

that up." I took his hand. "Let's try this again, Todd. I really do want to find some time to spend together this week. Look, my meeting Monday is at night. But I'm free right after school."

I just wish Todd still went to Sweet Valley High. It would sure make life simpler.

Wednesday evening
Dear Diary,
Everyone is talking about the Battle of the Schools, which Coach Schultz announced in an assembly this week. Events include traditional sports, such as swimming, tennis, and track; fun things, such as obstacle courses and relays; and academic events, such as the spelling bee and the College Bowl. Normally I'd do one of the academic events. But I could use something physical to vent all this frustration I'm feeling lately, so I've decided to sign up for the relay team.

Ten area schools—including Sweet Valley High as well as our traditional rivals, Big Mesa and Palisades—will be competing. Unfortunately, so will Lovett Academy.

I can't believe that I might end up competing against Todd. I hate to think of us on opposite sides of anything. The metaphor is just too obvious to ignore, especially after our fight last weekend.

When the competition was announced, Jessica managed to find a new way to endear herself to all our classmates. She's still obsessed with getting into Lovett, so she says she couldn't possibly participate on a Sweet Valley High team. So much for school spirit. And this from a cheerleader!

Sunday afternoon
Todd and I went to a party at the country club yesterday—a party thrown by Courtney Kane. It was every bit as awful as I'd imagined.

Things didn't start out that way. I spotted Ben Orson from Sweet Valley High and was thrilled to see someone who wasn't rich and obnoxious. But Ben was there as a caddie, and Courtney's friends gave me a hard time for talking to him. I can't believe the nerve of those people! Even Todd acted as if he hadn't recognized Ben.

Then there was Courtney herself. . . .

Courtney's date was Campbell Rochester IV—who said his name as if it should mean something to me. He had tried to get me to dance with him, even though he knew I was with Todd. The last time he asked, I told him no again, but Courtney overheard us. I knew I was in big trouble when I saw the tense way she was biting her lip. That's about as much rage as cool, elegant Courtney would ever allow herself to show in public.

A few minutes later she pulled me aside as I was searching for Todd to take me home. She backed me up against the side of the clubhouse. And that's when she got really nasty.

"You know, Elizabeth," she said, spitting out my name as if it tasted bad, "you might have been fine for Todd in the old days. But not anymore. Todd is somebody now, and you're not. Can't you see how well he fits in with this crowd? And isn't it obvious that you never will?"

"Todd is old enough to choose his own friends," I said bravely—though I secretly doubted it. "And if Todd has chosen to be with me, then that's none of your business. Besides, Campbell Rochester the Fourth seems more like your type. He's all yours," I said magnanimously. "I sure don't want him."

Courtney was practically sputtering. "You'll pay for that," she said.

"Like everything else here, it's probably over-priced," I retorted.

Courtney rose up to her full height and glowered at me for about a minute. Inside, I was shaking. But I met her eyes steadily.

"All I can say is, watch your back, Elizabeth Wakefield," Courtney whispered. "The world is a dangerous place."

On the way home, Diary, I was going to tell Todd about that little conversation. I kept remembering what Courtney had said about how well he fit in with the Lovett kids, and it scared me. Maybe she was right, I thought. Maybe he had moved on—outgrown me. Besides, if Todd was comfortable with people who are as mean and superficial as most of the kids at that party, then perhaps he wasn't still the guy I thought he was.

To be honest, I've been wondering if his values are changing. He talks about money a lot more than he used to. He's suddenly interested in sports like polo and golf. And it bothered me to see that he didn't stick up for Ben when some Courtney wanna-be made a snide comment about how I was "talking with the hired help."

It turns out (I hope) that I have nothing to worry about. On the way home, Todd confessed that he'd had a rotten time at the party too. He thought there were a few nice people there. But for the most part, his opinion of Courtney and her friends is the same as mine. I was more hopeful after I heard that. And I decided to keep Courtney's threats to myself, at least for now.

Tuesday night
I knew this stupid Battle of the Schools was a bad omen. I was even more sure of it when I found out that Jeffrey and I are on Sweet Valley High's relay team together. Then Todd told me he's on Lovett's relay team!

I thought things couldn't get any worse. They did. . . .

Todd and I met at the Dairi Burger Tuesday evening for a quick hamburger after both of our relay team practices. I was feeling pretty confused to begin with. And then Todd didn't help matters any by showing up a half hour late.

After we got our food, he started in on a monologue about the famous people's kids who went to Lovett, the school's expensive new computer center, and the school trip to China. Finally I asked him if we could change the subject. I wanted to hear about *him,* not his school. That's when he started telling me how hard this all was for him.

"You have no idea how much pressure I'm under," Todd told me. "Everyone expects me to just magically adjust to this whole new lifestyle. It happens to be pretty tough, Liz. And I'd appreciate a little more support from you, instead of all this grief you keep giving me about Lovett."

I felt tears in my eyes, and I blinked them away angrily. "I can't believe you!" I cried. "Why are you feeling so sorry for yourself? Because you have to get used to having your own screening room and a mansion to live in and a brand-new BMW?" You have to understand, I had weeks of repressed anger to get out. "I don't think it's your parents who care so much about Lovett Academy!" I said. "Let's be fair, Todd. You *like* being at Lovett! And you can't blame it on your parents."

Todd gripped the edge of the table so hard that his knuckles turned to hard white knobs. "Cut it out, Liz," he barked. "I mean it. Cut it out right now!"

Honestly, I didn't mean to hurt him. But I didn't like what I saw happening to my boyfriend. His values *were* changing. He was turning into the kind of person he'd always hated. And I loved him too much to let it continue without speaking my mind. "I have to tell you how I feel," I said weakly.

"Well, I'm sick of having you judge me," he snapped. "You know what? Maybe we should stop seeing each other—at least till we've figured out what we both want, since all I seem to do lately is disappoint you."

I felt as if the linoleum floor were tilting beneath me. "Stop seeing each other?" I repeated, stunned. "Are you sure that's what you want?" I whispered.

Todd's eyes were wide; his breathing was heavy. He looked as if he couldn't believe that the words had come out of his mouth. "I don't know," he said quietly. "I just know I can't stand fighting with you, Liz. If this is how it's going to be, arguing all the time, then maybe we should break up. From what you've been saying, it seems like that's what you really want."

Is it what I really want, Diary? I don't think so. I still love Todd. But maybe there really isn't any way to work this out. I don't know. I'm as confused as I was about breaking up with Jeffrey.

I do know that Todd is the one who's changed. And he's the one who broke up with me. So I absolutely will not swallow my pride and beg him to give me another chance, no matter how lonely I am.

That's easy to say, of course. But life without Todd will be bleak—especially if my disloyal twin actually goes through with her plan to transfer to Lovett. All along I assumed it was just one of her whims. But she seems so serious about it that I'm starting to get scared. I already lost my boyfriend to Lovett Academy. Am I about to lose my sister too?

Wednesday, 10:00 P.M.
I can't do anything right. Relay practice today was the worst! All I could think of was Todd. And then I did something so shameful that you, Diary, are the only one I can tell. I actually tried to get romantic with Jeffrey. . . .

My event in the relay was the rope climb. Unfortunately, that's not my best skill. In practice Wednesday, I was a total klutz. I was supposed to climb to the top of the rope, slide back down, and then run to the finish line. But I couldn't get enough of a grip with my hands and feet, and I kept sliding down, scuffing up my hands with rope burns.

I never would have managed to reach the top if not for Jeffrey. He was helpful and encouraging at practice, holding the bottom of the rope for me and giving me pointers as I struggled for the top. I couldn't tell if he was just being a good teammate or if he was being particularly friendly to me.

Anyhow, his coaching helped me get my mind off Todd and concentrate on that darn rope. And eventually I shimmied all the way up.

"We're going to be fantastic tomorrow," Ken Matthews said, slapping Jeffrey on the back. "I'm sure we'll be one of the top schools," Ken continued. He was the team captain; it was his job to be optimistic.

"Yeah," Jeffrey agreed with a sigh. "Lovett's the only school we have to worry about. They're really good. And they've got such fantastic sports grounds and facilities and coaches and stuff. . . ."

"Well, we've got the psychological edge," Ken said, grinning. "Right?"

My stomach knotted up at the first mention of Lovett Academy. I had managed to forget about it as I battled the rope. Now the events of the last few days all rushed back to me. I wondered if Todd was with his own team right now, practicing for the Battle of the Schools. He probably wasn't even thinking about me. He was probably glad to be free to spend all his time being with the right people and going to the right parties.

After my own practice was over, I sat on a bleacher to sort out my thoughts. My teammates headed for the locker rooms—except for Jeffrey.

"Are you all right, Liz?" he asked, sitting beside me. "You seemed distracted during practice."

I caught my breath at his caring tone. Maybe I hadn't been imagining things, I thought. Maybe he really had been being extra attentive. I turned to look into his eyes, and I couldn't hide the tears that must have been shining in mine. I shrugged. "I'm OK," I said weakly.

He put his hand on my arm, and my temperature shot up about a hundred degrees. "No, you're not," he said. "You've always been a rotten liar."

I smiled. "You're right," I said. "I *am* distracted." I watched the area in the middle of the track where the obstacle-course runners were hopping through a series of tires. It felt funny talking to Jeffrey, of all people, about the end of my relationship with Todd. Finally I took a deep breath and told him the truth. "Todd and I broke up yesterday," I said simply.

Jeffrey's eyebrows shot up, and I tried to read his expression. Mostly he just looked concerned, like a friend who hated to see me in pain. But I thought there was something else in his eyes. It might have been hope.

"What happened?" he prodded gently. "You'll feel better if you talk about it."

So I told him the whole story, and Jeffrey listened, nodding understandingly and making compassionate little noises in all the right places. In other words, he listened to what I was saying in a way that Todd hadn't done in weeks.

Suddenly I noticed the way his beautiful blond hair glowed in the sunlight. *He really is attractive*, I thought—just as handsome as Todd.

I held my breath as he placed his hand on the back of my head and drew me toward him in sort of a half hug. He kissed me, ever so lightly, on the forehead. And I breathed a whiff of that woodsy aftershave that I always liked so much.

I've heard that smells can trigger strong memories. Maybe that's what happened. Or maybe I'm just looking for excuses. But as soon as I smelled Jeffrey's aftershave, the last few weeks vanished. Todd was in Vermont, Jeffrey was my boyfriend, and we were as happy as we thought two people could be.

As I sat there on the bleachers, I placed my hand on Jeffrey's shoulder. Then I raised my face to his, and I kissed him warmly on the lips. For a split second Jeffrey responded. Maybe he was caught up in memories too. But then he pushed me away. And when I looked into his face, he was scowling.

"I'm sorry," I whispered. "I thought—"

"You thought?" he asked. "Don't you get it, Liz? You're too late! It was your decision for us to break up, not mine. You wanted to be with Todd. But now that it's over with him, you can't come running back to me! I still love you, Elizabeth. I always will. But I can't turn my feelings on and off like that!"

"But you were being so nice," I started lamely. "I thought—"

"Yes," Jeffrey admitted. "I guess I was paying more attention to you today than I have been lately—but only as a friend, because you seemed upset. Now I wonder why I bothered."

He jumped to his feet and stalked off toward the locker room. And I was left alone on the bleachers, feeling like the biggest fool on earth.

Dear Diary,

It's Thursday night. Everyone else is out celebrating, and I'm sitting alone in my bedroom. It feels like the end of the world. We had the elimination round of the Battle of the Schools today. As luck would have it, the relay race was the final competition of the day. . . .

Lovett and Sweet Valley High were neck and neck as the ten schools went into the relay race. It looked as if it would be the two of us competing against each other in the finals on Saturday. But both teams wanted to go into the championship round in first place, and this race—my race—would decide it.

Coach Schultz blew the whistle. Ken and the other nine egg race participants scrambled toward the finish line—each holding an egg in a teaspoon. It must have seemed silly to Ken, who was more accustomed to rushing down the field gripping a football, but he was a good sport. And all that practice as Sweet Valley High's star quarterback had honed his egg racing skills. Ken's egg wobbled a bit, but he easily beat the others to the finish line.

He tagged Jeffrey and Robin Wilson, who were tied together for the three-legged race.

By this time I had such an adrenaline rush that it was all I could do to hold myself back from sprinting to my nemesis, the rope. A few feet away, Todd was rubbing his hands together in preparation for his own rope climb. I tried to catch his eye to silently wish him good luck, but he refused to look at me. Instead, I noticed Jeffrey's wide grin as he and Robin clomped toward me, ahead of the other three-legged teams. They practically fell on top of me. I zoomed off toward the rope, which seemed to grow taller, like Jack's bean stalk, as I neared it.

Sweet Valley High was ahead, but now it all came down to me and Todd. If I won this race, my school would be in first place. I was sweating before I even started running.

Unfortunately, Todd hadn't earned the nickname "Whizzer" on the basketball courts for nothing. He whizzed past me, leaped onto his rope, and was at the top in three lunges. But I was right behind him on my own rope. None of the other climbers was even close. I shimmied up that rope faster than I'd thought possible. My sneakers hit the dirt just after Todd touched down, and I crossed the finish line one second behind him.

Later I tried to find Todd to congratulate him, but he vanished from sight every time I thought I spotted him in the crowd. So I guess he must have been avoiding me on purpose—a fact that was not lost on Courtney Kane, who by this time had become just about my least favorite person on earth. No—in the whole solar system. She caught up with me and smirked about Todd's conspicuous lack of attention to me after the race. Then she dashed away and disappeared into the crowd. As glad as I was to see her go, at the same time I was worried. It seemed safer, somehow, having her out in the open, where I could keep an eye on her.

As I walked toward the parking lot, I heard a voice call out, "Liz?"

I spun around and saw Jeffrey looking at me, a friendly smile on his face.

"I just wanted to tell you what a great job you did on the rope today. Thanks for helping get us into the finals."

I swallowed hard. I had single-handedly caused my school to come in second instead of first, and there he was, congratulating me! Why did Jeffrey have to be so wonderful?

"Oh, it was nothing," I mumbled. "But thanks. You were great too."

He was looking at me so compassionately that I wanted to throw myself into his arms and cry on his shoulder.

"You need a ride anywhere?" he asked.

Gosh, Diary, you won't believe the jumble of emotions I was feeling when he asked me that. I was happy that Jeffrey was paying attention to me and hopeful that he still loved me. At the same time, I wanted him to be Todd so much that it hurt. But all I did was shake my head. "Thanks," I told him. "I've got my car."

The truth was, part of me was still praying that Todd would appear in the

*parking lot and tell me our fight had all
been a terrible mistake and that he wanted
to be my boyfriend again, if I would have
him. Then we would clasp our rope-burned
hands together and lean into a deep, slow
kiss. And we would live happily ever after.*

Darn.

*I've missed my calling. Instead of jour-
nalism, I should consider a career in fiction.
Because that last bit is surely a fantasy.
Todd probably never wants to see me again.*

*Jeffrey, of course, had no way of reading
the thoughts that raced through my mind.
He gave me a parting smile and headed for
his own car. But something he said the other
day came back to me right then:* "I can't
turn my feelings on and off like that."

*Maybe Jeffrey can't. But Todd obvi-
ously can. I wish I could too.*

Sunday afternoon
*Yesterday was one of the best days of
my life. And I have Courtney Kane to
thank, of all people! Diary, don't you love
irony?*

My palms were sweating. My heart pounded in
my chest. Once again, the relay race was the last

event of the day. And once again, everything was riding on it. As the relay began, Sweet Valley High and Lovett Academy each had forty-five points.

I glanced over at Todd. To my surprise, *he* was looking at *me*. I turned away quickly. I couldn't afford to be distracted. The whistle blew, and my eyes locked on Ken, his egg held out in front of him as he dashed past the Lovett runner.

I heard cheers on the sideline. "Go, Sweet Valley High!" rose Amy Sutton's voice above the rest as she cheered Ken on. "Go, Gladiators!" she yelled again. Normally the screams of another cheerleader, Jessica, would be heard over everyone else's. But Jessica was making good on her promise not to root for her own school. Oddly enough, she hadn't seemed nearly as enthusiastic about Lovett since that morning. But I didn't have time to worry about my sister's loyalties, because Jeffrey and Robin were stomping toward me.

Jeffrey tagged me, and I dashed onto the course while Lovett's three-legged team was still lumbering toward Todd. Suddenly a new voice rose above the rest of the cheers: *"Come on, Lizzie!"* yelled Jessica. Twinship had won out over loyalty to Lovett. I grinned and leaped at the rope just as I glimpsed Todd beginning to run toward his own rope. I climbed, hand over hand, feeling strength streaming through my arms. And I suddenly knew that I would conquer that rope and win the race.

But something was wrong. I reached for the top of the rope, and it jerked downward once before catching. A split second later the world slipped out from under me. The rope broke, and I plummeted to the dirt below.

"Keep going, Todd!" called Courtney as everyone else went silent.

Then I was lying in the dirt with one arm twisted beneath me. Todd leaned over me, his eyes full of love and fear.

"Let me through!" screamed Jessica, pushing her way past the coach to kneel at my side.

I was a little dazed, but it took me only a moment to realize that I wasn't really hurt. I sat up and rubbed my elbow. "I'm fine," I said. "Really, I'm fine." I was speaking to Coach Schultz, who had just suggested calling an ambulance. But my eyes were on Todd.

The coach crouched beside me. "That wasn't the original rope," he said angrily. "I don't know how that old one got up there. Elizabeth, are you sure you're all right? You don't feel dizzy? Did you hit your head?"

"No, I'm fine. I landed on my arm, and it just feels bruised. Really."

Todd took my hand and held it tightly. "Liz," he

whispered, "when I saw you fall, when I thought something might have happened to you . . ."

"We need another event!" somebody yelled as soon as everyone was convinced that I wasn't hurt. "Let's have a tug-of-war!"

The coaches considered the suggestion for a few minutes and decided to go with it. A tug-of-war between the two relay teams would determine the winning school.

"We need a replacement for Elizabeth," Coach Schultz pointed out. I wanted to tell him I was OK to compete, but when I flexed my arm, I knew I was in no shape to pull on another rope.

"Let me!" begged Jessica, raising her hand in the air. I smiled gratefully. My sister seemed to have forgotten all about her desire to go to Lovett.

"Someone should take my place too," Todd said. "I don't think I want to be part of this anymore."

Courtney stared daggers at Todd, but another Lovett student volunteered to take his place. A few minutes later Todd's arm was wrapped tightly around me as we sat on the grass at the front of the crowd. The tug-of-war was about to begin.

At first Sweet Valley had the edge. Then Lovett pulled our team forward, inch by inch, toward the chalk line that marked defeat. Fans on both sides screamed as Sweet Valley pulled back harder. Ken was leaning so far back that he was practically lying on the ground. At the front of the line, Jessica's eyes were squeezed shut with effort.

"Pull! Pull!" Jeffrey yelled.

Jessica's face turned red and then purple. But despite her efforts, she was getting yanked closer and closer to the chalk mark.

Suddenly Todd jumped to his feet and screamed above all the other voices: *"Go, Sweet Valley High!"*

My heart soared. Ken's grin was electric, and Jessica's eyes shot open. Todd's support gave them strength, and the team pulled together with all its might. The Lovett players tumbled over the chalk mark.

Pandemonium broke loose on the Sweet Valley side of the crowd. We had won the Battle of the Schools!

I didn't find out until later, Diary, how close we came to losing. Jessica told me she'd spotted Courtney and a friend giving cues from backstage to Lovett's College Bowl team. And rumor has it that Courtney was the one who switched my rope for an old, frayed one.

In the end, everything worked out for the best. In fact, everything worked out terrifically! Todd and I are an item again. And Todd and Jessica both decided that Lovett's lack of sportsmanship is not their style! Todd is transferring back to Sweet Valley, and Jessica is going to stay!

Thank you, Courtney Kane! I couldn't have done it without you.

Wednesday

Dear Diary,

It's great having Todd back at school. I get such a thrill every time I run into him in the hallway or the cafeteria. I guess I truly feel whole again for the first time since he left Sweet Valley. If only I didn't have to see Jeffrey's soulful eyes every day in the halls. It seems as if everyone at school is in a great mood this week, except for him. And Terri Adams.

Terri is the statistician for the varsity football team. I can't say that I know her very well, but I like her a lot. She's smart and sweet, though she is a little shy and unsure of herself—except when it comes to football. I think Terri knows more about football than anyone at school, except maybe Ken.

And Ken just happens to be the reason for her rotten mood. Terri has a crush on

him. I think they'd make a great couple.
The problem is that Ken seems to have a
thing for Amy Sutton. I can't see it. Ken is
laid-back and down-to-earth. Amy is a
boy-crazy airhead. I wish Ken would come
to his senses. I guess even sensible guys are
easily fooled by long, perfect legs and a
dazzling smile. Poor Terri.

> *Late Saturday night*
> *Something horrible has happened. Sorry*
> *my handwriting is so jumpy, but I'm still*
> *shaking. . . .*

Amy hosted the victory party after the football
game Saturday night. I was too busy gazing into
Todd's eyes to notice a lot of what was going on
around me. But I did see Amy publicly declare her
and Ken's status as a new couple by kissing him in
front of everyone. Ken blushed. Terri, standing
nearby, nearly burst into tears.

Winston Egbert and his girlfriend, Maria Santelli,
had to leave early, and Ken offered to drive them
in his Toyota. Terri needed a ride too, so Winston invited her along.

It was raining, and the roads were slick. Ken
dropped off Winston and Maria. By the time he
stopped his Toyota in front of Terri's house, the rain

was falling in thick sheets. Terri invited him inside to wait out the storm. But Ken said he had to get back to the party.

> *Oh, Diary! If only Ken had accepted Terri's offer! If only he hadn't been on the road a few minutes later. We discovered the wreck nearly an hour later, when Todd was driving me and Jessica home from the party. . . .*

The rain was ending. Todd slowed the BMW when we approached the hill. Flashing lights reflected off the wet pavement. An ambulance was pulled up alongside the wreck of a white car. The car's front end looked like an accordion, and glass sparkled everywhere.

"Todd, isn't that a white Toyota?" I asked. "Like Ken's?"

"It's a Toyota, all right," Todd said.

A terrible feeling of foreboding washed over me. I strained to see the back bumper of the car, to prove to myself that there was no bumper sticker there that said Honk If You Love the Gladiators. But it was there. Or part of it, anyway—a big chunk of bumper had been torn away.

Suddenly I was shaking all over. "Uh, I think

you'd better pull over," I choked out. "I'm—I'm pretty sure that's Ken's car."

Monday

Ken is going to be OK, though the doctors still don't know the extent of the damage. He has head injuries, and his face is all bandaged up. He's in intensive care, but he regained consciousness yesterday.

People were walking around school today like zombies—everyone is so worried, Diary! Terri, in particular, was almost in tears. She asked me for all the details about the accident. I told her it was a drunk driver who ran Ken off the road. She's blaming herself for the accident, since he had just come from dropping her off. Of course, that's ridiculous.

I'm just glad that Ken is going to get better.

Wednesday night

Jessica and I visited Ken in the hospital this evening, and everything is terrible. Ken is blind! The doctors say he might regain all or some of his sight when the injuries in his brain heal. But nobody knows for sure. In a day or two they're sending

98

*him up to Hollyfield to a rehabilitation
center where he'll learn to live without his
eyesight.*

*Oh, Diary! This is all so unfair. Ken's
whole life has changed. I can't believe that
he will never again play football or see the
ocean or read a book.*

> *Sunday night,
> a few weeks later*

*I'm usually meticulous about my jour-
nal writing, but life at school has been
crazed. And Todd has been keeping my
evenings occupied. But something wonderful has happened, and I can't put off writing about it any longer. . . .*

Ken's first few days back at school were
tough. Everyone felt uncomfortable around him;
nobody knew what to say or how much help to
give him. And Amy dumped him for Scott Trost,
who replaced Ken as first-string quarterback. In
fact, the only thing that kept Ken from running
right back to the rehab center, he told me later,
was Terri.

During his very first day at school, most of his
classmates felt too awkward around him to say anything at all. Or, even worse, they kept telling him

how sorry they were. At lunchtime, he fled the cafeteria and sat outside by himself. Terri materialized out of nowhere, he told me later, like an angel. She sat down beside him and pointed out the wonderful smell of magnolias on the breeze. Then she filled him in on the latest football news. It was the first time all day that anyone had spoken to him as if he were just like everyone else.

A few days later she took him to the beach. He said he'd never felt so free as when he was running along the water's edge, the sun warming his face as his feet sank into the wet sand. He said that Terri had really changed his life—that she reminded him of all the things he still could do.

> As glad as I am to see that Ken and Terri are now a couple, something even better has happened too: Ken's sight is returning! It may take a while until he's completely cured, but things are definitely looking up.
>
> OK, I admit that there's one cloud on the horizon. And as usual, it's about six feet tall and blond, with sad green eyes. . . .

Jeffrey and I were sitting in the *Oracle* office Friday afternoon, discussing the photo possibilities for a story I was writing about Ken. It was still uncomfortable at times to be around Jeffrey when I knew how badly I'd hurt him. But I couldn't exactly run away every time he walked into a room—especially since we both worked for the newspaper. Actually, things were pretty good between us on Friday, relaxed and friendly. At least at first.

"I've got another photo idea!" Jeffrey exclaimed, pounding a fist against his steno pad. "Didn't Ken make a lot of jokes in your interview about how different it is to watch a football game than to play in one?"

"That's right," I said, scanning my notes. "He said he's in training to be a fan but that he'll need a lot of coaching to figure out how it's done."

"So let's get a shot of him sitting in the bleachers," Jeffrey said with a laugh, "all decked out in school colors, waving an SVH pennant!"

"Great!" I agreed. "And I'll borrow Jessica's pom-poms for him to hold!"

"That sounds like plenty of shots," Jeffrey said, consulting his list. "Are we missing anything?"

I pulled his pad closer and read through his notes. "Uh-oh, we sure are," I said. "We need a shot of Ken and Terri together. It's only natural, now that they're dating."

Jeffrey's face lost all expression as he made a note on his steno pad. "What setting?" he asked, suddenly all business.

I looked at him curiously. What had I said? "The beach," I replied after a moment. "They'll tell you exactly where. I think they've got a special spot they like to go to together."

Jeffrey's eyes clouded over, and I wished I could take back my last sentence. I knew he was remembering our own special spot, a little way up the shoreline from the Beach Disco. We'd spent hours there together, walking along the sand with our arms around each other as ripples of waves tickled our bare feet.

I feel so terrible about Jeffrey, Diary. I hate to admit it, but I still love him. And it tears me apart to see him so lonely, even after all these weeks. Any mention of a happy couple seems to depress him. He's such a great guy. I know there's a special girl out there for him. Sometimes I even wish it could be me.

Part 2

Dear Diary,

Life has finally settled down. Todd and I are more in love than ever, and we've both gotten back into our school activities. I'm even starting a new newspaper column, "Personal Profiles." My first "victim" is Patty Gilbert, who's a senior and one of the best dancers at school. I got to know her early this year, when I was the student director for the school variety show and she was the choreographer.

I saw her at lunchtime today, when I was telling a group of friends about my new column. . . .

❖   ❖   ❖

103

I was with Todd, of course. And also Bill Chase and his girlfriend, DeeDee Gordon—who just happens to be Patty's best friend. We were sitting around a table in the school cafeteria. Even Jessica dropped by to chat. DeeDee, a wonderful artist, was wearing a hand-painted T-shirt that we were going crazy over. She said she would actually be selling them at a crafts fair at the mall over the weekend.

The conversation was jumping from subject to subject, but we kept coming back to my new personal interview column for the *Oracle*—and I have to admit, Diary, that everyone loved the idea.

"Do you see Patty anywhere, DeeDee?" I asked, scanning the noisy, crowded room. "I want to talk to her about being interviewed for 'Personal Profiles.'"

"As a matter of fact, she's right over there," DeeDee said. I followed her gaze and saw Patty setting down her lunch tray at a table where Olivia was already sitting with a couple of the Droids, Sweet Valley's most popular rock band. Patty was pretty, slender, and graceful, with a perfect coffee-colored complexion and long black hair. "But don't expect her to talk any sense to you," DeeDee warned. "You know her boyfriend, Jim Hollis? He's a freshman at Pacific College, and he's coming home this weekend for the first time in almost a month. Need I say more?"

I laughed. With Todd's move to Vermont, I'd become an expert on long-distance romances. *Thank goodness that's all behind us,* I thought, glancing at Todd's handsome profile as he swiped a french fry from my tray. "I think I'll go talk to her right now," I decided. "I want to arrange an interview with her before the weekend gets here and we lose her for good!"

A few minutes later I pulled up a chair and joined the group at Patty's table. After explaining about the new column, I popped the question: "How would you like to be my first profile?"

Patty's dark almond-shaped eyes widened in surprise. "Me? Are you kidding? I'd love to!"

"Great. Tell you what, Patty. I'd like to get started as soon as possible. DeeDee said she didn't think you were doing much of anything this weekend—maybe we could get together on Saturday."

Patty's jaw nearly hit the floor. "DeeDee said *what?*" Then she must have caught my smile. She nodded. "She told you about Jim, huh?"

"Believe me, I know how you feel. You must be dying to see him."

"I am," Patty admitted. "I miss him like crazy. Four weeks is too long to spend apart."

Hear! hear! I said to myself. "I thought you two got together every weekend."

"Not recently," Patty admitted, squirming in her chair. "Jim's been too busy. We'll really have to make up for lost time."

We set the interview for Sunday, and I was sure that my "Personal Profiles" column was off to a running start.

> *Sunday evening*
> *My Patty Gilbert profile isn't going exactly as I'd planned. Poor Patty! She came over for brunch today, and she was so upset that we skipped the interview stuff for the first hour and just talked instead. . . .*

"After I talked to you on Wednesday," Patty began as we sat outside by the pool, "I found out that my sister was coming home from San Francisco this weekend too. I decided to try to change my plans with Jim so I'd be free to do stuff with my family, but I couldn't reach him at college before he left."

I held out a tray of bagels toward Patty. She selected one but then held it in her hand, forgotten, as she continued her story.

"I tried to explain the situation to him Friday

night when he got here, but he just blew up," Patty explained. "He accused me of putting my sister before him. And then *I* said all this jealous stuff, like, 'Where were you when I tried to call?' and so on. We had a huge, and I mean *huge*, fight," Patty concluded, her chin trembling. "Basically, we broke up then and there!"

I remembered the fight that had split up Todd and me not too many weeks earlier, and my heart went out to her. "But Patty," I ventured, "people often say things they don't mean in the heat of the moment. Have you tried to talk to Jim? Maybe it's not as bad as you think."

"No, it's worse," Patty said, shaking her head. She took a deep breath, and I realized that the story wasn't over. "Last night I went to the movies with DeeDee and Bill and a friend of Bill's from Santa Monica, Craig. Guess who was at exactly the same movie!"

"Jim?"

"Jim," Patty confirmed, "with a date."

Wednesday night

Dear Diary,

I almost feel guilty about being happy. Everyone's life but mine seems to be in some kind of turmoil.

I just got off the phone with Patty, and

107

she's totally mixed up. She's still con-
vinced that Jim has another girlfriend.
He's back at school now, but he won't
even return her calls. To make matters
worse, her sister, Jana, came to town be-
cause she's getting married and moving
overseas—right away. The whole family's
in chaos, trying to put a wedding together.
And Jana's too absorbed in wedding plans
to notice how down in the dumps Patty is.
So Patty feels as if she's lost her sister as
well as her boyfriend. She told me all
about a fight she had with Jana today. . . .

"Jana, hi!" said Patty as she walked into the
kitchen and found her sister waiting for a pot of tea
to boil. "I'm glad I caught you alone."

"Why? What's up?"

"Well, I just wanted to talk to you," Patty explained. "Something's been on my mind. You see, I
have this problem with—"

But Jana interrupted before Patty could tell her
she'd broken up with Jim.

"Problem!" Jana yelled, just as the teakettle
began to shriek. "Not another one!" Patty stared at
her sister in surprise as Jana continued. "There just
can't be any more problems!" Jana complained, re-
moving the kettle from the stove. She began a

108

long-winded tirade about caterers, gerbera daisies for the centerpieces, and the church organist. Then she threw up her hands. "So don't hit me with another problem!"

Patty told me she'd approached Jana with a warm feeling of sisterly love. Now that warmth disappeared, and her anger and frustration burst out, like the force behind a cork from a champagne bottle.

"I don't want to hear about the florists and the caterers and the dumb organist!" Patty shouted. "I'm sick and tired of hearing about this wedding! Don't you think anyone's entitled to a problem besides you?"

Now it was Jana's turn to be struck speechless.

"The wedding's all you care about!" Patty cried tearfully. "I might as well not exist anymore! I don't feel close to you. I don't even feel like we're sisters! Maybe you'd better get somebody else to be your maid of honor, Jana, because I don't want to have anything to do with your wedding! I never want to hear the word *wedding* again!"

But Patty's not the only one with a disaster on her hands. My disaster of a twin has done it again. At least Jessica's disasters are easy to laugh at. She doesn't even realize that I know about her current idio-

tic scheme. But I overheard a few telephone conversations and pieced together the whole tangled tale.

It seems that Jessica was doing DeeDee a good turn at the crafts fair on Saturday, watching her booth for a few minutes. While she was there, a guy named Vincent came by from a local gift shop and was interested in selling DeeDee's T-shirts at the shop. Unfortunately, he happened to be extremely good-looking. So Jessica—being Jessica—tried to impress him by passing herself off as the artist. She even set up an appointment to bring some of "her" hand-painted shirts by his store—without telling DeeDee.

As it turns out, DeeDee's T-shirts sold out. So Jessica is left with no examples of "her" work to impress Vincent. She's decided to paint her own, so she's been nosing around the artsier kids at school for ideas on how to paint T-shirts.

This I've gotta see. Jessica is the only person in southern California who is a more atrocious artist than I am. It will be entertaining to watch her try to put together an entire collection of hand-painted shirts in a week. And the best thing about

Jessica's situation is that she hasn't begged me to help her get out of it!

Sunday
You won't believe who Jim's "date" was! And it was Jessica, of all people, who made me understand what Patty really saw at the movies that night. Sometimes my sister's crazy schemes really do have a silver lining!

I barged into Jessica's room Sunday morning to retrieve the sunglasses she had borrowed without asking. She was hunched over her desk, trying to hide the fact that she was painting a T-shirt. Of course, I pretended I knew nothing about her loopy shenanigans. "What's with the art supplies?" I asked. "You're not going to paint your room again, are you?"

A few years earlier Jessica had gotten it into her head to paint the walls of her room a rich chocolate brown—the same color as a mud-wrestling pit. And she kept it almost as neat as one.

"Don't give me any ideas!" Jessica said. Then she abruptly changed the subject, obviously trying to deflect my attention from her artistic endeavors—if you can use the word *artistic* to describe what she was doing to that poor, innocent T-shirt. I'm not sure what effect she was trying for, but it

111

reminded me of an oil slick being devoured by muddy green spiders from outer space.

Naturally, I pressed her about the painting project. Jessica coolly shrugged it off as a casual whim, inspired by seeing DeeDee's work at the crafts show. "You know me," she said glibly. "I'll try anything for fashion!"

As I turned to go, I noticed a pair of silvery earrings dangling from her lobes—earrings I'd never seen before, with beads and tiny shells strung on them. I asked if they were new.

Jessica put a hand to her ear. "These? Yeah, I bought them last weekend at the crafts fair."

"I guess there's no chance you bought an extra pair for me?"

Jessica laughed and admitted that she hadn't. But then she said something that surprised me. "You know who could get you a pair if you really like them?" she said. "Patty Gilbert."

"Patty?"

"Yeah. Her boyfriend's cousin made them," Jessica said. "Jim Hollis's cousin. I forget her name, but I think she came up from L.A. for the weekend."

Well, Diary, the missing piece of the puzzle slipped into place with a satisfying click. Jim's cousin was visiting his family

*last weekend! Wanna take bets on the iden-
tity of the girl Patty saw at the movies with
him?*

*I ran right over to Patty's and told her
what I knew. The rest, Dear Diary, is up to
her.*

Tuesday night
*All is not well with Patty. She's been
trying to get hold of Jim to apologize for
jumping to conclusions. She still loves him
and wants to get back together with him,
but he won't even answer her calls. And I
always thought he was such a nice guy!*

*Jessica finally had to abandon the
T-shirt plot. . . .*

Jessica's T-shirts were so horrendous that Vincent,
the guy from the gift shop, knew he'd been had. She
tried to claim artistic experimentation or some such
thing, but finally Jessica resorted to something really
drastic—the truth. Minus the part about having a
crush on him, of course. The same day, Vincent
called Jessica's "partner," DeeDee, about making
some shirts for him to sell—the kind without green
space spiders.

I'm sure DeeDee realized that Jess was up to
one of her complicated schemes. But she was so

113

thrilled about having her work displayed in a store that she was willing to overlook it.

I'm just glad I didn't have to step in and tell DeeDee the truth myself. Even when Jessica does bad things, I don't like ratting on her.

Besides, I'm sick of being Glenda the Good Twin. I wish I could change my reputation. Oh, I don't want to do anything that's actually bad. But it would be nice to be a little less . . . predictable. To be more like Jessica.

Gosh, I can't believe I just wrote that! To be more like Jessica? That's a scary thought—especially after the Great T-Shirt Caper.

Is there a way to be unpredictable and relatively normal at the same time?

Sunday, 9:30 P.M.

Patty just called, and I haven't heard her so happy in weeks. Everything worked out for her and Jim.

First, Patty made up with Jana. I think it was the sight of her big sister trying on her wedding gown that brought on the thaw. Both of them realized they would regret it forever if Patty missed the wedding. But she still thought she'd lost Jim for good. Luckily, Jana intervened. Aren't sisters wonderful? Well, sometimes.

Jana tracked down Jim and discovered why he hadn't returned Patty's phone calls—he'd been away on a two-week geology field course. Jana told him the whole sad story and invited him to the wedding, as a surprise for Patty, and Patty and Jim made up right after the ceremony.

More good news—my first "Personal Profiles" column was a hit! Lots of people told me how much they enjoyed learning more about Patty. She says she feels like a real celebrity, with her picture in the paper. And Mr. Collins complimented me on the interview. I wonder whom I should profile next.

Don't you just love happy endings?

Wednesday evening
Dear Diary,

I'm sick and tired of being Elizabeth "Miss Perfect" Wakefield. Everyone expects me to be exactly the same all the time. I'm almost an institution, but it's my own

*fault—I have this annoying sense of right
and wrong. What a drag! I've always told
myself that it's because I'm a decent human
being with principles and ethics. But what
if I'm wrong about that? What if it just
means that I'm rigid and inflexible?*

*I can't believe I'm even saying these
things!*

*Consider a conversation that Jessica
and I had this afternoon at the mall. We
were crammed into a dressing room at
Lisette's, and I was trying on this to-die-for
strapless dress in a shimmery blue-green
fabric. . . .*

"You don't think it's too wild for me, do you?" I
asked Jessica as I craned my neck toward the mirror behind me to see what the dress looked like
from the back.

"No, not at all," Jessica replied. "It's perfect for
you."

I sighed. "I know," I said sadly. I'd fallen in love
with the dress the moment I saw it on the rack. It
would be exactly right for the big dance coming up
at school. But my conscience got the best of me, as
usual. "It's way over my budget," I said, reaching
behind my back to unzip the dress. "I really can't
afford it."

"What's the problem?" Jessica said. "Just charge it on Mom's account. You can worry about paying for it after you have it. Mom won't mind when she sees how great you look in it."

For a moment I was actually tempted. Unlike Jessica, I seldom borrow money from my parents for clothes. My mother probably wouldn't have minded. But borrowing without asking first just felt wrong. I shook my head. "That's the way *you* would do it," I told Jessica. "Not me."

Then Jessica said something that has come back to haunt me many times since then. "Elizabeth Wakefield," she scolded, "if you spend your whole life being so principled, you'll never have any fun."

Is she right, Diary? Am I a drone? Would I have more fun if I was a little less responsible and a little more selfish? Maybe I should make a point of forcing myself to do something spontaneous now and then.

Gosh, listen to me. If I have to "make a point of forcing myself," then just how spontaneous would that be? I'm hopeless. Jessica, on the other hand, has no problem acting on impulse. A few minutes after we left Lisette's—with me taking one last regretful glance back at the blue-green dress—she dove headfirst into another wild, Jessica-like stunt. I knew we were in trouble when she spotted a new business at the mall, a computer dating service for teens. . . .

"Oh, no, you don't, Jessica!" I warned, playing my usual, predictable, boring-but-responsible big-sister role. I reminded her of her last experience with a dating service, when she'd set up herself and our older brother, Steven, with a couple of characters out of a bad horror movie.

As always, Jessica impressed me with her overwhelming confidence in the face of past disasters. So I followed her through the door, eager to see what she was getting herself into this time. I was a little worried when she grabbed a questionnaire for me as well as one for herself. But as we went into a private booth to fill them out, she revealed her plan.

"It's not really for you, Liz. Don't worry," she whispered. Then she uttered the sentence that, coming from Jessica, always struck me with a mixture of fear and curiosity: "I've got an idea."

She said she'd realized what she'd done wrong the last time she used a dating service—she'd told the truth about herself. If she wanted to date a different type of guy, she'd have to represent herself as a different type of girl. Or two different types, to be exact.

"See, what I'll do now is fill out two forms with different names. Then I'll put different answers on each. That way I'll get a better range of responses. Isn't that brilliant?"

I groaned. "Brilliant, Jess. Just brilliant."

Then she introduced me to her two new personalities.

Different was an apt description. Daniella Fromage was an intellectual who liked foreign films, modern poetry, French cuisine, and world travel. Magenta Galaxy was a wild rocker who was into fast cars, loud music, and wild clothes.

Jessica smiled gleefully when she finished filling out the forms. "Aren't they perfect? I couldn't decide if I wanted a really sophisticated, cultured guy or a wild, daring type. This way I'll get both!"

I thought the plan was preposterous, even by Jessica's standards. But she can't pull it off without my help—at least when it comes to answering the phone. I can imagine my father's reaction when some punked-out,

119

inarticulate biker calls the house to ask for Magenta Galaxy!

Oh, well, if I'm stuck being boring and respectable, I guess it's a good thing I have a twin like Jessica. At least she's entertaining.

Sunday

Jessica's going all out on this latest campaign of hers. She's researching the tastes and lifestyles of both Daniella and Magenta to prepare for the first two dates she's got set up. Suzanne Hanlon is teaching her about foreign films and Impressionist art. And Dana Larson, from the Droids, is showing her how to take a walk on the wild side. The weird thing is, Jessica is working on both of her alter egos at the same time! Her bedroom looks like a split personality having a garage sale—neon jewelry and CDs by the Psychedelic Overtones are all mixed in with posters of French paintings and maps of Europe.

Her plan still sounds ludicrous to me. But in a strange way, it's starting to make sense. Not that I'd ever admit it to her. In fact, I tried to tell her a few minutes ago that she's making a mistake. . . .

"You're trying to turn yourself into something you're not," I told her.

"I may not be that person yet, but I could be," she replied. "Why shouldn't I go for something I want? You never get anything if you don't take a chance!"

I bit my lower lip. "I know. That's not what I meant. It's just that—" To be honest, I don't know what I meant.

"Just what?" Jessica demanded. "Do you think I'll blow it?"

"No," I said, feeling a blush creeping over my face. "I wasn't trying to insult you. I just don't want you to end up getting hurt."

Jessica shook her head. "You always say that, Liz. You never take risks. You just play it safe so *you* don't 'end up getting hurt.'"

"So?" I asked. "What's wrong with that? What's wrong with knowing your limitations?" Suddenly I felt embarrassed and guilty. She made me sound so dull and spiritless. Deep down, I guess I was jealous of Jessica's courage. Maybe you only have limitations if you set them yourself.

"That's so typical of you, Liz," Jessica said. She jumped up, walked to the mirror, and began vigorously brushing her hair. "It's just like that dress you wanted so much for the dance. You *know* it's perfect for you. But because it doesn't fit your budget, you just make yourself forget about it."

121

I met her eyes in the mirror, not knowing how to respond.

"So you won't get it," Jessica went on. "But now you'll be disappointed with whatever you do wear to the dance, because you'll always wish you had gotten that dress."

Am I really a coward, Diary? Am I turning into a bore? I need to follow Jessica's lead. I need to adopt a new motto: Dare to Be Different!

If only I could figure out how.

Wednesday

The Good Twin
Early to bed and early to rise
Responsible, sensitive, loving, and wise
I do what I'm told and never am late
So slow to anger; never show hate.
Trapped in a box built on unspoken lies
While inside, a tiny flame sputters
and dies.

Friday night, late
I told Todd tonight about how stifled I'm feeling by my good-girl image. He didn't get it. . . .

*   *   *

Todd and I were sitting in the front seat of his car at Miller's Point. We'd gone to a movie, but it was so bad that we left halfway through. Now we were looking out over the lights of the valley, holding each other close and kissing. I guess I should have left well enough alone. But even a deluxe make-out session with Todd wasn't enough to distract me from my gloomy thoughts.

"Is something wrong?" he asked finally.

I shrugged. "Jessica's got her first date as Daniella Fromage tonight. Tomorrow she turns into Magenta Galaxy."

Todd rolled his eyes. "I should have guessed it was your psycho twin who's got you worried," he said. "Don't be concerned about Jessica."

"I'm not—" I began, but Todd continued before I could finish.

"Jessica is a certified kook," he said, "but she can take care of herself. This latest scheme will bomb like all the others. She'll mope around for a day, then she'll find a new ridiculous stunt that will make her forget all about the trials and tribulations of Daniella and Magenta."

"That's not it," I said. "The thing is, I think Jessica might have the right idea this time. I wish I could do the same thing."

Todd stared at me. "You're joking, right?"

"No, I'm not."

"You want to invent some lunatic alter egos to become, in order to pick up guys?"

I laughed weakly. "No, of course not. But I feel an urge to do something . . . I don't know. Outrageous, I guess."

"I won't complain if you want to borrow that black leather miniskirt of Magenta's," he told me, "as long as it's for my eyes only!"

"That's not what I mean," I said. "Don't you ever feel as if you work so hard to live up to everybody else's expectations—to your own expectations—that you lose touch with who you could become?"

He cocked an eyebrow, and I knew he didn't have the slightest idea what I was talking about.

I tried again. "Todd, I know I have this image of being a good girl—the perfect twin. And it's stifling me! I want to be more daring. I want to be less predictable."

Todd placed an arm around my shoulder and laughed. That's right, Diary. He laughed! He said that I have a perfect image because I am perfect and that a weekend of hearing about Jessica's dating disasters would cure me of my restlessness.

How's that for a sensitive boyfriend?

Saturday afternoon
(a week later)

Dear Diary,

I finally did something wild and crazy—I got my hair permed! It was totally impulsive. I was in the mall today to buy that gorgeous blue-green dress for the dance. (I know, I can't afford it. But Jessica offered to help me pay for it, and I decided to bite the bullet. God only knows what kind of favor she'll expect in return.)

Anyhow, on my way to Lisette's, I happened to walk by Shear Glamour, the beauty salon. There was a sign advertising a special on temporary perms. So I waltzed right in there and took a risk! To tell you the truth, I haven't decided yet if I like it. One thing I do know—it's different! And if I decide that I hate it, it's no big deal. It will last only two weeks. OK, so I guess that means I'm not exactly Evel Knievel in the risk-taking department. But I had to start somewhere.

So far, everyone who's seen my new curly hair hates it. I can tell they do— although most people are too polite to come right out and say so. Well, almost everybody hates it. . . .

I finished my shopping and stopped at Casey's for a soda. As I was sipping it, Jeffrey walked by, carrying a to-go drink from the counter. He looked at me and did a double take. "Wow!" he cried. "Liz, you look great! You know, for a minute I actually thought you were Jessica. She's always the one to try out new hairstyles."

I gestured to him to have a seat, and he slid into the bench across from me.

"So how did you know it was me and not Jessica?" I asked, curious.

Jeffrey shook his head. "I couldn't say for sure. I just took a second look and recognized you instantly. Something about your eyes, I think. So what made you decide to have your hair curled? And how do *you* like it?"

"To tell you the truth, I haven't decided whether I like it," I said. "I only got it done an hour ago. But I do like the *idea* of it, if you know what I mean."

Jeffrey sipped his drink. "I'm not completely sure I do," he admitted. "Can you explain?"

I couldn't help comparing that conversation with the one I had with Todd at Miller's Point last week. Todd definitely came out on the bad end of the comparison. Instead of looking at me as though I

*were out of my mind, Jeffrey seemed truly
interested in understanding what I was
trying to say.*

I told him how frustrated I'd been about being
expected to be perfect all the time. I talked about
wanting to take chances and try new things.

"I know what you mean," he said. "When I first
got interested in photography at my old school in
Oregon, my friends on the soccer team thought I
was crazy. Athletes didn't work on the school newspaper—it just wasn't done. But it was something I
wanted to learn about. I don't know—I just felt
I needed to stretch myself in that direction."

"You *do* understand!" I marveled. "But how did
you choose that direction in the first place? I know
I want something different, but I don't know
what."

Jeffrey smiled. "A new hairstyle isn't enough?"
he teased.

"No," I said seriously. "The hair is more of a
symbol. I had to show that I can break away from
my old image. But it's only a quick fix. I still need
to find a way to prove to myself that I have the
courage to take a real risk—to explore something
different."

Jeffrey nodded approvingly. He told me about
getting his first camera—and discovering a whole

new side of himself. "For me," Jeffrey said, "expressing myself in an artistic way was the real risk. Of course, you do that all the time, in your writing."

"Maybe I need to think of something more physical," I said. "You know, I don't remember feeling frustrated like this while we were practicing for that relay race!"

"So it's settled," he said. "Next week you're trying out for the football team!"

"Somehow I don't think Sweet Valley High is ready for that," I said.

After talking with Jeffrey, I felt a lot better. I wish I could make Todd understand as well.

*Still Saturday afternoon,
a few minutes later*
I knew Jessica would make me pay for loaning me half the money to buy that dress, but I didn't think she'd get me so soon! I sure wish I didn't owe her a favor. You'll never believe what I just agreed to do. I don't believe it myself.

Jessica has been dating two different guys she met through that dating service. Daniella is soaking up culture with Pierre, and Magenta is having a wild and crazy time with Brett. Unfortunately, Daniella and Magenta got their wires crossed today, and somehow Jessica ended up with two dates for the same night. Worse, she's commandeered me into being her double! She's got this harebrained plan that includes each of us sitting with one guy in different rooms of the same Chinese restaurant.

How does she come up with these things? It's hard to believe that somebody who looks so much like me could have such a twisted mind.

Don't get me wrong—having a twin is great. But having an identical twin is a curse! Will I survive this night? I just may murder Daniella and Magenta before it's over!

Sunday, 8:45 A.M.

Dear Diary,

Last night was like an episode of The Twilight Zone. As usual, Jessica's "brilliant plan" collapsed around her ears. . . .

We both wore black leotards and black skirts that night, and Jessica rolled her hair to be as curly

129

as mine. Magenta wears a blue streak of temporary color in her hair, so we both had to have that too.

But I began the evening as Daniella, in Suzanne's gray cropped jacket and elegant jewelry—and a black beret to hide the blue hair. Jessica wore Magenta's crazy jewelry. We planned to meet in the bathroom every fifteen minutes to exchange accessories, catch each other up on our respective topics of conversation, and swap guys.

> *Dressing as Daniella made me feel like ridiculous, like a little girl playing dress-up. But it was nothing compared to how ridiculous I felt as the evening wore on. And on. And on.*

Pierre was tall and slim, with a sensitive face, a deep tan, and light brown hair. But good looks couldn't compensate for his snobby attitude, I realized quickly. He kept dropping the names of high-class places he'd been. And I soon discovered that he didn't know nearly as much about high society as he let on.

"Do you spend much time in Paris?" I asked, in response to a comment he'd made about the Louvre.

"Mmm." Pierre nodded as he sipped his water and opened his menu. "I love the Riviera. I spent most of my childhood there, and I go over as often as I can."

I stared at him blankly. "Paris isn't on the Riviera," I informed him.

Pierre almost choked on his water. "What?" he gasped. Then he laughed awkwardly. "Oh, what I meant was, I spent most of my childhood going back and forth *between* Paris and the Riviera."

"Oh," I said. I was skeptical. But I reminded myself that I didn't have to like this guy or even believe his bragging. I just had to eat a nice Chinese dinner and fill in for Jessica—or Daniella—for as long as necessary. Luckily, the waiter showed up then, so I didn't have to continue trying to carry on a conversation. I ordered my favorite Chinese dish, ginger chicken, and then made up a story about having to make a phone call. It was time for our first switch.

I paced in the ladies' room, waiting for Jessica. This was the silliest, most idiotic escapade she had ever dragged me into. Being adventurous was one thing, I told myself. Making a fool out of yourself was another.

Jessica burst through the door and started yanking off Magenta's multicolored bracelets and a necklace made of fluorescent fish.

"What were you and Brett talking about, just so I know?" I asked as we swapped accessories.

"Oh, classic rock and roll," she said. "You know, the Beatles—all those ancient bands."

I could handle that, I decided. Then I emerged from the bathroom as Magenta Galaxy.

Brett was attractive in his own way. He had a tousled, bad-boy look. But he seemed nervous.

"I'm back," I announced, sliding into the seat across from him.

He nodded. "Great."

It seemed that Brett was a man of few words. In fact, after a few minutes of trying to draw him into a conversation about rock music, I was beginning to wonder if he was capable of stringing words together to make a sentence. He looked up with obvious relief when the waiter appeared. He wasn't the only one. I didn't even know if Jessica had ordered yet, so I decided to order ginger chicken again. Brett ordered sweet-and-sour pork, which seemed pretty unadventurous for a guy who liked to live on the edge.

After the waiter left, we continued talking—haltingly—about rock music. Brett started saying something inarticulate about the Doors. "Their music is still great after twenty years," he added. "Take—oh—" He broke off, searching for an example. "'Sympathy for the Devil,' for instance."

I blinked. "Isn't that a Rolling Stones song?" I asked.

"Oh!" Brett replied, blushing. "Yeah, I meant

that's an example of a great *Stones* tune."

Jessica and I switched places a couple more times, but the charade was getting harder to keep up. Once Jessica showed up as Magenta while still wearing Daniella's expensive watch. She was mad at me for ordering ginger chicken; I guess I'd forgotten that she hates ginger. Before long, we were both feeling frazzled. The novelty had definitely worn off.

To me, both of our dates seemed like morons. I couldn't figure out what my sister saw in either one of them. Finally I blew up and told Pierre that I thought he was a fake. Jessica was mortified when I broke the news to her in the ladies' room. Both our dates ended a few minutes later.

Sunday afternoon
Jessica was totally ticked off at me for a while, but everything's OK now. Through yet another bizarre set of coincidences, Pierre and Brett both ended up at our house this afternoon—at the same time that Suzanne and Dana both dropped by, separately, to pick up some of the stuff Jessica borrowed.

It turned out that Pierre and Brett had

been doing the same thing as Jessica. Both were pretending to be different from who they really were in order to meet a different kind of girl. And in the end, each met a girl who was a much better match for him than Daniella or Magenta. Yes, you guessed it, Diary. Pierre—whose real name is Pete—ended up with Dana. And Brett was attracted to Suzanne from the moment he saw her.

By then Jessica didn't even care. She had just come from playing tennis with Cara Walker and was swooning over some guy she'd met on the courts.

I have to admit that I enjoyed being wild and crazy for once. Well, I enjoyed some of it. But now I think I'm about to branch out in a different way. What Jeffrey said about trying something physical made a lot of sense. After school tomorrow, I'm going to start researching a new hobby for myself. What'll it be, Diary? Scuba diving? Hang gliding? Mountain climbing?

Look out, Sweet Valley High!

Sunday night

I found my new hobby! I bought all kinds of magazines on adventurous topics, and I went to the sporting goods store to look at equipment. Well, it turns out that risk taking is expensive in more ways than one! I had no idea how much a hang glider or mountain climbing gear costs!

Hmmm. My parents are downstairs arguing so loudly I can hardly hear myself think. They were both kind of quiet at dinner. I wonder what the problem is. Oh, well—as I know from recent history with Todd, the course of true love never does run smooth. Mom and Dad argue so seldom that it's easy to blow it out of proportion when they do get mad at each other. I guess whatever it is will work itself out.

What was I saying? Oh, my new sport! I had given up hope of finding something both adventurous and affordable. Then I saw a sign advertising surfing lessons. So I drove over to the Moon Beach Surf Club. . . .

As I entered the room, a boy with lime green zinc oxide on his nose spun around and pointed a finger in my face. "And *she's* the one!" he cried to his companions, two boys and a girl. "Congratulations. You win the prize."

His name was Sean Blake, and he'd just bragged

to his friends that he was such a good surfing instructor that he could teach anyone to surf in less than a month—and have them surfing well enough to win a big competition that was approaching.

Sean was tall and lean, with sun-streaked hair, well-defined muscles, and a tan that was straight out of a suntan oil commercial. The girl's name was Laurie MacNeil, and the other two boys introduced themselves as Sammy and Dave.

To win his bet, Sean is willing to give me free lessons three afternoons a week. I'm a little worried about the time commitment— I'm so busy already, between schoolwork, my new column for the Oracle, *and trying to spend time with Todd. Plus Mom's been tied up with some pretty important projects at her interior design firm, so I've taken on some extra chores at home. But it's only for a month. And it will all be worth it, to prove that I can be as much of a risk-taker as Jessica.*

Oh, I almost forgot to mention that I'm keeping the surfing lessons a secret from everyone. I'm telling people that I have a marine biology project at Moon Beach. How about that for the perfect Elizabeth Wakefield? A real, honest-to-goodness little white lie. Jessica would be proud of me.

*And I can't wait to see the expressions
on my friends' faces when the announcer at
the surfing competition calls my name!*

Tuesday night

Dear Diary,

I had my first surfing lesson today!

*Of course, I had to cancel a tennis date
with Todd that I'd completely forgotten
about. I felt bad about that, especially
since I lied and told him I had to work on
my marine biology project. His reaction to
that almost made me glad I was deceiving
him!*

Todd chuckled. "A *marine biology* project!" he
exclaimed. "How much safer can you get?"

"Don't you mean how much more *boring* can
you get?" I asked pointedly.

Knowing how I'd been feeling lately, Todd
should have realized that he'd said exactly the
wrong thing. He was not racking up points for
sensitivity.

*Sean is awfully confident of his ability
to transform me into an expert surfer. He's
also a little bit too friendly at times, if you*

*know what I mean. For example, he
wanted to help me rub on some sunblock
today. But so far it's pretty innocent. I
guess I can fend him off, if only he'll teach
me how to surf.*

*I found out today that it's a lot harder
than it looks! I arrived at Moon Beach full
of optimism, but before I even got my feet
wet, I got a reminder of how dangerous
surfing can be. I was the one who wanted
to take risks, though. . . .*

As Sean and I walked toward the water, we
watched a surfer riding a sparkling wave offshore.
The sky was the color of a robin's egg, and the ocean
shimmered with blue, green, and silver, rimmed
with white foam. The surfer soared gracefully along
the edge of one perfect wave, so smoothly that he
could have been flying.

Suddenly something went wrong. The board
flew out from under the boy, and he went sprawl-
ing into the waves. He surfaced a moment later,
unhurt, but by then *I* didn't feel so well.

"Did you see that wipeout?" Sean asked. "Let
that be a warning to you that there's more to surfing than riding the curl. Safety always comes first.
OK?"

He showed me how to use the ankle strap on

the purple board he was lending me from the surf club. "That way," he explained, "you'll never lose your board. But that doesn't mean your board can't pearl, and if—"

"Pearl?" I asked. "What does that mean?"

"When your board shoots up from under you and goes flying into the air, that's called *pearling*— like what happened to the guy who just wiped out. And pearling is one of the most dangerous things about surfing. The board can come down on top of you and give you a pretty good whack on the head. That's how most surfing fatalities happen."

I gulped as I pulled off my T-shirt. I was getting more and more nervous by the minute.

"To prevent pearling," Sean said as he pulled a stick of wax from a canvas bag and started waxing the board, "just make sure the nose of the board doesn't dip under the water."

I watched the ocean as he lectured me on the proper technique for waxing a surfboard. The waves were huge and powerful, and I suddenly wasn't sure if I was cut out for surfing. I considered backing out—telling Sean I'd changed my mind. Nobody would know the difference. And I could go on playing it safe for the rest of my life.

Come on, Liz, I urged myself. *You came out here to prove a point. So prove it!*

"OK, Liz," Sean called. "Let's hit the water!"

My first lesson went well, despite my misgivings. I was pretty relieved when Sean told me I wouldn't be standing up on the board for a while. But even riding on my knees was a thrill, once I finally managed it. . . .

I knelt on the surfboard and paddled out until I saw the perfect wave approaching. Then I turned my board toward shore and waited until I felt the swell lift the board. The wave roared beneath me, and I could barely hear Sean's instructions.

"Turn left!" he shouted from the shore.

I paddled desperately to the left. And then it happened. The board dipped gracefully and then slid along the wave. I was surfing! I couldn't believe it. The ride seemed to last forever. I was vaguely aware of Sean, Sammy, Dave, and Laurie applauding from the shore. But mostly it was just me, the surfboard, and that awesome wave.

"That was a great job, Liz!" Sean said as I emerged onto the beach a few minutes later, dripping but happy. He grabbed me in a hug, and I pulled away.

Sean bounded off into the water himself, to show us how an expert did it. I spoke to Laurie for a minute as he paddled out.

"Are you a surfer, too, Laurie?" I asked.

"No," she said. "I just hang around at the club-house."

I was still so excited about my ride that I was ready to convert the world. "You should give it a try sometime," I urged. "It's a terrific thrill!"

"I love watching Sean surf," Laurie said. "He's the best."

We all watched while Sean caught a wave and began surfing it into shore. As he did, he walked toward the nose of the board—"hotdogging," Laurie called it. Then he did something I'd never seen before—something that impressed Dave and Sammy immensely. He moved to the very tip of the surfboard, so that his toes curled over its edge, and he squatted down low, just under the curl of the cresting wave.

"He's hanging ten!" Laurie cried. I watched her face as she gazed at Sean, and I realized that she liked him as more than just a friend.

"Are you guys a couple?" I asked.

"Uh, sort of," Laurie replied.

I was glad to hear it, Diary. If Sean is spoken for, then he doesn't really mean any-thing by the passes he's making at me. To some guys, flirting with girls is as natural as breathing, I guess—sort of like the way

Jessica is with boys. If he meant anything by it, he certainly wouldn't be hugging me on a public beach in front of his girlfriend!

Speaking of Laurie, I could have sworn I caught a glimpse of her a little later, after my lesson. A girl was alone in the water, trying to ride on her knees on a surfboard—just as I'd done. Except she wasn't having much luck.

But it couldn't have been Laurie. She said she doesn't surf. I guess it was someone who just looks like her.

Thursday night
I am so psyched about surfing! Today, after some false starts, I stood up on the board. What a feeling!

I was in the water, mesmerized by the sight of a beautiful wave rolling toward me like something out of a Japanese painting. I turned toward shore, and my adrenaline spiked as I felt my board slide along the wave. Then I rose slowly and carefully to my feet. The board was a little shaky beneath me, but I was in control. I glanced backward and saw the wave's white crest curling toward me as the board sped along without any effort. I was doing it! I was standing up and surfing! As soon as I realized

I was up, I wiped out. But every time after that, I got a little bit better.

By the time we finished the day's lesson, I felt as if I'd really accomplished something. I also found myself eager to know everything there is to know about surfing. Did you know, Diary, that there are surfboards worth five thousand dollars? Sean actually has one. He took me to his house after the lesson and showed me his collection of rare boards. I loved learning about surfing history and techniques. But then Sean spoiled it by inviting me to come inside and watch a movie or something.

I don't know, Diary. Maybe it was innocent, but it felt a lot like he was asking me on a date! What can he be thinking? I mean, he has a girlfriend! Thank goodness Todd doesn't know.

Sunday

As I said a few days ago: It's a good thing Todd doesn't know about Sean. Todd's jealous enough about my fictional marine biology project! We had a date last night, and he was all bent out of shape because he says my project is taking too much time away from him. He reluctantly agreed to come to my marine biology presentation, but he's sure it's going to be too dull for words. I almost told him the truth. I hate to see him as grumpy as he's been lately. But I want my surfing debut to be a complete surprise to him and everyone else!

Besides, his reaction steams me. I mean, what if it were a biology project? If I'm this excited about any project I'm working on, isn't it Todd's obligation as my boyfriend to at least act interested? Shouldn't he be thrilled to see me working at something that makes me happy?

Wednesday, 10:30 P.M.

Oops. It's a week and a half since I've written. I've been too busy surfing and studying and working on the newspaper and trying to fit Todd into the cracks between it all.

Today was an incredible day on the beach. Sean and I rode the same wave! Believe me, that's a big accomplishment for a beginning surfer. But something weird happened in the clubhouse afterward. . . .

Sean reached into his canvas bag and pulled out a small white box with a pretty bow. "I have something for you," he said, "in honor of your dedication to surfing."

I was so surprised and flattered that I didn't even stop to think about how inappropriate it was for me to accept a gift in light of the advances he'd been making. I lifted the lid and pulled out a layer of cotton. Underneath was a tiny silver charm in the shape of a surfboard. "This is great!" I exclaimed. "I haven't gotten a new charm in a long time!"

Before I knew what was happening, Sean was hugging me. Then he tried to kiss me, and I pushed him away.

"I thought you liked me!" he said.

"I *do* like you," I assured him. "But what about Laurie?"

Sean seemed puzzled. "Do you mean Laurie MacNeil?" he asked. "What about her?"

"I thought she was your girlfriend," I told him.

He said that she wasn't—that they had known each other all their lives and that they were just friends. I found myself wondering if he'd bothered to let Laurie know that they were just friends. But that wasn't any of my business. Todd was.

"Sean, I have a serious boyfriend," I said. "We've been together a long time."

"Oh," said Sean. He was afraid I'd want to stop coming to the lessons, but I wasn't about to quit after all my hard work. Not over a silly miscommunication. He wouldn't even take back the present.

In the end, everything turned out fine. "Don't worry, Liz," Sean told me as I prepared to leave. "I know I just wiped out in a major way. I won't hassle you at all—except about the finer details of surfing. Promise."

Saturday, almost midnight
So much has happened today—and all of it bad. I hardly know where to begin. . . .

The weather had been stormy for two days, and we'd had to cancel my surfing lessons. But Saturday was clear, and I was determined to get back to the waves, even though they looked a lot rougher than I was used to. Sean suggested that we might want to skip it for the day, but I thought I could handle it. Bad choice.

I paddled out on my board and waited for a wave. Finally I saw the one I wanted. It was enormous, with a gleaming white top. But when its swell lifted me from behind, something felt wrong. The

146

wave tossed me around like a piece of driftwood; I could barely control the board. I managed to stand, but I knew right away that I was in trouble.

Then the wave crashed over me. I gasped for air but found only saltwater. The surfboard slipped away, and I struggled to the surface to catch my breath. Suddenly something slammed against the side of my head, and everything went blurry. I was sinking deeper and deeper into the wave. I kicked my legs frantically, but a strong current grabbed me from below and pulled me deeper, as if a great anchor were dragging me to the ocean floor. *I'm caught in a riptide,* I thought helplessly. Then I fainted.

The world was still blurry when I opened my eyes. Warm air filled my lungs. I was no longer caught in the wave. I was lying on the sand, and Sean was leaning over me, giving me mouth-to-mouth resuscitation.

For the first time, I realized that I could have died in that wave. I began to cry. And I reached up to embrace him, holding on tightly, as if he were a life raft.

It took me a few minutes to collect myself, but soon I realized that I was all right. The surfboard had conked me on the head, I'd gotten caught in the current, and Sean had swum out to rescue me. Now he checked my pupils to see if they were dilated, but he told me they looked normal. He kissed my nose. "No concussion," he said lightly.

He assumed I'd want to give up on surfing after nearly drowning, but I shook my head. "I don't give up that easily," I told him.

Ten minutes later we walked slowly up the beach. Sean's arm was around my waist, and I didn't object. I felt shaky enough to need the support.

He asked me to dinner, but I told him I had a date with Todd. And as I said it, I realized how much I was looking forward to it. Todd was right: We hadn't been seeing enough of each other lately. And after this frightening day, it would feel so good to curl up safely in his arms.

I did accept Sean's offer to drive me home. But when I saw Todd's BMW already in my driveway, I panicked and had Sean drop me off two houses away.

We were too late. When I opened the door to my house, Todd was waiting inside the front entrance, his arms crossed. I was still shivering from cold and fear, and I almost fell into his arms for a warm, safe hug. But something in his face stopped me.

"I'm just here to tell you that I have an extra-credit project I have to work on tonight," he said flatly. "So I can't take you to dinner." He slammed the door behind him when he left.

Monday at lunchtime he confronted me in the cafeteria. I told him that everything would be clear after my marine biology presentation on Saturday.

He crossed his arms sullenly. "Let me tell you," he said, "this had better be one special presentation."

Monday night

I didn't have a surfing lesson this afternoon, and Todd was still too upset with me to want to get together. Of course, that made me upset too. I hate hurting him like this, Diary! But I have my heart set on surprising him this Saturday—if he's still my boyfriend by then.

By the time I got home from school I could hardly hold back the tears, and so I hung out in my room for a while. Mom was late, though, and Dad was reminding her over the phone that she had promised to be home early. His voice was getting louder and louder. Their argument only reminded me of the problems between me and Todd. And that was the last thing I wanted to be reminded about.

So I jumped in the Fiat and drove up to Jackson's Bluff, a cliff that overlooks the

shore, near Big Mesa. After a while the
warmth of the sun and the steady roar of
the waves lulled me into relaxation. I ab-
sentmindedly began reviewing what I'd
learned about tides and reefs by mentally
mapping out the bay below me.

Suddenly I sensed that I wasn't alone. I
spun around, hoping for no logical reason
to see Todd standing behind me. I was flab-
bergasted when I saw who it really was. . . .

"Jeffrey!" I said. "How did you know I was
here?"

My former boyfriend shook his head and
stepped toward me, the sun casting a halo around
his blond hair. "I didn't," he explained. "I just like to
come here sometimes to look out over the ocean."
He touched the camera that hung around his neck.
"I was hoping to get some sunset-over-the-Pacific
shots in a little while. But I can do it another time if
you want to be alone."

"No!" I said, patting the rock beside where I
was sitting. I was surprised at how glad I was to see
him. "I'd really like it if you would join me."

Well, I ended up spilling the whole story
to Jeffrey, and I felt a lot better afterward,
even though it seems weird telling Jeffrey,

of all people, about my troubles with Todd.
He didn't offer any solutions—just sympa-
thy and a good ear. But he promised he
wouldn't tell a soul about the surfing. And
he said he'd be at Moon Beach Saturday to
cheer me on.

Saturday night, late
Veni, vidi, vici. *As Julius Caesar said, I*
came, I saw, and I conquered. Well, sort of.
But my main mission was accomplished.
Nobody knew what hit them when they
saw me on the waves today! Here's what
happened. . . .

As it turned out, word got around school that there would be a surfing competition at Moon Beach on Saturday. Jessica decided that the sight of handsome surf bums was a fitting compensation for being forced to watch my marine biology presentation. And even people like Lila Fowler, who wouldn't be caught dead at anything involving science, were planning to show up.

Before the competition, I overheard a conversation that changed my entire plan for the day. Laurie was talking to a friend, and I know I shouldn't have listened. But I'm glad I did. I finally found out the truth about what's going on between

Laurie and Sean: nothing. But she *wants* something to happen. In fact, he'd been starting to get interested in her—right before *I* entered the picture. So Laurie had been teaching herself to surf, just to impress him. She was sure she would lose him forever if I showed her up in the competition.

As for my own love life, I was terrified that Todd wouldn't even come. I scanned the bleachers. Jessica, Amy, and Lila were checking out the surfers. Winston and Maria were perched right behind them, with DeeDee and Bill. Bill would be a tough audience, I knew. He'd won quite a few surfing competitions himself. Even Bruce Patman was there, sitting with his friend Kirk "the Jerk" Anderson and scoping out the women in bathing suits. And just before it was my turn to surf, I spotted Todd, who was handing Enid a soda as he sat down beside her.

I nearly jumped out of my skin when the announcer's voice boomed through the loudspeaker: *"And our next competitor is . . . Elizabeth Wakefield!"*

Screams erupted from the Sweet Valley section of the bleachers. First they were screams of disbelief. But when I strode to the water's edge, clutching my borrowed surfboard, my friends' cries became cheers of support, with Jessica's and Todd's voices rising above the rest.

The swell of a perfect wave caught me. The board slid along it, exactly the way it was supposed to. I was thrilled to feel the power of the ocean carrying me along. I rose quickly to my feet and rode like an expert for a few seconds. But I knew what I had to do. As everyone watched, I pretended to lose my balance, and I sprawled into the surf with a giant belly flop.

Laurie was next in the competition, and she did beautifully—as I'd known she would. I saw Sean's face as he watched her, and his eyes widened, as if he were seeing her for the first time. I smiled to myself and picked my way back along the beach toward my friends. Jessica was the first to reach me.

"You were great!" she cried, tackling me with a monster hug. "But I still can't believe it was you!" Then she told me how glad she was not to have to sit through a marine biology program. "Your wipeout was the most hysterical thing I've ever seen!" she howled. "Your legs were flying up in the air, and you did a few flips, and—I have to say it, Liz— you looked like a total klutz!"

"Some sister you are!" I said, snapping her with my towel and then wrapping it around my waist.

Then Todd and Enid were upon me. "Well," I asked, suddenly feeling uncertain, "what do you think of my big surprise?"

Todd squeezed my hand. "What do I think? I think it was the funniest wipeout I've ever seen. But I know you had to have a lot of guts to get up there in the first place." At that moment, the rest of the gang came rushing up to shake my hand and congratulate me on, as Winston put it, my "valiant attempt." I felt happier than if I'd won first place. On the edge of the mob, I spotted Jeffrey. He gave me a discreet thumbs-up before he disappeared into the crowd.

In the parking lot a while later, Bill Chase caught up with me, and I let Todd and Enid walk ahead. "Why did you decide to wipe out like that?" Bill asked. "It was the strangest thing I've ever seen."

I was amazed. "You could tell that I wiped out intentionally?" I asked.

Bill shrugged. "Of course I could tell. And I could also tell that you're a really good surfer, just by the way you got up on the board. I mean, you did *that* like a total pro. If you had just finished your ride, you might have gotten first place."

So what if everyone else thinks I'm a klutz, Diary? At least they think I'm an adventurous and unpredictable klutz!

And now that I've proven myself, I feel pretty good about going back to being good old perfect Elizabeth.

Sunday evening
I've never believed in ghosts, but today
I saw one! OK, so it wasn't a real ghost,
but it was just as much of a shock.

Steven had arrived home from college the night before, and the two of us were at the mall. First he dragged me into the Sports Shop to learn about hang gliding lessons. He said he got the idea from reading all those outdoor adventure magazines I'd brought home.

Next it was *my* turn to drag him—against his will, I might add—into the Unique Boutique. When a sales clerk approached us, we were both stunned into silence. She looked exactly like Steven's old girlfriend, who had died of leukemia several months earlier. She had the same big eyes and the same slim figure. She wore her tawny mane of long, curly hair in the same style. She could have been Tricia Martin's ghost.

Speaking of ghosts, Steven's face was about the color of one. "Tricia?" he whispered.

"No, my name's not Tricia," the girl said. "It's Andrea. Can I help you?"

I just heard Steven on the phone with Andrea, making a date for tomorrow night. Only I happen to know that he already had a date to go to the movies with Cara Walker, whom he's been dating for quite a while now. I hope Cara doesn't find out why he's breaking their date.

Friday

Today was one long nightmare. Some of it is minor annoyances: The Fiat keeps breaking down, and I have an English paper due Monday. If that were all, I'd be on cloud nine! But my life—my family, specifically—is an utter mess!

First there's my brother, who's chasing a ghost. Steven is obsessed with Andrea. He's been out with her several times this week, and when they're not together, he's mooning over her.

He claims that he knows Andrea is her own person and not some sort of reincarnation of Tricia. But at the same time, he tries to force her into a mold. Some of it is silly things, like assuming Andrea should order chocolate ice cream instead of vanilla, because chocolate was Tricia's favorite flavor. And he's always picking out parallels that don't mean anything at all—for instance, he thinks it's amazing that Andrea likes to walk on the beach, just as

Tricia did. Give me a break! This is southern California. Everyone likes to walk on the beach.

I hate what Steven is doing to Cara. He keeps canceling dates with her. And when they're together, he's distant and preoccupied—as though he holds it against her that she doesn't look like Tricia Martin! Cara knows something's wrong between them, but she doesn't understand what it is. She asked me today if I know what's going on, and I had to lie, because I promised my brother I wouldn't tell. Poor Cara looked so sad and confused!

I'm angry with my brother about the way he's lying to and cheating on such a warm, caring girl—a girl he still claims to love. And I hate having to lie to her myself.

But Steven isn't the only one with a screwed-up relationship right now. To borrow (liberally) from Macbeth, something much more rotten is going on in the state of Wakefield.

It's my parents, Diary. They're practically at each other's throats! I don't understand it. Usually our family is like a Norman Rockwell painting. But lately it seems more like the Addams Family! I know that all couples argue from time to time. But in the past, my parents did it in private—never in front of us kids. And they didn't stay mad for long. Now they can barely hold a civil conversation.

For instance, listen to what happened a few days ago, when Steven told them he was signing up to learn more about hang gliding lessons. . . .

My mother was concerned. "Steven, I don't know about this."

"What do you mean?" Steven asked. But he knew exactly what she meant. I was in a motorcycle accident a few months back, and Mom's been nervous ever since then about our taking risks. That was one of the reasons I'd kept my surfing lessons a secret. And hang gliding seems a lot more dangerous than surfing.

"Honey," she said carefully, "I know you're old enough to make your own decisions—"

"So let him make them!" my father interrupted. "He's a big boy, Alice!"

"Ned, I just want him to know how I feel about it."

"No! What you want him to do is feel guilty about worrying you, and *not* do it," Dad retorted. Then he said to Steven, "My opinion is, go for it while you have the chance!" He added bitterly, "It won't be long before you can't afford to take any risks at all!"

I don't know where that last bit came from. Neither did Mom, apparently. "I'd like to know what you mean by that," she said in a voice that sounded hurt and defiant.

"He's young," Dad replied wearily. "He doesn't have any obligations to get in his way. That's all I'm saying. If he wants some adventure, I say he should be able to have it."

Steven cut in to tell them he hadn't even decided for sure if he wanted to take lessons. He was only going to an orientation program.

"See?" Dad practically snarled at Mom. "He's already backing off! Good work, Alice."

Mom told Steven that she didn't like the idea of his trying something so dangerous but that she wouldn't hold him back if he really wanted to do it. And then Dad—in an obvious effort to annoy her— jumped in and offered to pay for the lessons and equipment.

I know, Diary. It sounds like Dad was being a real jerk. And he was—as much as I hate to say it about my own father.

But the tension between them isn't all Dad's fault. Mom's been insensitive too. Lately she's been so engrossed in her job that we never see her! She comes home late without letting Dad know. She's always canceling plans with him. And when she is home, she chatters nonstop about the exciting new projects she's working on—as if her career is more interesting to her than her own family!

My father, on the other hand, seems to be working on totally routine cases at his law firm. It must be frustrating for him. But when Mom spends her whole life at work, Dad starts going to his own office on weekends and staying late at night too. I don't know if he's trying to get back at her or if he wants to prove to her—or to himself—that his job is important too. Or maybe Dad just figures it's not worth coming home if Mom's not around to spend time with him.

Friday, a week later

I went out with Todd tonight. But even the Droids' loud music at the Beach Disco wasn't enough to drown out the echoes of my parents' angry voices. And when I wasn't thinking about them, I was remembering the tears in Cara's eyes as she begged me to tell her why Steven is ignoring her.

It didn't take Todd long to pick up on my mood. He suggested that we leave, and I *gratefully walked with him to the parking lot.*

I'm starting to wonder if relationships are worth the trouble. Yes, Todd and I are in love. But so are my parents—presumably. Todd and I are happy together. But until lately, my parents were too. How do I know if our happiness will last? How do I know we won't start hurting each other?

I just worked out a haiku that's been twisting around in my mind since I got home from my date. Haiku is a form of Japanese poetry that Mr. Collins has been teaching us about in English class:
Why was I frightened
and empty inside, when all
you did was kiss me?

.

Saturday afternoon
Steven and Cara broke up! Jessica called her a little while ago and learned the whole story. . . .

Cara found out about Andrea and tried to make Steven see exactly what I've been telling him: that spending time with Andrea can't bring Tricia back, and that it's unfair to expect Andrea to live up to the memory of a dead girlfriend.

She asked Steven if he planned to continue

dating them both. She said she had a right to know. But Steven accused her of being possessive. A minute later he broke up with her.

When he gets back from his hang gliding lesson, I plan to sit my big brother down and tell him what's what. Unless Jessica murders him first. She's even more ticked off at our dear brother than I am.

Late Saturday night
I'm almost too upset to write this. I'm sitting in the dim corridor of Fowler Memorial Hospital. My brother is behind a cold steel door, struggling for every breath he takes. My mother's fears about hang gliding were justified—Steven had a terrible accident. He lost control of his glider and crashed to the ground.

Jessica is beside me, sobbing. My parents sit nearby, their faces as white as the blank, sterile wall behind them. The doctor came to talk to us a little while ago. She said it's still too early to know whether Steven will be all right. . . .

"His left arm is broken," Dr. Nichols told us. "But we took care of that easily enough. And the contusions, cuts—we can deal with that. But it's the head injuries we can't be certain of. When we see the X rays, we'll have a better idea."

"When will he wake up?" my mother asked in a hoarse voice.

Dr. Nichols shook her head and took off her glasses. "That's hard to say," she said slowly. "He might be unconscious for just a short while, or it could be a matter of days."

My father's face got even paler, and I noticed that he reached automatically for my mother's hand. "Can we see him?"

"Yes," said the doctor. "But I have to warn you—his face is quite bruised and swollen."

Jessica took a shaky breath, and I squeezed her hand.

It was awful, walking through that door and seeing my brother so helpless and still. The room was dim except for a light near the bed. In its harsh glow, the cuts and bruises on Steven's face looked garish and unreal, as if they'd been painted on. His arm was in a cast. And the gauze bandage that was wrapped around his head shone threateningly in the light.

"Oh, no!" Jessica breathed, her voice full of tears.

*I remembered Ken's accident and the head
injury that could have left him blind for life.
I can't believe it's all happening again. What
if Steven goes blind? What if he slips into a
coma? What if it's even worse than that? Oh,
Diary, he has to survive. He just has to!*

*Ironically, this nightmare has brought
my parents together for the first time in
weeks. . . .*

My mother bent over Steven's bed, and I saw a
tear fall onto his pillow. "Steven?" she said in a
pleading voice. "My little boy!"

Daddy wrapped his arm around her shoulders and
pulled her close. "He'll be OK," he said in a ragged
voice as he smoothed her hair. "He'll be all right."

I turned to the doctor, who stood tactfully near
the door. "Can we stay here? With Steven?"

Dr. Nichols nodded. "It might be a long wait,"
she warned gently.

Sunday afternoon
*Steven is going to be fine. He's still pretty
sore, but he's conscious now. And his head
injury is not serious. He'll be able to come
home sometime this week.*

But no more hang gliding.

❖   ❖   ❖

164

Monday

The Wakefield sisters strike again! We were determined to find a way to get Steven and Cara back together. I mean, it's so obvious that they're meant for each other. And we knew Steven was still in love with Cara. When he was delirious, it was Cara's name he called—and Tricia's. But not Andrea's.

So we came up with a spur-of-the-moment plan.

It wasn't meddling, really. We just gave Cara and Steven a little push. . . .

Jessica let it slip to Steven that she had seen Andrea at the movies with another guy. Amazingly, right after Jessica said it, Andrea jumped out of a convertible in the hospital parking lot below. As Jessica, Steven, and I watched through the window, Andrea kissed the guy who was driving the car. Then she started up the walkway to visit Steven.

That's when Jessica and I played a hunch. We ran out to the pay phone in the corridor, called Cara, and asked her to come.

I'm embarrassed to recount what we did next, Diary. I know it was wrong. Maybe my recent frustration with being perfect Elizabeth was still nagging at my

brain, urging me to break my usual stan-
dards of conduct. . . . Nah, it was probably
just Jessica.

For whatever reason, I succumbed to
temptation, and I stood with Jessica out-
side of our brother's hospital room door,
eavesdropping on his conversation with
Andrea. . . .

Steven confronted her right off the bat about the
guy in the convertible. Andrea didn't make any apol-
ogies. She reminded him that the two of them hadn't
known each other for very long and that they'd never
agreed not to date other people. And while she was
sympathetic about Tricia, she made it clear that she
couldn't go on living in a dead girl's shadow.

"Steven, you've never really seen me or heard
me or gotten to know *me, Andrea*," she said gently.
"You want me to replace Tricia for you, and I can't
do that."

"I do see you," Steven said, but his voice lacked
conviction.

"Steven, I'm really, really sorry about Tricia,"
Andrea told him. "I know you must have loved her
a lot, and I realize you still miss her. But I found
someone who likes me for who I am, not for who I
remind him of."

They spoke for a few minutes more, but in the

end it was clear to both of them that things were not going to work out between them. Andrea left, leaving Steven with just enough time to reflect on what a mess he'd made of things. Then Cara arrived.

Jessica wanted to eavesdrop on their conversation as well, but I had to draw the line somewhere. So I dragged her away, and we waited in the hospital lounge. We gave Steven and Cara plenty of time to work through what had happened and to realize that they were still in love. When we were sure they must be finished, we crept back to Steven's room and gingerly pushed open the door—just in time to witness the tail end of their reunion.

"I still love you, Steven," Cara whispered.

"I love you, too," Steven said, reaching up with his right hand to pull her close. *"Ow, my arm!"*

I yanked Jessica out of the way and pulled the door shut.

> *Wednesday, 9:30 P.M.*
> *Steven came home today. But what should have been an evening of laughter and love turned dismal. It didn't start out that way. . . .*

The whole family was on the back patio, along with Cara, for Steven's welcome-home celebration Wednesday evening.

"When do we get to eat?" Steven asked.

Mom's eyebrows arched comically. "But Steven," she said, "your doctor prescribed a diet of boiled fish, rice pudding, and lima beans."

"A fate worse than death," Jessica gasped as she, Cara, and I all grabbed our throats and groaned in agony. Prince Albert barked, as if to say that he hated lima beans too.

"No, come on, Mom," Steven said. "Dr. Nichols didn't really say anything like that, did she?"

Mom shrugged. "Doctor's orders!"

"Right," said Cara. "If you want to get your strength back, you have to eat lots of nutritious foods, like tofu—"

"Steamed cabbage," Jessica interrupted.

"Cod liver oil," I added.

"You guys!" yelled Steven.

"Now, give him a break," Dad said. "Whatever you want, Steven, you just name it, and it's yours."

"Whatever you want, as long as it's steak," Mom said cheerfully. "That's what I got."

"You could always go out for something else," Dad suggested, an edge creeping into his voice. I caught Steven's eye and winced. "After all, it *is* his first night home. He should have something special."

Mom laughed, but she didn't sound as if she thought it was funny. "Thanks for volunteering my time to go shopping," she said, her voice growing sharper. "I'll be happy to prepare the *steak* any way Steven wants it."

Now even Jessica was casting worried glances at me. Cara was staring at her hands.

"Steak would be fine, Mom," Steven said quickly.

There was some awkward conversation about how to prepare the steaks. Then Jessica rattled the ice cubes in her glass, as if signaling the start of a new subject. "Hey, you know what?" she piped up. "Maria Santelli's father is running for mayor!"

Dad looked up. "Peter Santelli? I'm surprised he didn't tell me. We've known each other for years. He's done a good job as city planning commissioner, and I think he'd make a good mayor."

"Maybe I can interview him and Maria for the school paper," I said, glad that the mood in the backyard had relaxed. You never knew what would set my parents off these days. "You know," I elaborated, "how it feels to have a father in politics— that sort of thing."

Mom sighed. "Something you'll never know firsthand, thank goodness."

"I don't know why you say that," my father retorted. The temperature dropped by about thirty degrees. "I'd hate to think I'll never do anything for this community. It's not as though being a lawyer until the end of my days excites me."

Mom threw her hands up in exasperation. "If it makes you so unhappy, Ned, then stop being a lawyer!" she burst out. "Don't take it out on us!"

"Oh, right!" Dad exploded, standing up. "Just like that! Quit my job? Good thinking, Alice. Steven's in college, and the girls will be there soon." He stalked into the house.

Mom sank into her chair and glowered at his retreating figure. I noticed her twirling her wedding band around and around on her finger.

"Mom?" Jessica asked quietly. Her voice caught, and I knew she was holding back tears.

"Excuse me, honey," Mom said. Her voice sounded hollow. "I'll be right back." She rose from her chair and walked resolutely through the sliding glass door.

Teardrops are blurring this page, Diary. I don't understand what's wrong between my parents. Why did they have to ruin such a special evening? Is there something I could have done to make it better?

What is happening to my family?

Part 3

Tuesday

Dear Diary,

Last night the whole family went to a fund-raising dinner for Mr. Santelli's campaign. Steven's still home from college, recuperating from his injuries and researching a prelaw project on legal ethics, so he was able to go too.

We were all so psyched about the candidacy! Then we woke up this morning and saw the front page of today's newspaper. Mr. Santelli has been accused of accepting bribes as city planning commissioner! . . .

"That's absurd," Dad said. "Peter would never accept a bribe. Not in a million years. I can't

171

imagine who could make an allegation like that."

"Neither can I," Mom said. "But it's rotten timing. Even if the charges are dropped, one accusation can destroy a campaign."

Even when they were united in their belief in Mr. Santelli, my parents couldn't resist sniping at each other. "Well, it isn't over till it's over, Alice," Dad said, his voice growing nastier. "Don't start assuming Peter's out of the race. It's exactly that kind of reasoning that will cost him votes!"

Jessica and I had to get to school, so we didn't hear much more of the conversation—thank goodness. I wish my parents could let it rest for once.

On the way to school, I kept worrying about Maria. I can't imagine what it must be like to have the whole town read about your father being accused of a crime. . . .

At school, everyone was talking about and pointing and staring at Maria. I was at my locker before homeroom when I heard Jessica, at her own locker, gabbing away with Lila and Amy about Peter Santelli.

"That's it!" Lila exclaimed. "He's finished. History. Done for!"

"My mom thinks it's going to be the biggest

story at the station," confided Amy, whose mother is a television sportscaster. "She says unless Mr. Santelli can clear his name, there's no way he'll be able to win the election."

Lila grasped Jessica's arm. "Hey! There she is!" All three of them turned to watch Maria, who was walking down the hall with a grave expression on her face. The corridor was crowded, but people parted around her, as if they didn't want to get too close. I tried to catch Maria's eye to give her a sympathetic smile, but she never looked my way, and I was juggling too many books to run after her.

"Poor thing," Amy commented cheerfully as Maria disappeared into a classroom.

Jessica sighed. "It would've been so much fun, knowing the mayor's daughter."

"I was even going to invite Maria over for dinner sometime soon, just to get to know her better," Lila revealed, shaking her head. "I guess now there's no reason to do that."

As the three of them moved on to another topic, I slammed my locker door and chased after Maria.

Friday, 9:40 P.M.
Mom and Dad have both been working
like crazy all week. Mom just got a huge

173

project at work—her firm is putting together a design proposal for the interior of the new wing at the Valley Mall. And Dad is defending Peter Santelli in his bribery trial.

It turns out that ten thousand dollars was deposited into his bank account early this week—but Mr. Santelli says he doesn't know how it got there. Dad believes him, and so do I. A lot of people don't. He might have to drop out of the mayoral race now. But things could get a lot worse than that—if this goes to trial and he gets convicted, Maria's father might go to prison!

Everything at home has been doom and gloom lately—with the tension crackling like lightning between my parents and with the depressing developments in Mr. Santelli's situation. I saw Todd on the school lawn after last period today, and he really was sweet. I'm lucky to have a boyfriend who cares about me enough to put up with my recent bad moods. He reminded me that we've had problems in our own relationship—and that we've managed to work through them. He convinced me that my parents could do the same.

As he drove me home from school, I thought of a small contribution I could make toward the relief effort. It's been ages since the family had a relaxing meal, with all of us together. So I decided that I would make a nice family dinner tonight. Too bad I didn't have a nice family to go with it.

I did all the work myself, so that no-body else would have to lift a finger. But Mom and Dad couldn't have cared less. . . .

The first problem was that Steven had a date with Cara, so he wasn't even going to be home for our evening of family togetherness. Still, I figured that the four of us could have a nice meal together. But Mom was supposed to be home from work by six-thirty, and she wasn't. By seven she still hadn't shown up. Ten minutes later Dad announced that it was time to eat.

"Shouldn't we wait for Mom?" Jessica asked. I wish she could have left it alone, but that's Jessica for you. Dad got this grim look on his face, but I ignored it and served dinner. I hadn't made any-thing fancy—just hamburgers. I'd thought that keeping the food simple would allow us to concen-trate on the conversation.

As it turned out, there wasn't any. For five min-utes all I could hear was forks clinking against stoneware. Then the back door burst open and Mom rushed in.

My mother looked a little frazzled, but she had a big smile on her face. When she saw that we were already eating, she glanced at her watch. "Oh, no!" she cried. "You poor things—you must have been famished!" She slipped out of her blazer, dropped her briefcase, and collapsed into a chair across from me. "I'm so sorry, but we went into a meeting at five, and I couldn't get away. Not even long enough to make a phone call."

Then she told us her good news: She had been selected to head the design team for the mall proposal! She started telling us all about it, and Jessica and I did our best to keep up our end of the conversation. Finally Mom noticed Dad's silence.

"Ned," she said, frowning suddenly, "you haven't said anything."

Dad came right out and told her that being team leader sounded too time-consuming. "I'm sorry to say this, Alice," he said, "but right now—especially with my commitment to Mr. Santelli—is it really such a good idea for you to be taking on this much extra work?"

My mother's face turned pink. "It will mean some extra work, Ned. But this is the kind of project I've dreamed of for years! You know that!"

Dad's expression was dark, but he kept his voice low. "Let's discuss this later, Alice," he said.

"There isn't anything to discuss," she replied. "I already told them I'd be happy to do it."

After a few minutes of dead silence, my mother took a deep breath and changed the subject. "How was work today, Ned?" she asked lightly.

Dad grunted. "Fine," he snapped.

Things only got worse from there. Mom reminded us all about the annual design firm outing on the senior partner's boat.

"This Sunday?" Dad asked. "I thought it was *next* Sunday."

My mother's eyes grew wide. "You know it's this Sunday, Ned," she said, her voice rising. "And you know how important it is for us all to be there!"

"Well, I'm afraid I have a conflict. I told Peter Santelli that I'd spend the entire weekend working with him on preparing his defense. The trial is due to start on Monday."

My mother blinked. "You didn't tell me the trial was starting so soon," she said. "At any rate, we have a commitment, Ned. It isn't going to look very good if we cancel out."

"*We* don't have to cancel out. *I* do," Dad insisted.

They went on in that same vein for a few more minutes, neither one budging an inch. Finally

Mom jumped to her feet and stormed out of the room.

Sometimes I'm so angry at both of them that I just want to scream! Can't they see what they're doing to each other? Can't they see what they're doing to me and Steven and Jessica? Why can't they just work things out?

Wednesday afternoon
Jessica's being manic. So what else is new? Sometimes she's as bummed out as I am about the fireworks between the "parental units" (as Winston Egbert likes to say). But an hour later I'll see my mirror image floating around the house like a helium balloon, with a big smile on her face.

I think my twin's giddier states are induced by this stupid teen party line she's been calling for the last few weeks. It's one of those gimmicky telephone things. You call and spend truckloads of money to chat with people you don't know. In fact, I can hear her in her bedroom right now, gabbing away with some guy whose voice she's fallen in love with. With her luck, he probably has pimples and belongs to the chess

178

club. That would sure disillusion her.

I warned her about how expensive those party lines can get. But you know Jessica! Live now, pay later. Well, I've got enough on my mind without worrying about the moment of truth when our next phone bill shows up. Though I hate to think of her doing anything that could make our parents more irritated than they already are.

Mom and Dad act like strangers. They're not fighting openly anymore. They're barely even talking. And when they do talk, they only say as much as they absolutely have to. Or they downright lie to each other. . . .

Last night before Mom came home from work, Dad told me and Jess that Mr. Santelli's trial was going very badly.

"It's going to be a tough case to win," he said, his forehead wrinkling. "There's a lot of incriminating evidence. Most of it is circumstantial, but I don't have anything solid to cast doubt on it. And the publicity because of the mayoral race only makes it worse."

I shook my head. "But I thought he was considered innocent until the prosecution proved him guilty," I said, which shows you how naive I can be.

"That's the way it's supposed to work," Dad said. "But in politics, it seems as if it's the other way around. *I* know Peter's honest. But how do you prove that somebody *didn't* take a bribe?"

A little while later Mom showed up. When she asked him about the trial, the whole case had miraculously turned itself around in the last ten minutes.

"Everything's great!" Dad lied. "All my prep work has paid off. Looks like an easy acquittal!"

Today I was supposed to see Todd after school. Lucky him. His big date with his girlfriend consisted of pushing a shopping cart around the supermarket for me. I felt bad about that, even though Todd was a good sport. But I had no choice, Diary. We hardly had any food left in the house. If I don't do the grocery shopping, who will?

Thursday morning
Last night I was so depressed about my parents that I called Todd and begged him to take me away from all this. So he picked me up and we drove to Miller's Point. We got to talking, and Todd said some pretty heavy stuff. It sorted of

freaked me out. It started as I tried to explain how my parents' problems are affecting me. . . .

I leaned against Todd's shoulder and gazed out the windshield at the night sky, trying to find exactly the right words to express what I was feeling. "It makes me worry about whether loving someone really is enough," I said. "I mean, my parents always had a good marriage. I didn't know that could evaporate so quickly."

"It probably hasn't evaporated at all," Todd said. "Everyone's relationship goes through tough times. I bet it will all blow over in a few weeks."

I shook my head. "That's what I thought at first," I said. "But Todd, it only gets worse! Did I tell you about breakfast this morning? Mom and Dad actually carried on a whole conversation by directing every comment through me, Jessica, and Steven. It was like they couldn't bear to talk to each other—not even about bank statements and furnace repairs! I've never seen them so cold to each other."

"That would never happen to us, you know," Todd said, squeezing my shoulder.

"But how do you *know?*" I asked. "How does anyone ever know for sure?"

"It's all a matter of keeping communication

channels open," Todd explained. "If you really work at it and care about each other, instead of being tied up with your jobs and other things, you can still have a good relationship. Even after twenty years of marriage, you and I will find the time every day to really *talk* to each other."

Suddenly his arm around my shoulders felt oppressive. *Marriage? Me and Todd?* I suddenly felt myself transported to Moon Beach the week before the surfing competition, as the water closed in over my head and nearly drowned me. I couldn't breathe.

I gulped hard. Then I pulled away from Todd and fiddled with the controls on the window.

Todd placed a hand on my arm. "Liz, what's wrong?"

"Marriage?" I asked in a quavering voice. "How can you even think about us getting married?"

Todd reeled as if I'd slapped him. "How could you *not* think about it?" he asked. "We've been dating for so long, and we've been through so much. I always just assumed—I thought we both assumed—that someday we would take that step. Haven't you ever even considered the idea?"

"Well, sure I have," I admitted. "But it's too far in the future to think seriously about it. And lately I'm not sure I ever want to get married," I said. "To anyone." I turned back to the window so he wouldn't see the tears that were forming in my eyes. "It's too risky."

"Elizabeth, you shouldn't feel that way. You can't let your parents' problems rule your own life. If we love each other, we'll find a way to make it work."

"My parents probably said that too," I pointed out. "And so did Enid's parents, and Lila's, and Amy Sutton's, and Aaron Dallas's . . . think of all the kids we know whose parents are divorced! Do you think all those couples started out any different from us? At one time they were all in love too. And look where it got them."

"I can't believe I'm hearing this," Todd said.

I looked at his forlorn expression and immediately felt sorry. It was true that I felt a huge weight bearing down on me when he talked about our getting married someday. But he'd been so sweet and understanding lately that I couldn't bear to hurt him. And we had years before we had to think seriously about a lifelong commitment.

"I'm sorry, Todd," I said. "I do love you, and I can't think of anyone else I'd rather be with— ever! But this is a rotten time for me to be thinking about marriage, even marriage way in the future."

Todd took a deep breath and nodded. "I'm disappointed to hear you talk this way," he said. "But I guess I understand—considering what you're going through at home." he said. "I think you'll change your mind once it all blows over."

"Maybe," I agreed. But I doubted it.

Sunday night
Todd hasn't said anything more about marriage, thank goodness. And he's still being incredibly nice to me. He knows how upset I've been, so he took me to the Lotus House for a nice Chinese dinner. I actually had an OK time—despite having vivid flashbacks of my "double date" there with Brett, Pierre, and Jessica Magenta Daniella Wakefield. Todd was a much more relaxing companion. And I didn't have to worry about making sure a beret was covering a blue streak in my hair!

By the end of dinner, Todd had me feeling much calmer about being an innocent bystander in the Wakefield Wars. Then the waitress brought out some fortune cookies. The slip of paper in mine read, Stay calm in troubled waters.

Is that ominous or what? As soon as I arrived home and said good night to Todd, I walked into the house to hear my parents yelling at each other.

What is happening to my family?

Tuesday

Last night I tried to plan another family-togetherness meal. I went all out this time— spaghetti and meatballs with my famous tomato-mushroom sauce. I shouldn't have bothered. It was even more of a disaster than last time.

Dad was depressed because the judge threw out Mr. Santelli's case today, without a ruling. I guess it's better than being found guilty, but now his name will never really be cleared in the minds of the public. His chances of being elected mayor are blown. And Dad's blaming himself for the judge's decision.

Mom was late again. And by the time seven o'clock rolled around, the spaghetti had turned into a big, gloppy mess. So Dad said we would just have to eat frozen dinners.

But the worst was his reaction when Mom rushed in a few minutes later and sprang her big news . . .

"Guess what!" my mother exclaimed, waving a

bottle of champagne. "We did it! We got the project!"

She was so excited that her proposal for the mall had been chosen that she didn't even notice Dad's stony expression. She threw her arms around him, despite the stack of frozen dinners he was holding. "Ned, I'm so happy!" she cried.

"You may be happy," Dad said in a voice that was colder than the frozen dinners in his hands. "But you're also extremely late, Alice."

She tried to apologize for not calling. And she seemed genuinely sympathetic when he told her that Mr. Santelli's case had been thrown out of court. But she also reminded him that she'd be working even longer hours now that she had won the mall contract.

"I'm glad you've gotten what you wanted, Alice," my father said in a low, controlled voice. Then he threw the frozen dinners onto the counter and stomped out of the kitchen.

Saturday evening

Dear Diary,

Today was as strange as they come.

I guess I should backtrack. The entire week was crummy!

Tuesday night Mr. Santelli called Dad to say he'd decided to drop out of the race. Mom's been too wrapped up in her design project to show Dad any sympathy. Jessica's so obsessed with Charlie, the mystery voice on the teen chat line, that she hardly notices any of us.

Mom got a car phone so she could be reached about the mall project at any time, anywhere. She didn't even tell anyone she bought it. When Dad saw the thing, he just stared at it as if it were accusing him of being a failure in life. The crowning touch was last night, at a big-deal reception of an attorneys' group Dad belongs to. The whole family went, and I hoped it would give my father a chance to feel good about his career. Instead, all his attorney friends ignored him and congratulated Mom on the mall project. We left early.

I'm happy that my mother's career is going so well. But I sure wish it could have happened at a time when Dad's wasn't at such a low point!

Then there was today. Todd and I were sitting in my backyard, having brunch by the pool. He was trying to be supportive, but I felt as if he were a million miles away. He keeps telling me that the situation isn't so bad and that I shouldn't feel so awful about my family. But it is bad. And I do feel awful. I know he means well, but *telling me not to feel the way I feel isn't a lot of help. It worked for a while, but as my parents' differences drag on, it gets harder and harder to believe that the problems will just go away.*

I guess it's not fair of me to expect that Todd could say anything that really would make a difference. I mean, there's nothing Todd can do to get my parents talking to each other again. All he can do is be a supportive boyfriend. And I know he's trying his best to be that.

After Todd left, I fled our "happy home" for the library. I always feel more peaceful when I'm surrounded by books.

And Diary, Jeffrey was there. . . .

I reached over my head to pull a volume of Emily Dickinson's poetry from the stacks. Through the open bookshelf, I caught a glimpse of blond hair and a familiar face.

"Jeffrey!" I exclaimed.

"Elizabeth?"

An instant later he was rounding the corner into my aisle. He looked as handsome as ever, with his soccer player's body and deep green eyes. But his eyes lit with concern as soon as he saw me. "How have you been?" he asked. "You look tense."

188

I led him deeper into the stacks, where nobody would overhear us.

"I'm all right," I told him.

"No, you're not," he said.

I laughed weakly. "No, I'm not," I agreed.

"I've been told I'm a good listener," he said with a smile.

"Wait a minute!" I said. "*I* was the one who told you that—it was that day on Jackson's Bluff, before my surfing competition."

"See? So I have it on good authority. Tell me what's wrong, Liz. I'm your friend, remember? I hate to see you upset. If Wilkins isn't treating you right—"

I shook my head. "No, it's not Todd. He's trying to help, but he can't seem to understand that the situation really is serious. It's not going to blow over."

"What situation?" Jeffrey asked, squeezing my arm.

I took a deep breath. I'd forgotten how easy Jeffrey was to talk to. "It's my parents."

Jeffrey raised his eyebrows. "Your folks have always been so cool," he said. "What's the problem? Are they giving you a hard time about something?"

"Nothing like that," I said. "Mom's career is taking off, and she's so obsessed with it that she's put the family on the back burner. That wouldn't be so

189

bad, except that Dad's in the dumps about the whole Santelli thing. I think he was already afraid that his career had stalled."

"That's rough," Jeffrey said. "Are they arguing a lot?"

"Some," I said. "And when they do, it's horrible—as though they don't even speak the same language. Most of the time they don't even talk to each other anymore."

Jeffrey leaned against a shelf of Chekhov plays. "And how do *you* feel about all this?"

"I'm not sure," I replied honestly. I was beginning to remember why I had loved Jeffrey so much. "I wish my mother would be more sensitive to my father's needs right now. And I wish he would show some support for her success."

"I see what you mean," Jeffrey said. "There are always two sides to any argument."

"Or *war*, in this case," I said. "You know, I can't get Jessica to understand that at all. Most of the time she sees our parents' feud as a great opportunity for her to ignore her chores and break the usual household rules. But when she does get upset, she seems to blame Mom for the whole thing!"

"And if I know you," Jeffrey said quietly, *"you're* too fair to take sides like that."

I nodded. "I can't take sides," I agreed. "But

I don't know if it's fairness. *Confusion,* more likely!" I covered my face with my hands. "I keep thinking there should be more that I can do to help!"

Jeffrey held me close for just a few seconds and patted my back. "You have every right to be confused," he said. "It's a confusing situation." Jeffrey stepped back and looked at my face. "The thing you have to accept is that this is a problem between your parents, Liz," he told me. "You didn't cause it. And there's nothing you can do to fix it— except loving and supporting them both, the way you always do."

"We were right," I told him. "You *are* a good listener."

I know, Diary: What Jeffrey said sounds so simple. But I didn't realize how badly I needed to hear it. I wanted to kiss him right there in the middle of the library!

Now I'm back home, trying to study the French and Indian War. But thoughts of the Ned and Alice War keep intervening. So do thoughts of Jeffrey. He was wonderful at the library today.

I hadn't realized how much Todd has been downplaying the problems between my parents—and downplaying my anxiety about it. I tell Todd what I'm feeling, and he gives me sympathy. But we don't really talk about it. Jeffrey gives me permission to confront my feelings. And trying to express them like that helps me to understand what's going on in my own mind. Does that make any sense?

Maybe I should prescribe a session with Jeffrey to both my parents!

Seeing him today made me wonder: What would my life would be like if Todd still lived in Burlington and Jeffrey and I were still a couple?

After Jeffrey left the library, my mind raced back to a night on the beach before Todd moved back to town. The sea breeze was warm, and the sky overhead was like velvet. Jeffrey's arm encircled my waist, and I nuzzled against his shoulder. When we kissed, I felt as if we were rocking gently on the waves and then flying through the starlit night.

Diary, I wonder if Jeffrey still remembers that night. I wonder if he ever thinks about me and what we used to be to each other.

Here's a snatch of a poem I'm working on:

> *Do you still love me*
> *as you did*
> *the night the stars sang*
> *to the ocean*
> *and my heart swelled*
> *like the tide?*

Oh, gosh, Diary, I have no business writing things like that! In a way, I'll always feel affection for Jeffrey. But Todd is my real love. My one love. So what was I thinking?

Sunday afternoon

I can't believe what Jessica just told me. She says that Bruce Patman's father just asked our father to run for mayor! Could it be true? Or is Jessica exaggerating some innocent comment she overheard?

I know that Mr. Patman and another man stopped by a little while ago to see Dad. Mr. Patman is one of the richest men in town. He's got a lot of influence in political and business circles. After the two men left, Dad said he needed to talk to Mom about something. But she was just jumping into the car to go to the office (yes, on a Sunday). He snapped at her about working on the weekend and said he would talk to her some other time.

I've sworn Jessica to secrecy. It will only make matters worse between them if Mom finds out something like this from us before Dad tells her himself—if what Jessica thinks she heard is really true.

Tuesday, 11:00 P.M.

Jessica's upset about our annual family trip to Lake Tahoe, coming up this weekend. We usually stay in a cabin with no phone. She may suffer from withdrawal symptoms if she has to spend a whole weekend without talking on the teen party line.

Personally, I can't wait for this weekend. A few days alone in the woods is just what our family needs. Unfortunately, Mom is starting to talk as if she can't spare the time for us. . . .

"I don't see how I'm going to manage to juggle everything," my mother said, as if the long-awaited weekend was just one more burdensome obligation. "Everyone else in the group is planning to work this weekend. I wonder—"

I felt an alarm buzzer go off in my head. "Mom!" I wailed, sounding about seven years old. "You can't back out of the trip. You need a vacation. We all do!"

"Oh, sweetheart, I know," my mother said. "But I'm really buried in this stuff. I'm not sure it's a good idea for me to go away for the whole weekend. Maybe if I came up a day later than the rest of you—"

"Alice," my father interrupted in a no-nonsense voice, "there are other things in life besides work."

Mom bit her lip. "I'm sure I can get through most of this by Friday, anyway," she said.

"And another thing," Dad reminded her. "We're going to have an understanding before we even set foot out the door on Friday: no work up in the mountains. The point of this weekend is to spend time together as a family, right?"

Mom agreed, but she sounded tentative. I'm scared, Diary. My intuition tells me that this weekend in Tahoe is my parents' last chance to salvage this family. Maybe I'm being too melodramatic. But I really believe that everything depends on it.

I hope they don't mess it up.

Wednesday night

I convinced Mom's assistant to tell Mom that she has to go this weekend. It wasn't easy. Julia called to leave Mom a message this afternoon, and I found out that Mom hadn't even told her coworkers about our trip! Once Julia knew about it, she wanted to tell Mom they couldn't possibly get along without her for three days! That would have made up Mom's mind for her real fast.

I had to think quickly. And I ended up violating a sacred law of Wakefield vacations: I gave Julia the phone number of the inn near the cabin we'll be staying in. I didn't want to, but it was the only way I could get her to agree to make Mom go.

I hope I did the right thing. No, I'm sure I did the right thing. Dad would freak if he knew I was giving out that phone number. But he'd be a lot more ticked off if Mom canceled out on our trip. Now I'm keeping my fingers crossed for a real family weekend. I just know it's going to be great.

Sunday night

We arrived at the cabin Friday evening,

*and everything started out like a dream.
All five of us took a swim in the lake as
soon as we got there. And Mom and Dad
were actually talking to each other. OK, so
they weren't talking about anything more
important than pine needles and grilled
fish. But it was a start.*

*That warm, fuzzy feeling lasted about an
hour. Then the cold pricklies took over. . . .*

We were all hanging out by the grill, putting
dinner together. That's when Jessica opened her
big, fat mouth. "This place is beautiful, isn't it?" she
said, slipping a sweatshirt over her head. "Daddy,
don't you think Sweet Valley needs a beautiful inn
and cabins like this? Maybe when you run for
mayor—"

I poked her in the ribs—not nearly as hard as I
wanted to. Dad dropped the charcoal with a loud
thud. And Mom and Steven stared, open-mouthed,
from Jessica's face to Dad's.

"Whoops," Jessica said with a nervous giggle.

"How on earth—" Dad began.

But Mom's voice rose above both of their com-
ments. "Run for mayor? What are you talking
about, Jessica?"

"I haven't the faintest idea where you heard
that, Jessica," Dad said. "But I haven't made any

decisions yet about whether or not to run."

"I can't believe this!" Mom said, her voice full of hurt and bitterness. "Do you mean to say that you are seriously considering running for mayor— and that I don't even know about it? Did you plan on mentioning it to me? Or were you just going to save it as a surprise?"

I was shocked that he hadn't told her himself. It had been almost a week since Mr. Patman talked to Dad. I'd just assumed that my parents had discussed it in private but hadn't made a decision.

"Alice, I tried to find time to talk to you," Dad said wearily. "But you've been so busy."

"That's preposterous!" Mom cried. "I know I've been busy, but you could have told me how important it was that we talk. You could have said *something*." She looked pale, and I felt horrible for her. But my sympathy ebbed a bit when she lashed out at Dad a moment later. "I think it's a ludicrous idea!" she announced. "You don't have any political experience. Who even suggested that you think about it?"

Naturally, that made Dad angry too. So he yelled back at her about how qualified he was and how Mr. Patman seemed to think he was right for the job. And then they both clammed up and hardly said a word for the rest of the night—except for when he caught her going through some of the mall files she wasn't supposed to have brought with her. You can bet he had a few choice words for her then!

Saturday morning Mom didn't want to come canoeing with the rest of us. I guess she and Dad were still at war over the mayor thing. But I decided to make the best of it, and the canoe trip turned out to be fun. We got back to the cabin to find that Mom had prepared a picnic lunch for us all—a peace offering, it seemed.

For a few minutes I thought we really would still have the relaxing weekend we needed so badly. Mom and Dad started talking to each other. And Dad began to say he would probably turn down the mayoral nomination because it would take him away from the family too much. It seemed that they had reached a truce. Then the hostilities resumed.

A boy about my age pedaled a bicycle down the path. I noticed Jessica appraising him and could almost hear a "too geeky" verdict in her head.

"Mrs. Wakefield?" the boy asked, puffing from the exertion. "I'm from the main inn—I'm the owner's son—and my dad asked me to tell you there's a telephone call for you. They say it's urgent."

A knot formed in the pit of my stomach.

"Urgent?" my mother asked. "Who could possibly be calling me here?"

Dad had been passing paper napkins around the table. Now he stopped, and I could see his jaw tensing. "I thought we agreed we wouldn't tell a soul where we were going to be," he said evenly. His face was reddening.

"We did," my mother answered. "And I didn't. Nobody knew."

"They said it had to do with some sort of design project," the messenger said, glancing uncertainly from one adult to the other.

Dad slowly crumpled the napkin in his hand until it formed a small, tight ball. When he threw it down on the table, I felt as if he were unleashing something dark and ugly. "Great, Alice," he said bitterly. "Thanks a lot for honoring our promise! It's not bad enough that your job is ruining life at home. Now it has to ruin our life here too!"

The messenger's mouth dropped open. Mom rescued him. "Go on ahead," she told the boy. "Tell them I'll be there as fast as I can." But her eyes were blazing. Her face had gone completely white.

Later I confessed to Mom that I was the one who had given Julia the phone number. She told me not to worry about it—that none of this was my fault. But I still feel responsible. And most of all, I didn't want Dad blaming her for Julia's phone call.

I'd like to say that the weekend only got better from that point on. But the truth, Diary, is that it got worse. Much worse . . .

We all went horseback riding on Sunday morning, but Mom got another call from Julia. When she caught up with us on the trail later, it was only to say that she would have to ride back to the inn and catch a bus back home.

My father's eyes filled with fury, and he blasted her. "It's astonishing to me to see how little respect you have for this family right now, Alice!" he barked. His chestnut horse did a nervous little dance beneath him, and Dad jerked on the reins. "You've always been the one who's said that family commitments come first."

"They do come first!" my mother cried. "But I can't abandon the design team, either. They need me!"

My eyes filled with hot, stinging tears. "We need you too, Mom," I choked out.

"Look," she replied, "I've asked all of you before, and I'm going to ask you again. I have to work extra hard now that my firm has been chosen for this project. I need your support and patience right now. I don't like being apart any more than you do."

Dad opened his mouth to say something, but Mom didn't give him the chance.

"I have to go now," she continued firmly. "I'm going to ride back to the inn and let them take the horse for me. Mrs. Jenkins said she'd give me a ride to the cabin to get my things."

My father could rein in his horse but not his emotions. "I'm sorry I even bothered to worry about how running for mayor would affect the family!" he said in an accusing tone. "Since you obviously couldn't care less, why should I?"

I gasped. It was hard enough to believe that such terrible things could come out of my parents' mouths. But it was *impossible* to believe that my mom and dad would talk that way in front of us kids.

"For your information, Alice," he continued in a cold, hard voice, "you're not going to be the only one with extraordinary commitments anymore. I'm going to tell Henry Patman that the answer is yes. I'll run for mayor! So what if I won't be home anymore? It obviously won't make any difference at all to you!"

My ears were ringing. Breakfast churned in my stomach. Steven, Jessica, and I all stared at each other. Despite the amount of sun we'd gotten that weekend, my brother and sister were both as pale as ivory. Neither of my parents seemed to remember that we were there.

"Do whatever you please!" my mother retorted. "I'll see you tonight at home."

"Alice, if you take off right now, you're doing more than just walking out on a weekend," Dad warned. "You're walking out on me and the kids too. Why don't you just stop and think for a second what that means."

I held my breath.

"Are you threatening me?" my mom asked, outraged.

Dad's voice became very quiet, but his words were chilling. "All I'm saying is that I can't stand this anymore," he said. "If you leave now, you're leaving me. You're leaving our marriage."

The world seemed to spin. "Mom, don't!" I screamed.

With one last look at the man she'd been married to for twenty years, my mother turned her horse around and cantered away from her family.

That's the end of the story. It might also be the end of the Wakefield family. My parents are separating! And it's all my fault! I cried all the way home from Tahoe. I feel so guilty and so helpless. Why did I give Julia that phone number? How could I have been so stupid? Will my family ever forgive me, once they know the truth? I'm afraid to admit to them that I was the one who screwed up. Mom says she forgives

203

me, but I think she's just trying to be nice.

Can I ever forgive myself?

Saturday morning

My family was horseback riding together this morning, in a honeysuckle-scented glade filled with birdsong. Sunlight danced in my mother's hair. She galloped toward Dad on a graceful white horse, its mane streaming in the wind. And love shone through Dad's eyes as his own mount raced to meet her. The horses slowed to a walk and then stopped, touching noses. My parents dismounted, with joyful smiles on their faces. They ran to each other and embraced. Then they reached out their arms to envelop me and Steven and Jessica—and, for some reason, the messenger boy on the bicycle. The sun was warm on my face, and I couldn't stop grinning.

Unfortunately, that was only a dream. In reality, it's drizzling outside. And my father is moving out of the house today.

Saturday night, late

Dear Diary,

I'm the worst person on the face of the

planet. Not only did I drive my parents
apart, but I also cheated on Todd!

I want to run somewhere far, far away
and never come back. I don't deserve to
have people around who care about me. All
I can do is hurt them. . . .

It was the worst day of my life. Mom left the
house at the crack of dawn, as if she wanted to
walk out on Dad before he had the chance to walk
out on her. By the time I woke up, he was all
packed, with stacks of boxes and a few odd pieces
of furniture waiting in the garage to load into his
own car and Steven's. The three of us went along
with him to his new apartment.

Dad's place isn't far away, Diary. But
it might as well be in China. Or
Burlington, Vermont. It's small and sterile
and totally unhomelike. I couldn't bear to
leave him there. But he said he had plenty
to keep himself occupied, with his mayo-
ral campaign. Jessica and Steven had to
drag me out of the place.

Jessica mystified me all day long. "It's
not the end of the world," she said philo-
sophically this morning. She even had the
nerve to suggest that it would be fun to

visit him in his own apartment. Fun? My sister is a psycho.

By evening I just wanted the day to end so I could lose myself in sleep. But Todd was over, watching a rented video with me. Except that I wasn't paying much attention to him or the movie. . . .

"Are you going to tell me what you're thinking?" Todd asked. "Or do I need ESP?"

I put a handful of popcorn in my mouth to keep from having to answer him. It was cheddar cheese flavor, my favorite. But even my taste buds were depressed; it might as well have been that foam stuff that shipping companies use as packing material.

Todd was staring at me, waiting for an answer. But my eyes filled with tears, and I just shook my head. What was there to say?

Todd reached for the remote control. "Listen, you don't want to watch this junk," he said, flicking off the movie. "Tell me what you're feeling instead."

I stared at the television screen, even though it had gone dark. "You want to know the truth, Todd?" I asked finally, slowly. "What I really feel—way deep down—is guilty."

"What could you possibly have to feel guilty about?" he demanded.

"A lot of stuff . . . ," I began, but my voice trailed off. I could admit in the pages of my diary that I was responsible for my parents' ruined marriage, but I couldn't admit it out loud. I couldn't force the words out. So instead, I shook my head and pushed my boyfriend away. "I can't describe it," I told him. "Never mind."

Todd looked hurt, and I hated to make him miserable too. But I couldn't bear to hear myself say that my parents' separation was my fault. And I was afraid that Todd wouldn't love me anymore if he knew the truth about me.

Todd left early, and I tried to go to bed. But it was only eight-thirty, and I kept tossing and twisting until the sheet was wrapped around me like a rope. Finally I gave up. I jumped to my feet and paced back and forth across my room. I needed someone to talk to. Someone who would sympathize, but who had enough distance from my family to say sensible things back to me. Someone whose love I didn't have to fear losing.

I reached for the phone, ready to punch in Enid's number. But Jessica's voice protested at me through the receiver. She was probably talking to Charlie and the rest of the teens on that stupid chat line of hers. I slammed down the receiver. Then I realized that it didn't matter if I called or not. Enid, I remembered, was visiting her aunt.

Suddenly I knew who I could talk to: Jeffrey. But did I dare? After all, *I* was the one who had dumped *him*. Running into each other at the mall or at the library was one thing. But after what I'd done to him, was it right for me to seek out my former boyfriend when I needed a shoulder to cry on? What if I called Jeffrey and he told me not to come?

I shook my head. Whether to call first was a moot point. The only way to get Jessica off the phone would be to wrestle her to the ground. And I didn't have the energy to start another Wakefield War. I decided to drive to Jeffrey's house unannounced. He could decide whether to let me in or turn me away.

"Elizabeth!" Jeffrey exclaimed when he opened the door. He was clearly surprised to see me.

But one look at my anguished face was enough. Without saying another word, he pulled me close and held me for a few seconds.

"My parents are home," he warned apologetically, after I'd collected myself. "And I have a hunch you'd rather talk in private. Come around back with me. I know a place where we can be alone."

A few minutes later we stood on the edge of the woods behind Jeffrey's house. "Voilà!" he said with a flourish. "Welcome to my private counseling office."

I looked up to where he was pointing. "A tree house?"

Jeffrey shrugged. "I helped the two little boys next door build it. They said I could use the place anytime I want to."

For the first time in what seemed like weeks, I actually laughed. "You're kidding!" I said.

"No, I'm not!" Jeffrey said, grinning. "I really did help build it—the floor and ceiling, at least. Andrew and Nick did the walls themselves." The outside lights from nearby houses cast a faint glow, dimly illuminating the tree house. The triangular platform nestled between three trees, about eight feet off the ground. Another platform six feet above it formed a roof, and a patchwork of scrap plywood, cardboard, and various unidentified materials enclosed two sides.

"It's good to see you smile," Jeffrey said. And suddenly I knew why he'd suggested the tree house as a meeting place. He knew the oddity of it would lighten my mood. "But we really don't have to go up there if you'd rather not."

"No!" I said, touched. "I think a tree house is a great idea. So what if it's a little surreal? So is everything else about my life lately."

Jeffrey gestured to the wooden rungs that were nailed to a thick tree trunk. "After you, Ms. Wakefield," he said. "But be sure you wipe your feet before you walk in the grand front entrance. The butler would be so distressed if he had to polish the floors again."

A few minutes later I was sitting on Jeffrey's sturdy wooden platform with my back against a tree—which seemed safer than leaning against Andrew and Nick's so-called walls. After admiring Jeffrey's handiwork, I lapsed into silence, grateful that the darkness would hide my tears. Jeffrey sat with me for several minutes, not saying a word. But it was a comfortable, friendly silence—not like the cold, forbidding silences that had become business as usual back home on Calico Drive.

Thinking about home made my tears flow more freely, and I couldn't hold back a sob. When Jeffrey grasped my hand, I realized how badly I'd missed the feel of his strong, callused fingers enveloping my smooth, slender ones. It seemed so natural, having him hold my hand. In a funny way, sitting alone with him in that strange little tree house, I felt more at home than I had felt lately in my family's four-bedroom split-level.

When I managed to stop crying again, Jeffrey encouraged me to talk. So I did. I told him about Julia and her phone calls to the inn at Lake Tahoe. I described my parents' final argument during the horse-back ride—and my father's ultimatum. And I broke down when I talked about leaving my dad alone in a one-bedroom

*apartment that looked as if nobody had
ever lived in it.*

As always, Jeffrey listened to me. I mean *really*
listened. He asked questions, gently probing me to
tell him what I felt deep down. And he let me
know that it was OK for me to feel angry, frustrated, confused, and afraid.

"I'm no expert in this stuff," he acknowledged.
"But I remember trying to help Aaron hold himself
together during his parents' divorce. I know how
tough it can be on the kids." Aaron Dallas, another
soccer player, was Jeffrey's best friend. They'd
known each other from soccer camp even before
Jeffrey's family moved to California.

I nodded, remembering how Aaron had vented
his anger and frustration on me, Jeffrey, and anyone else who got within range. "I guess I understand a little better now why Aaron behaved the
way he did. I've had the urge to punch things lately
too," I admitted. "But I've held it in."

"Don't," he said simply.

"Don't punch things?" I asked. "Or don't hold
it in?"

"Don't suppress your feelings. If you feel like
punching something, lock your bedroom door and
whack your pillow until the feathers fly. You may
feel silly, but you'll definitely feel better."

I smiled through my tears. "I just might try that."

"Good," he said. "But I still don't understand why you think your parents' separation is your fault."

I banged my fist against the wooden floor. "Don't you see?" I exclaimed. I hadn't been able to admit to anyone else who was really responsible for my parents' separation. But with Jeffrey, I felt safe saying anything. And the fact that it was too dark to see his expression made it easier for me to admit the truth.

"I knew I wasn't supposed to give Julia the phone number at the inn, but I gave it to her anyway!" I said. "And then, because Julia called, my mom told my father she was going home. And *he* said that if she left Tahoe, she'd be leaving the marriage! *She left!*"

"That's right," Jeffrey said. "*He* gave her the ultimatum, and *she* cut her trip short. Liz, they both made their own decisions. You didn't have anything to do with it."

"If I hadn't given Julia the phone number, none of it would have happened," I said glumly.

I caught a slight movement in the dark as Jeffrey shrugged. "Maybe things wouldn't have happened in exactly the same way," he said. "But if it hadn't been that, it would have been something else. From what you say, this has been coming for at least a couple of months—and that's probably just the tip of the iceberg. In private, they've probably been having problems for a lot longer than that."

"But I should have—"

"From everything I've seen about kids in this kind of situation," Jeffrey said slowly, "it's perfectly normal for you to *feel* guilty. But you need to understand that you're *not* guilty. Of anything. You did everything you possibly could. It's not your fault that it wasn't enough."

"It should have been enough," I said faintly.

Jeffrey shook his head. "Liz, a lot more than one wrecked weekend went into your parents' decision to split up for a while. Nobody jeopardizes a twenty-year marriage because of a few badly timed phone calls!"

A few minutes later my ex-boyfriend preceded me down the ladderlike steps to solid earth. I followed carefully. But two feet above the ground, I reached down with my foot for the lowest rung—and missed it. Jeffrey caught me as I started to fall. He turned me quickly in his arms so I was facing him.

"Are you all right?" he asked. Now that we were outside again, the lights from nearby houses revealed the concern and tenderness in his face. When I looked into Jeffrey's eyes, the reality of my relationship with Todd melted away like mist. The months we'd been apart melted away too, and I could almost hear the crash of ocean waves, as I had the night Jeffrey kissed me on the beach, under the stars. I raised my lips to his, and we fell together in a passionate embrace full of the longing of all that time spent apart. All the time spent denying the emotions that neither of us had been able to banish from our hearts.

I could feel both our hearts pounding as we kissed under the trees. For those few minutes Jeffrey and I existed in our own private time and place. The forest was enchanted; anything was possible.

We both returned to earth at the same moment. We pulled apart and stared at each other, stunned and trembling. "We can't," I said, shaking my head. Tears cascaded down my face once more. This time I didn't try to stop them. "Jeffrey, we can't!"

He nodded. "I know," he whispered. "I know."

"Never again," I sobbed. "I'm sorry." Without looking back, I sped across Jeffrey's backyard, toward my car and home.

Thursday night
Everything's a mess. I screwed up my English paper on Othello. *At least Mr. Collins is letting me rewrite it. I got in trouble with the newspaper too. I totally forgot an interview I was supposed to do. Penny Ayala had to apologize for me. I*

can't concentrate in any of my classes.

And I keep pushing Todd away. So far he's been patient, but I think he's reaching his limits. To be honest, I'd almost welcome being single again. The way things are going, I'd probably just ruin our relationship eventually. It would be less painful to break it off now than to wait until we do something serious like getting married. Look at Mom and Dad.

I heard Mom crying in front of the television the other day, though she said she wasn't. And I miss Dad so much! With him gone from the house, I feel like a piece of myself has been torn out.

Steven defends Mom at every turn, and Jessica keeps running to Dad whenever Mom disciplines her or asks her to do a bit of work around the house. I've tried to support both parents. But nobody seems to notice—except Jessica, who accuses me of being a goody-two-shoes.

Speaking of Jessica, the phone bill came yesterday.

Yep, you guessed it. That party line of hers added up to more than three hundred dollars worth of calls! Jessica won't be getting an allowance again until she's sixty.

She's in the dumps about the money she owes Mom and Dad. But the fact that they're separated hardly seems to faze her at all. I don't know how she manages to go on gossiping with Lila and flirting with Charlie and practicing cheers with Amy, as though life is fine.

Life is not fine. Life is the pits.

Love is the pits. I remember an old rock song that captures my feelings on the subject exactly: "Love stinks."

Friday night

Dear Diary,

Todd and I are finished—just like my mom and dad! School let out early today because of a teachers' meeting. And Todd was waiting for me outside of English class.

He was leaning against a row of lockers with his jeans jacket slung over his shoulder. And for just a second I felt butterflies in my stomach, the way I'd felt when we first met. He was wearing the blue and wine plaid flannel shirt that usually makes my fingers itch to touch him. He was so cute and so sexy that for a few minutes I forgot that I don't believe in love anymore. . . .

216

"Hey, remember me?" he asked, giving me a hug. "I just thought I'd come charm you to death and see if I couldn't convince you to fall in love with me all over again."

"Todd, you're amazing," I said, and I really meant it. I fell into step beside him in the hallway. "I don't know what I would have done this past couple of weeks without you. Really."

"Good," Todd said with a grin. "That means I did the right thing buying tickets to see Sondra Gray at the Palace tonight."

Suddenly I felt that wave wash over my head again, as if I were drowning. "Tonight?" I asked him when I'd caught my breath.

"Yeah, tonight," he said, his eyes twinkling. "What's the matter? Do you have another date?"

I wasn't sure why I didn't want to go. Sondra Gray was one of my very favorite folk singers. But he hadn't even asked. He'd just taken it for granted that I'd want to go out with him.

I know I wasn't being fair, Diary. Todd and I have always had kind of an unspoken agreement to go out on Friday nights. I've always assumed it, the same as he did today. But I suddenly had this horrible memory of something pulling me down, down, down. I

217

*couldn't breathe, and I couldn't even re-
member who I was.*

*Then I had another mental image: my
mother sitting alone in front of the television set, sobbing. . . .*

"Todd, listen," I said abruptly. "I don't feel like
going out tonight. I've had a long week. And to be
honest, this is the first Friday since Dad moved
out, and . . . well, I don't know. I just don't think
it's right leaving my mom home by herself."

Todd was quiet for a moment, and I knew I'd
hurt him. "OK," he said at last. "I guess I'll see if I
can get a refund on the tickets. So what are you
going to do, Liz? Just hang out with your mom and
watch TV?"

"We'll think of something. I'm sorry, Todd.
But—"

Todd snapped his fingers. "Wait a minute!" he
said. "What if I can get an extra ticket? Then we
could ask your mom to come with us!"

I shook my head, annoyed. Why couldn't he get
it through his head that I just didn't feel up to a
night on the town? "No, thanks," I said, a little too
shortly. "Mom's going to be tired. And she wouldn't
enjoy the Palace anyway."

But he just wouldn't let up. Next he tried to get
me to go out with him on Saturday night. I told him

I needed to spend the weekend at home. Todd didn't buy it. He thought I needed time with him as well.

I swear, Diary, I suddenly felt as if Todd and I had taken on the parts of Ned and Alice Wakefield in the movie version of my future autobiography: Alice says this other part of her life is too important to neglect right now. Ned says it's not more important than spending time with him. Then comes the part when Ned asks Alice to make a choice—and she does. . . .

"What scares me," Todd said—raising his voice, although we were still standing in the bustling hallway at school—"is that I'm not sure anymore whether you even want my support! I can't tell if you want to stay with me or not. You don't confide in me anymore. I have the feeling that you'd rather go through all this on your own." He balled one hand into a fist and rammed it into his palm. "Do you want me around, Liz, or don't you?"

For a moment I felt dizzy and weak. I thought I would cry or scream or faint. I couldn't believe it was happening. Then my emotions went numb. Todd's words seemed unreal, as if I were sitting in the movie theater watching a movie about myself. A strange sense of calm blanketed me.

"You're right, Todd," I replied finally. "I have been acting like a jerk. I guess I've been kidding myself. I'm too confused right now to be in a relationship. I don't even know what I want anymore."

Todd's eyes got huge and scared. "You can't really mean that."

"You said it yourself, Todd. I'm too involved in what's going on with my family right now to have enough time for you. And let's face it—I haven't been myself lately." I took a deep breath. "You know what? I think I'm so scared about what's happening to my parents that I just don't feel ready to care about anyone. Not even someone as wonderful as you."

Todd blinked, as if he was trying not to cry. Deep inside of me, a tiny little voice asked if I knew what I was doing. But I did *know* it. I just didn't *feel* it. And that absence of feelings—of painful, confusing emotions—made me feel calm and lighter than air.

I'm not talking about a giddy, helium-balloon kind of buoyancy, Diary. It was more of a dried-up weariness, as if you could puff on me and I'd waft away in a hundred tired white fluffs, like dandelion seeds.

I think I did the right thing in speeding

up the inevitable failure of my relationship with Todd. In real life, there is no happily-ever-after; every love ends eventually.

Mr. Collins asked us today to think about why Shakespeare wrote a tragedy about marriage. Now I know what I'll say when I rewrite my essay: Shakespeare wrote *Othello* that way because marriage really is tragic. And I'm never, ever going to have a chapter about it in my own future.

Now pain and loneliness have replaced the nothingness I felt this afternoon. I know my decision is for the best. But my heart feels as though it just took a nosedive from a high altitude and smashed into the ground. Now it's lying on the pavement in a million glittering pieces.

And all the king's horses
and all the king's men
couldn't put Elizabeth together again.

Wednesday, 11:20 P.M.

Dear Diary,

I'm taking on the single life with a vengeance. It was Jessica's idea, really. I was telling her late last Friday night about breaking up with Todd, and she suggested that I play the field for a while.

"Why not?" I asked myself. Dating other guys would divert my mind from my family's problems. It would keep me from thinking about Todd—and Jeffrey, added that nagging little voice in my head. And it just might be fun, as long as I kept it light and decidedly unserious—no thoughts of love, no commitments, and no strings attached.

If you don't go too deep into the ocean, I figured, the undertow can't drag you down.

I wore a very Jessica-like denim miniskirt to school Monday. And it worked! Before first period ended, I already had a date with Paul Jeffries for that night. Enid warned me that Paul's a womanizer with a terrible reputation, but that seemed about right. I didn't deserve a boyfriend as sweet as Todd or one as wise as Jeffrey. Paul was fun. And that's all I was after.

Tuesday I had a date with Steve Anderson. Today I went to the beach with John Campbell. And I'm meeting Paul at the mall tomorrow!

To be totally honest, the novelty began to wear off by about the second date. I mean, all those first dates can get tedious—having to work through all the "So, I hear you're on the tennis team" conversations that you can't really avoid at that stage. It's not as comfortable as knowing what to expect from the guy you're with—being able to read each other's moods and thoughts. But the dating was absolutely necessary if I was going to make it through the next few weeks. It was helping me to avoid seeing both Todd and Jeffrey.

And it was helping me to avoid the truth I didn't want to face: that my parents split up because of me.

Jessica and Enid both seem worried about me. I can't blame Enid. I should be confiding in her more. She's my best friend, and she really does care. But it's easier not to be too close to anyone right now. As for Jessica, she's probably just jealous of all the dates I've had! I think I might even be out-Jessica-ing her in the last few days. Jess never did like sharing the spotlight.

Thursday evening

Dear Diary,

Today what was left of my life crashed and burned. Steven and Jessica confirmed what I've believed all along: Mom and Dad's separation was my fault. . . .

I arrived home to find my brother and sister both on the front doorstep, Steven reaching for his keys. I was surprised to see him home.

"Where have you been, Liz?" Jessica demanded. "Out with someone new? Or have you decided to take it easy and have just four dates this week?"

Frankly, I was stunned by how catty she sounded. "Wh-what?" I stammered.

Steven stared at her too. "Isn't that kind of out of line, Jessica—even for you?"

"I was at Enid's," I said pointedly.

"Well, all I know is that everyone's been talking about you at school," Jessica informed me. "It's one thing being on the rebound and going out on a date or two, but you've seen three different guys in the same week! People think . . . well, *you know*." She raised her eyebrows. "Maybe you should take it easy."

"You're the one who told me to play the field in the first place!" I protested.

"Playing the field is one thing. Going for all the players at the same time is another!"

Through the whole exchange, Steven had been staring back and forth between us, opening and closing his mouth like a guppy. "What happened to Todd?" he finally choked out.

"Todd and I broke up," I told him.

We all went inside, and Jessica jumped right back into it. "Even Amy Sutton thinks you've gone overboard," she told me in the front hallway.

I ignored her. "Steven, how did you manage to make it home again? It's so great to see you!" I was still trembling from my argument with Jessica, but I tried to pretend everything was normal.

"He came home to take care of Mom," Jessica said, an edge to her voice. "Didn't you, Steven? But he's forgotten that he ever had a father. Ask him when he last talked to Dad—even on the phone."

Steven looked Jessica right in the eye. "I've taken just about enough of this from you. If you say one more time that I haven't been in touch with Dad—"

"You haven't!" Jessica shrieked. "You're lying if you say you have!"

"Stop it, you two!" I begged. I tried to get them to see that it wasn't right to take sides. But my good intentions backfired in my face.

"And *you're* the perfect one, I suppose," Jessica said acidly. "Why should this time be any different from usual? I'm impulsive and Steven's stubborn, and only Elizabeth is perfectly reasonable." She glared at me. "Why don't you stop and listen to yourself for once? You sound so self-satisfied!"

"That's a really rude thing to say, Jess," Steven said. "You owe Liz an apology."

"I do not!" Jessica insisted. "I'm sick and tired

of Liz acting like she's so perfect all the time!"

"I don't act that way!"

"You do so!"

"Quit it, the two of you!" Steven yelled. "Can't you act your age? You're sixteen, not six."

It only kept getting worse. Steven told us the only reason he was coming home so often was that he didn't think Jessica and I were capable of getting along with each other and helping Mom out. And Jessica exploded at him about that.

"It's the two of *you* who are both acting like six-year-olds," I snapped at them. "Steven, you jump all over Jess. And Jess, you do the same to him. Can't we at least try to pretend to be a family, since we're all we have left?"

Jessica accused me of acting perfect again. And this time, Steven agreed. "Jessica's right, Liz," he said, shaking his head. "You shouldn't act so self-righteous."

I could feel my face turning red with anger. "Who's sounding self-righteous?" I asked.

"You are!" they screamed in unison.

"Cut it out," I muttered, barely able to control my voice. "I don't want to hear another accusation!"

"No one's accusing you," Jessica said. "In fact, we've been covering up your mistakes for weeks! No one ever mentions the fact that *you're* the one who gave our phone number at Lake Tahoe to Mom's assistant. You're the one who wrecked the weekend for all of us. If it weren't for you, Mom and Dad would probably still be together!"

We all stared at each other in shocked silence. My terrible secret was finally out in the open.

Steven turned to me with a puzzled frown. "Did you really do that?" he asked. "Why would you have given the phone number to Julia? Didn't Mom and Dad say they didn't want to be disturbed?"

I felt the color drain from my face. "I didn't . . . I mean, I had no idea. . . ."

"You just didn't think!" Jessica accused. "And it's thoughtless acts like that one that can destroy a family!"

Steven was still staring at me. "Well," he said uncomfortably, "I'm sure that wasn't such a big factor, Jess. Mom and Dad didn't split up because of that weekend. It isn't fair to make Liz feel rotten about it."

"But that's my point!" Jessica said. "Nobody makes her feel rotten about it. Everyone acts like it didn't even matter, when the truth is, it did! Look at poor Daddy. Here he'd gone to all that trouble to make sure the weekend was as great as it always used to be, and Mom got dragged away practically as soon as we arrived." She glared at me and just about spat out the last words: "All because of you!"

"It wasn't my fault!" I pleaded, trembling. "I didn't know that anyone from the office would actually call! And I had no idea Mom would have to leave early!"

Jessica shrugged. "Sure," she said. "Tell yourself whatever you want. But look what happened. Mom left Tahoe, and she and Dad decided to split." She snapped her fingers. "Just like that . . . the whole marriage was over. So don't go acting so perfect, Liz. You're the one who's to blame for this whole stupid mess!" Then Jessica burst into tears.

"I don't even know what to say," Steven whispered as he put his arm around her.

"She's ruined everything!" Jessica wailed.

I was crying by then too. But Steven made no move to comfort me. In fact, he and Jessica had turned away, as if nursing a private grief that didn't include me. I couldn't bear to watch. Instead, I turned around and ran upstairs.

I sat at my desk trying to calm my breathing, but tears were running down my face, and that same old drowning feeling washed over me again. This time there was no surfing instructor to rescue me from the wave, and no Jeffrey to squeeze my shoulder and say all the right things.

For a moment I actually heard Jeffrey's voice in my head: "A lot more than one wrecked weekend went into your parents' decision to split up. Nobody jeopardizes a twenty-year marriage because of a few phone calls."

But he was wrong. Jessica and Steven made that perfectly clear. I'm to blame for everything. I don't even deserve to live in the same house with the people whose lives I've ruined.

Friday night, late

I'm writing this from Enid's house. If my parents' separation is all my fault, then maybe they'll get back together if I'm not around. I wanted to take a bus to Dallas to stay with my aunt and uncle and cousin Jenny for a while—or to my grandparents' house in Michigan. But Enid begged me to come to her house for a few days instead.

Her mom was happy to let me stay, but she insisted that I let my parents know where I am. I did. Well, sort of. Enid helped me write a letter and drop off copies both at my father's apartment and at the house on Calico Drive. I'll transcribe the letter here.

229

"Dear Mom, Dad, Jessica, and Steven:
I want you to know how sorry I am for
what's happened. I know I'm to blame for
everything. I don't feel right living at home
now, as you can probably understand. But
please don't worry about me—I'm staying
with a friend, and I'm absolutely fine. I
promise I'll call you as soon as I feel ready.
I love you all—and again, I'm so, so sorry.
Love,
Elizabeth"

Friday night actually turned out to be fun.
Without telling Enid or her mother, I left the
phone off the hook so my family wouldn't be able
to get through to me. And Enid and I stayed up
way too late, watching videos and eating too much
popcorn. I had forgotten what it feels like to be in
a house that isn't full of tension.

Enid tried to talk to me about Todd. She said
he was still in love with me. But I'd seen him three
times that week with a cute red-haired sophomore
named Allison.

"It's better this way," I told Enid. "Look, what
possible good could have come out of my relationship with Todd? All that would happen is that we'd
break up when we went away to college!"

❀   ❀   ❀

Some kinds of pain are avoidable, Diary. And I mean to avoid them as much as I possibly can.

I bombed an English midterm today, on Othello and some other literature we've been reading this term. Mr. Collins asked us about the fragility of love, as seen by the different writers we've studied. The authors were all of the "better to have loved and lost than never to have loved at all" school of thought.

I couldn't think logically enough on the topic to put my thoughts to paper in class. But if I could have written that exam, I would have said that the authors were wrong. Love is fragile—so fragile that people shouldn't let themselves feel it, unless they know for certain they won't get hurt.

> *Saturday night*
> *Finally, a light at the end of the tunnel. I'm back home. . . .*

To my astonishment, the first person I saw when I walked into the house was my father.

"Liz!" he cried, lifting me off the ground in a big bear hug. "I'm so glad you're all right! You had me scared out of my wits," he whispered.

"I'm sorry we said that stuff to you, Liz," Steven apologized in a low voice after Dad put me down.

"You only said what you felt," I replied.

"That's not really true," he said. "I wasn't angry at you, but at the whole situation," Steven told me. "I didn't mean it."

Even though I still felt that the separation was my fault, everyone apologized to me, including Jessica.

"Listen," Dad said finally. "I guess we didn't handle this very well a few weeks back. Your mother and I were both so upset ourselves that we didn't do a very good job of talking it out with the three of you. Neither of us bothered to explain to you why we were temporarily separating."

Temporarily, I thought. Did that mean they might still get back together?

"Your mother and I knew we weren't getting along the way we wanted to. We knew we needed some time apart. And we thought this was the best way to handle it."

There were so many things I needed to know— so many questions I wanted to ask. But something told me that my parents didn't know the answers yet either.

"We're all just going to have to be patient with one another," Dad said, as if he'd read my mind. "But your mother and I both hope that all of you will be open about your feelings. It's only natural that every one of us will feel some guilt and anger about this. We just need to make sure we get those feelings out so we can deal with them. It's keeping them bottled up inside that makes us go crazy and start thinking things that aren't true," he said, looking at me.

I felt a wave of relief wash over me. "So you guys would have decided to live apart anyway . . . even if I hadn't given Julia the number of the place in Tahoe?"

My mom wrapped her arms around me. "Oh, sweetheart!" she cried. "You weren't to blame for anything! You were only trying your hardest to keep us together!"

For the first time in weeks, I didn't feel so numb anymore. And it hurt, like the prickly feeling in my foot when it's gone to sleep and begins tingling back to life. But at the same time I felt happy. I realized again just how much I loved my family. More than anything, I wanted my parents to live together again and to be happy.

It's strange, Diary, to think of my parents as independent people with lives of their own, outside of us kids—even outside of each other. I'm not responsible for everything that happens to them. And as relieved

*as that makes me feel, it also scares me—
because I have no control over what will
happen next. I can cook meals and buy the
groceries and be supernice to both of them
and refuse to take sides. But in the end,
none of it will factor into their decision to
get back together or remain apart.*

*I guess that means that my own life is
the only one I can control. And look what a
mess I've made of it! I miss Todd like crazy,
but after the way I behaved, I doubt he'll
ever want to see me again. Todd was no
more responsible for my parents' breakup
than I was, but I took it out on him—just
as surely as I took it out on myself. It
wasn't fair of me to resent him for not
being some sort of psychology expert. He
was trying his best to love me and support
me. And I wasn't giving him a chance.
Well, I made my bed (short-sheeted it, is
more like it)! Now I'm going to have to lie
in it.*

Sunday
*Jessica had another brainstorm today.
But I won't complain about this one—it
got me and Todd back together. . . .*

I thought Steven was a lunatic, the way he dragged me away from my studying this afternoon, insisting that I needed some fresh air. He wouldn't take no for an answer, so I let him shove me in his car. To be honest, I was a little curious about just where he was taking me, and why.

When we got to Secca Lake, I still had no idea what was going on.

"Over here," Steven said in a low voice, leading me to a stand of pine trees overlooking the picnic area. He pulled me behind a tree and pointed. My heart began to pound. Todd was sitting at the fourth picnic table. And *I* was with him!

Of course, I knew instantly that it wasn't me. (It's not for nothing that people say I'm a brain!) By the process of elimination, that meant it had to be Jessica. But why was Jessica sitting with Todd at Secca Lake? And why was she dressed exactly like me—with blue jeans and a white cotton sweater that my twin would have called boring under normal circumstances, and with her hair in a French braid, as mine was that day?

"Listen," Steven whispered.

"I was way too hasty," Jessica was saying in her impersonating-Elizabeth voice. "I think all the anxiety about my parents was what made me do it. And if you want to get back together . . . well, so do I!"

Todd's mouth dropped open. And for an instant I was horrified. How could Jessica humiliate me this way? She'd come crawling back to Todd, pretending to be me. And now he would let her have it, assuring her that he never wanted to see her—or me—again.

"I want to go to the costume party with you," Jessica told him.

"Liz, I can't believe my ears!" he said. "That's wonderful. I mean, well, of course I want to get back together with you! I love you more than anything in the world!"

Tears gathered in my eyes. Todd wasn't the only one who couldn't believe his ears! And I felt such overwhelming gratitude toward my brother and sister that I hugged Steven as tightly as I could.

Suddenly Jessica jumped up from the table under the pretense of needing to get something from the car. She grabbed my hand as she rounded the clump of trees. "Liz," she whispered, squeezing it tight, "he's waiting for you."

I hugged Jessica and then hugged Steven again. Then I thanked them both. Steven handed me a long-stemmed red rose and gave me a little push toward Todd.

"So," I heard my sister whisper as I slowly walked toward my boyfriend, "all's well that ends well."

I'm happy that I'm back with Todd, Diary. But I'm not so sure that all's well. I'm not even sure that the mess between us has ended. Even as Todd held me close this afternoon, I couldn't help thinking of Jeffrey. And as we discussed our plans to go to the Pi Beta Alpha costume party next Friday, I couldn't help wishing I were going with Jeffrey.

Am I a terrible person, Diary? Is it awful of me to want to have two terrific guys? I know, after the last few weeks, that I can't live without Todd. But I also know that I can't stop thinking about Jeffrey. I love them both. And I have no idea what to do about it.

Friday night
Tonight started out just as I'd planned. Todd and I went to the PBA dance, dressed as Romeo and Juliet. And I really did have a good time with him. Jessica, on the other hand, was less than thrilled with her evening. Another one of her so-called brilliant schemes blew up in her face. She finally met Charlie, the guy from the teen party line, but he was more interested in her friend Amy. . . .

"I've had it with men!" Jessica confided in me at the dance. Her hair was covered with silver stuff for her intergalactic-princess outfit, and she impatiently yanked off the foil and crumpled it in her hand. "From now on, I'm going to be a completely different person," she vowed. "No more phone lines or dating agencies or crushes or any of that stuff! It's too big a waste of time."

Todd and I just looked at each other and grinned. Jessica had given up men before. Generally it lasted about as long as it took for her to catch sight of another attractive one.

This time, she said, she would devote herself to politics instead. Dad's mayoral race was in full swing, and she knew he would need all the help we could provide.

> *But Jessica's announcement was not the most surprising event of the evening. I'm afraid that I'm about to do something very wrong, Diary. Very, very wrong . . .*

After the dance, Todd and I stopped at the Dairi Burger for a snack. And there in a corner booth, sitting all by himself, was Jeffrey.

Our eyes met as I walked behind Todd toward our favorite table. I held Jeffrey's green-eyed gaze for a long moment, my mind replaying the memory of our kiss beneath the tree house and the stars. I don't think Todd noticed Jeffrey sitting there. And I didn't want him to. When we reached our table, I made sure that Todd's back was to Jeffrey's table. I didn't look at Jeffrey again, but I was conscious of his eyes on me while Todd and I ordered french fries and root beer.

As I made conversation with Todd, I tried to imagine what Jeffrey was seeing and thinking. Todd and I were dressed as Romeo and Juliet. We moved together and talked together with an ease that screamed out: *We're a couple!* Even a stranger would have picked up on it. At one point Todd took my hand across the tabletop. But I thought of Jeffrey's watching eyes, and I let go of Todd's hand as soon as I could.

"Elizabeth, is there something wrong?" Todd asked.

I smiled weakly at him. "Nothing new," I said honestly, looking down at my hands.

He patted my shoulder. "You know that there's nothing you can do about the situation at home right now," he reminded me. "Your parents will work it out on their own."

I nodded, relieved that he hadn't guessed the truth about my preoccupation.

When Todd left to call his folks a half hour

239

later, I looked up across the tables between us, into Jeffrey's face. We held each other's gaze for a full minute, and I realized that I was holding my breath as well. Jeffrey stood up resolutely, threw a few bills on his table, and walked toward me.

He paused at my table for the briefest of moments. As he did, he placed a hand on my shoulder. He started to pull it away and move on, but I surprised myself by calling him back. "Jeffrey," I said. The nearby booths were empty, but I lowered my voice to a whisper. "I want to see you," I blurted out, shocked to hear the words coming out of my own mouth.

Jeffrey stopped and looked at me, his eyes full of anxiety and hope. He bit his lip and nodded. "Me too," he said.

I yearned to touch him—to take his hand in mine and squeeze it hard. But I knew that I couldn't. Not in public. I adjusted the wimple of my Juliet costume instead.

"Meet me at Miller's Point in an hour," he suggested, his eyes full of meaning.

My heart was pounding so hard I knew it must be drowning out the Jamie Peters song on the jukebox. I glanced up at Jeffrey's handsome features and soft blond hair. Then I quickly looked down at the table.

"Think about it," Jeffrey said gently. "If you decide not to meet me, I'll live with it," he whispered, bending down low. "But I can't take any more of this yes-and-no stuff between us. If you don't come tonight, I'll take that as your final decision. And I'll never bother you again."

He straightened quickly and walked out of the restaurant. And I plastered a smile on my face in preparation for Todd's return.

> *Todd took me home a few minutes later. At my front door, I gave him a quick kiss and pretended to be tired, to make him leave. Then I changed out of that medieval torture chamber I called a costume. Now I'm sitting at my desk, debating with myself about whether to go to Miller's Point to meet Jeffrey.*
>
> *But I have to go. I have no choice. From the moment Jeffrey touched my shoulder in the restaurant tonight, I knew I would see him again. I hope I'm not about to do something that I'm going to regret. . . .*

> *Saturday, 8:00 A.M.*
> *As soon as I opened my eyes this morning, I knew that last night was the biggest mistake of my life. . . .*

I arrived at Miller's Point ten minutes late. I was terrified that Jeffrey had already given up on me and left. But through the shadows, I could make out the shape of his car, parked under the trees.

When Jeffrey leaned across the seat to open the door of his car, light spilled across the interior. "Get in," he said, his voice rough with emotion.

For several long minutes we sat in silence, gazing at the view. The lights of Sweet Valley sparkled in the canyon below, and it was hard to tell where the town ended and the starlit sky began. Those same stars had wheeled above us on that long-ago night when we kissed on the beach.

"What do you really want, Elizabeth?" Jeffrey finally asked.

I shook my head. "I don't know," I whispered tearfully.

Jeffrey's hand rested on my shoulder, and from it, warmth seemed to spread through my entire body. "I think maybe you do know, deep down," he said.

As usual, Jeffrey was right. "I want Todd," I admitted, as much to remind myself as to tell Jeffrey the truth. "I love him so much, Jeffrey."

"Is that all you're feeling right now?" he asked quietly, brushing a hand against the side of my face.

I shook my head again. "No, of course not," I told him. "I want you, too Jeffrey. I don't know how to explain it. Todd is so important to me. My life would be empty without him. But there's another part of me that he can't seem to reach—a part that needs *you*."

Jeffrey smiled. "That's about what I figured," he said. My tears were falling like raindrops now. "Liz, I can't bear to see you so miserable," he said, holding his arms out as if to hug me. "Let me help you."

I shook my head. "No!" I cried. "It's wrong, Jeffrey, and we both know it. It was wrong for us to get carried away that night under the tree house, and it's wrong for me even to be here now. I should just go home," I added. But I made no motion to leave the car.

"I love you, Elizabeth," Jeffrey said, taking my face in his hands. "I never stopped loving you, and I never will."

"But Todd—" I began.

"Todd isn't here right now," Jeffrey said. "Only you and I are here. And you can say that it's wrong. But all I know is that nothing ever felt so right."

He pulled me close and hugged me to his chest. At first I tensed up, but then I felt his heart beating against mine, and I smelled his aftershave. All thoughts of Todd vanished—as if he'd never moved back to California. When Jeffrey and I kissed, it was as if we were the only two people on earth. Something melted deep inside me, and a delicious warmth washed over my body. We kissed for a long, long time.

When we finally pulled apart, Jeffrey and I gazed steadily into each other's eyes.

"I have to see you again," he said in a husky voice. "I don't care how or where, but I have to see you."

I meant to tell him no—that it was risky, that it was wrong. But when I opened my mouth, something entirely different came out. "So do I," I said. I held his gaze for another moment, until that warm, tingling feeling started up again. If I stayed in that car one minute longer, I knew I would once again bury myself in his embrace. Instead, I tore my eyes from his, jumped out of the car, and stumbled back to the Fiat.

His car was still there—a dark, motionless blob in my rearview mirror—as I sped away toward home.

I can't stand myself, Diary. I'm being cruel and unfair to both Jeffrey and Todd. I have to end this deceitful chapter in my life. No more Jeffrey! I won't even look at him or talk to him in school. And I'll never allow us to be alone together—not ever again. It's too risky, Diary. I don't know how I'll find the strength to avoid him. But it's the only way—because I know I don't have the strength to resist the look of love in his eyes.

Actually, that's not going to work. I have to see Jeffrey one last time. And I have to see him alone. I have to tell him that there can't be anything between us, not ever again. After the way I've led him on, I owe him at least that much honesty.

Wednesday night

Working on Dad's mayoral campaign is a great learning experience. Maria Santelli has been wonderful about helping me and Jessica stuff envelopes and make phone calls down at campaign headquarters. It must be weird for her, after her own father had to drop out of the race. And I know that a lot of kids at school are still giving her a hard time about it. But she says that my dad is working for the same things her dad was working for—protecting the environment and helping the poor. I think she's doing the right thing.

Jessica had some ridiculous idea about setting my dad up with Amanda Mason, an attorney who's working on the campaign. Luckily, it turned out that Amanda is engaged to be married. So now Jessica is scouting around for another woman to take Mom's place in Dad's heart.

And here I am, trying my hardest to get my parents back together. I admit that I've done some scheming of my own, setting up "accidental" meetings and phone calls between the two of them—so far with no luck. But Jessica is just as determined to help both our parents find new love interests. She says there's no way they're going to reunite and that I might as well admit it and help them get on with their lives.

The one person I don't like at campaign headquarters is Mr. Knapp, the man who came to the house with Mr. Patman to convince Dad to run. The guy gives me the creeps. He's insensitive and too ambitious, and I don't think he really cares about the issues Dad believes in. He worked on Maria's father's campaign, and she doesn't trust him either—though he does know a lot about politics.

Jessica says we're being paranoid and that anyone as rich as Mr. Knapp can't be all bad. My sister's logic is awe-inspiring. As far as I can see, the only good thing about Mr. Knapp is his nephew, Terry, who's also helping my dad get elected. Terry is about *our age. And he can't stand his uncle either!*

On another thorny subject, I'm meeting Jeffrey after school tomorrow. It won't be pretty.

I walked around the side of Jeffrey's house, my legs trembling with every step. He'd said he'd be waiting in the tree house for me. But I knew he'd misunderstood my reasons for wanting privacy.

"Jeffrey!" I called up the ladder when I reached the structure on the edge of the woods.

His face appeared above me, and I steeled myself against the warm, tender feeling that rose up inside of me at the sight of the tree-filtered sunlight dappling his hair. I took a deep breath and climbed toward him.

When I reached the platform, Jeffrey reached out his arms to embrace me, but I shook my head. I sat down heavily, my back against a tree trunk. Jeffrey crouched beside me, a concerned look on his face.

"I can't see you anymore," I blurted out.

"But you have to!" Jeffrey pleaded. "I mean . . . don't you love me?"

I nodded, feeling the tears forming behind my eyes. "I do," I said. "That's why I can't see you anymore."

"That makes a lot of sense," Jeffrey said. "And if

you didn't love me—what then? It would be OK for us to see each other?"

"Yes!" I said. "I thought we could be friends. But we can't—at least not right now. Neither of us could handle seeing each other and not being able to . . ." I stopped, unable to complete the thought, and buried my face in my hands.

"To do this?" Jeffrey asked, gently pulling my hands away from my face and kissing me tenderly. He wrapped his arms around me and nuzzled my neck. "And this?" he whispered.

For a moment I wanted to surrender myself to his kisses. But Todd's chocolate brown eyes appeared in my mind, hurt and confused. I pushed Jeffrey away. "Don't!" I cried. "Please!"

Jeffrey jumped up and paced the three steps across the tree house, his feet echoing hollowly against the planks. He turned and paced back. But the gesture seemed almost ridiculous, given the size of the place.

"Don't you understand, Jeffrey?" I said in a low voice. "It's not right!"

Jeffrey shook his head. "I don't care what's right," he said. "I only know that I want to be with you—any way I can."

"So do I," I said. "But I can't do it. You have to accept that."

He knelt in front of me and took both my hands in his. "Do *you* accept it?" he asked in a serious tone. "Can you tell me honestly that this is really what you want?"

I looked into his eyes and shook my head. "No," I whispered. "I can't. But it's what I have to do."

Afterward, I felt so guilty about being at Miller's Point with Jeffrey the other night that I drove straight over to Todd's house. He seemed surprised to see me—especially when I explained that I'd dropped by just to remind him just how much I love him. The truth is that I dropped by to remind myself. But we snuggled and kissed for a few minutes, and then I went home.

As far as I'm concerned, Jeffrey is a part of my past—not my present. I'll never again kiss him or feel his arms around me. And I'll never, ever tell anyone I was unfaithful to Todd—anyone besides you, Diary.

Todd will never know that I deceived him, but I'm still determined to make it up to him. I'll be the best, most loving, most faithful girlfriend that anyone ever had.

Except deep inside my heart, a little part of me will always belong to Jeffrey.

Saturday night
Tonight was weird. No, it was weirder than weird. It was surreal. Dad was taking

me and Jessica out to dinner. And as a special treat, he took us to Chez Sam, one of the classiest restaurants in town. I should have known something was up when Jessica kept trying to change his mind about the restaurant, even though she was dying to go there only a few days ago. As soon as we walked into the dining room, I knew why. . . .

"Ah, Mr. Wakefield!" the maître d' exclaimed in a French accent as soon as we arrived. "Mrs. Wakefield is already here."

Suddenly I knew just what Jessica was up to. I grabbed her arm—hard—and fell back a few steps behind Dad and the maître d'. "What did you do?" I hissed. "Who did you fix Mom up with?"

"You'll see," Jessica mumbled.

Did I ever! There was my mother, eating dinner with my favorite teacher, Mr. Collins! Mom's eyes opened wide when we walked into the room. My knees began to wobble, and I thought I might faint. I'd been so sure that deep down, my parents really wanted to get back together. But was Jessica right? Had they given up hope for their own relationship? Had they decided to, as Jessica kept putting it, "get on with their lives"?

"Well, this is unexpected," my father said mildly. *That's the understatement of the year,* I thought. I was having trouble catching my breath.

"It sure is," Jessica said with a weak little laugh.

I was furious with my sister—and with my mother. *How could she?* I tried to convince Dad that we could go somewhere else, but he said there was no reason to. So we sat down and ordered our food, keeping our eyes averted from the table in the back of the restaurant.

After a long, uncomfortable ten minutes, Mom and Mr. Collins stood and walked over to us.

"Hi, Mom!" Jessica said cheerfully. "Hi, Mr. Collins!"

"How are you, Ned?" Mom asked. Her smile was genuine, and she didn't look the least bit embarrassed. She gave my shoulder a little squeeze, as if to say, "Don't worry." I actually began to relax a little. Maybe Mom and Mr. Collins were only eating together as friends. Mr. Collins had been through a divorce himself. And I knew from personal experience how helpful he could be when somebody had a problem.

"Why don't you join us?" Dad said easily. "It's not a private party."

Mr. Collins looked at my mother with a question in his eyes.

She shrugged. "What do you think, Roger?" she asked. "Should we get the waiter to move us over here?"

For the second time that evening, I thought I was going to faint. My parents were about to have dinner together—and we had Jessica to thank for it!

I was surprised at how comfortable everyone became after only a few minutes. We talked about Dad's campaign, mostly, and my parents were smiling and communicating, just as they always had. Except for having my English teacher sitting next to me, it was just like going out for dinner with my parents in the old days—the days when all four of us would later climb into the same car and drive home to the same house.

The evening didn't end that way. In fact, it ended kind of badly, considering how well things had been going. After the check was paid, Mr. Collins stood up and told us, "We were planning to catch a nine o'clock movie. Why don't we all go?"

I looked at my father, pleading silently with him to say yes.

"Sorry," Dad replied. "I still have work to do tonight." He smiled at Mom. "It was nice to see you."

Mom and Dad both seemed perfectly happy about the way the evening had gone. And Jessica couldn't stop talking about what a great guy Mr. Collins was. But I was so depressed that I called Todd as soon as we got home. I had to talk to someone about what had happened tonight. I was hoping I could go over to his house, or maybe meet him at the lake for a private talk. I guess I was just feeling weird about the whole evening. I wanted someone to hold my hand and tell me that it was OK.

I felt a little thrill go through me when I heard Todd's sexy voice on the phone.

"Can I see you tonight?" I asked hopefully. "It's been kind of a weird evening."

"Aw, I'm sorry, Liz," Todd said. "But my dad and I are shooting pool. I know it sounds corny, but he's been out of town on business all week, and my mom's visiting her sister. He really had his heart set on a father-son kind of evening."

I gulped. "Are you sure you couldn't take a thirty-minute break?" I asked.

"Liz, is something wrong?" he asked. "I mean, I'd hate to let my dad down. But if it's important—"

"No, don't change your plans for me," I said, trying to make my voice bright. "We can talk tomorrow."

After we hung up, I lay down on my bed and stared at the ceiling, trying to sort out my feelings. Mostly I felt lonely. Enid had a date tonight, or I would have called her. And there was nobody else I could talk to about what had happened. Dad doesn't act the least bit jealous; I doubt he would understand my fears. And Jessica thinks Mom and Mr. Collins are the best couple since peanut butter met jelly.

After a while I dozed off for a few minutes, and I dreamed that I saw Jeffrey's face outside my window, looking in with love in his eyes. Only he was wearing a Romeo costume, like the one Todd wore to the dance last week. When I awoke, I only felt worse.

Why am I so lonely, Diary? Why am I so scared?

Saturday night, later

It's ten-thirty now, and Jeffrey is on his way over here. No, I'm not kidding. He called and pleaded with me to see him. How could I say no? He sounded so sincere. And I felt so alone. But now I'm nervous. I don't know what's going to happen.

I hear a tapping at my window. Jeffrey said he would throw pebbles at the glass and then climb up the trellis. . . .

❖ ❖ ❖

When I pulled back the curtains, there was Jeffrey, standing in the backyard with the moonlight glistening in his hair. He held up his hand, and I saw a long-stemmed rose grasped in his fist, the flower a velvety black in the night.

I listened for any sound that would indicate someone was awake, but as far as I knew, my mom was still out with Mr. Collins, and Jessica had gone to bed early. Did I dare let Jeffrey into my room?

For a moment I considered stealing downstairs on tiptoe and meeting him outside. But I was afraid my mother would hear me. So I slid the window open and raised the screen. I raced to the door that led to the bathroom and Jessica's room and turned the knob to lock it. Then I waited, trembling, while Jeffrey climbed the trellis with the rose clutched in his teeth.

He swung his body through the open window. "Just like climbing up the ladder to the tree house," he whispered through the rose, which turned out to be a beautiful, deep red. He pulled it from his teeth and handed it to me. "Don't worry about your family discovering us," he assured me. "We'll be so quiet that nobody will hear. And I parked my car a block away."

"I can't believe you're here," I whispered. "It's so romantic—like that scene from *Romeo and Juliet.*"

"But soft!" Jeffrey whispered, quoting from the

play. "What light through yonder window breaks? It is the east, and Elizabeth is the sun."

My heart melted at his words. I've always been a sucker for Shakespeare. And Jeffrey, unlike Todd, was also a fanatic for literary classics.

For a moment we just gazed at each other in the dim light from the reading lamp on my desk. He was so handsome that it made me dizzy just to look at him. And I was so tired of being bitter and cynical about love. Something in me—my resistance? my conscience?—dissolved.

"I don't know what's going to happen, Jeffrey," I warned him, whispering. "I can't promise you—"

He put his finger to my lips. "Shhh!" he said. "I'm not asking for promises."

I kissed his finger and then trailed a line of kisses up his arm to his neck and then his face. Then I pulled him to me and we held each other tightly. "Let's treat tonight like a beautiful dream," I whispered over his shoulder. "A last dance."

Jeffrey nodded, gazing into my eyes. Then he sat on the bed and pulled me down beside him. I laid the rose across my pillow. Jeffrey reached over to switch on the clock-radio. Soft jazz, turned way down low. Then he pulled me to his chest and kissed me until I was breathless. . . .

Oh, Diary! It was the most amazing thing—like something out of a romance novel. Jeffrey and I sat there on the edge of the bed, sharing these long, deep kisses that made every part of my body feel like singing. . . .

For a few seconds Jeffrey and I thought that the sudden tapping noise was some weird percussion track of the music on the radio. But then I knew it was coming from the window. I stared at Jeffrey, and he shook his head, as puzzled as I was. Who could be tapping at my window at midnight?

I motioned him to stay put on the bed, and I pulled aside the curtain again. I gasped. "Omigosh!" I hissed. "It's Todd!"

Sure enough, Todd stood on the lawn, in the exact same spot where Jeffrey had stood twenty minutes earlier. Like Jeffrey, he was throwing pebbles at my bedroom window. Suddenly the reality of what I'd been doing came crashing down around me. I was acting against everything I believed in.

"Quick!" I whispered to Jeffrey. "Hide in the closet!"

"Why should I hide in the closet?" he demanded. "Isn't it time you told him the truth?"

I shook my head. "Please, Jeffrey!" Todd was already climbing up the trellis. For a moment I silently cursed my choice of boyfriends. If I had to fall in love with two guys, why did they both have to be so athletic? A lot of people would have had trouble making it up to the second story. These two were better than Spiderman.

"Please, Jeffrey!" I repeated. With every second, Todd was climbing closer and closer to the window. Jeffrey stared at me for a moment as if trying to read my emotions. Finally he nodded and slipped into the closet.

A minute later a head of brown, wavy hair came into view through the window. "Todd!" I whispered. "What are you doing here?"

"I missed you," he said with a grin as he jumped through the window. "The pool game broke up a while ago, and Dad went to bed. Besides, you seemed depressed when you called earlier. I wanted to make sure you were all right. So I sneaked out of the house to come see you."

I smiled, placing my body directly in front of Todd so that he couldn't walk any farther into the room. "That was sweet of you," I said. "But I'm fine now, so maybe you should go. My sister's in her room, asleep. If she should wake up and hear—"

Todd placed his finger against my lips—just as Jeffrey had done a few minutes earlier. "Shhh!" he said. "She's not going to hear a thing." He took my hand and led me to the bed. "I'll stay for only a few minutes. I'm glad you're still up. What were you doing?"

I shrugged. "Uh, just reading and listening to music," I said.

Todd picked up the rose from where it lay on my pillow. "Where did this come from?" he asked, a hint of jealousy in his eyes.

"Uh, Dad took me and Jessica out for a special dinner tonight," I said. "He brought us each one."

Todd put his arm around me and nuzzled my neck, but I was painfully aware of Jeffrey, crouched in the closet. "Dinner tonight was the weirdest thing," I said quickly, hoping to distract Todd from making out. "That's why I called you earlier. I was upset. You see, my mom was there at the restaurant, and she was with a date—"

"Shhh," Todd said again. He covered my mouth with his own and began to kiss me. I kissed him back, a quick peck. Then I jumped up and began pacing the room—being sure to stay away from the closet door.

"You'll never guess who Mom's date was," I said with a nervous laugh. Todd reached for my hand and pulled me down beside him again. "It was Mr. Collins—"

"Not now," Todd said. "I know how upsetting

259

that must have been. So let me take your mind off it." He began to kiss me again. For a moment I tried to pull away, but his kisses became more insistent. And frankly, I found myself kissing him back, almost against my will.

Why did Todd have to be so sexy?

After a few minutes I heard Jessica's footsteps in her room. I pushed Todd away, horrified. Now I was in real trouble. Jessica would no doubt see the light shining under my door. I imagined the scene if she walked in and found me and Todd sitting on the bed, kissing. And what if she discovered Jeffrey in the closet as well? Jessica would never be able to resist blabbing the story to everyone she knew. Dread washed over me in cold, dark waves.

I heard water running in the bathroom. A moment later the doorknob rattled. "Lizzie?" Jessica called. "Are you awake? Why did you lock the door?"

"Go away," I said in a sleepy, you-just-woke-me-up kind of voice. "Can't a person get any rest around here?"

"Why are you sleeping with the lights on?" she asked.

I yawned. "I don't know," I said, trying to sound disoriented. I have to admit that it wasn't difficult, given how strange a night it had been. Suddenly I realized that I was very, very tired. "I guess I fell asleep reading," I said. "Can we talk about this to-morrow? I'm beat."

"Whatever," Jessica said with a yawn of her own. "Good night." I waited until I heard the door close on her side of the bathroom.

"You have to go, Todd!" I hissed, pushing him toward the window. *"Now!"*

Todd shook his head. "Not yet," he said. "Not until I do *this* once more." He enveloped me in a huge, sexy, full-body hug that made my skin tingle and my legs feel weak. And he kissed me until I relaxed and kissed him back with a fervor that took both of us by surprise. I didn't remember about Jeffrey hiding in the closet until I pulled away and looked up at Todd's heartbreakingly handsome features. I swallowed hard. My face must have turned as red as Jeffrey's rose, which still lay across my pillow like an accusation.

"Please," I whispered to Todd. "You have to leave!"

He misinterpreted my urgency. "Chill out, Liz! It's not the end of the world if Jessica catches us to-gether," he reminded me. "Knowing your sister, she'd be more impressed than horrified. Besides, you've certainly got enough dirt on *her* to keep her quiet about it!"

"I guess you're right," I agreed, wishing he'd just get out. "But still—"

Todd nodded. "I know," he said. "I'm going. But I want you to fall asleep remembering one thing: I love you."

He looked at me expectantly, and I had no choice but to answer weakly, "I love you too."

Then Todd climbed out the window and swung himself easily down the trellis.

As soon as I lowered the sash, Jeffrey sprang out of the closet. I jumped, almost as if I were surprised to see him there, and I guiltily yanked the curtains shut, in case Todd looked back up at the window.

"I don't understand you at all," Jeffrey whispered, his eyes more angry than I'd ever seen them.

"Please listen to me," I begged, though I had no idea what I was going to say.

Jeffrey shook his head and strode across the room to the window.

"No, Jeffrey!" I pleaded. "At least wait until Todd's had a chance to get away from the house."

Jeffrey glared at me with a look of hatred that chilled me deep inside. Tears were running down my face, but I hardly noticed them.

"Are you going to say anything?" I asked. I held my breath while I waited for an answer, but it never came. Jeffrey just threw me another icy stare as we faintly heard Todd's BMW start up out front.

Then he stepped over the windowsill and disappeared from view.

> *Earlier I decided to treat tonight as if it were a dream. Now I wish it had been. Oh, Diary, where are my senses? How could I have let either Jeffrey or Todd into my room at night? And how could I have sat here on my bed, making out with Todd, when I knew that Jeffrey could hear every moan and sigh? How could I hurt him that way? What kind of a person am I to do such a thing?*
>
> *I may have pushed Jeffrey too far this time. What if he tells Todd everything? What if I've lost them both?*

> *Sunday morning*
> *Between the unexpected gathering at Chez Sam and the unexpected gathering in my bedroom, I'd have thought that last night couldn't possibly have gotten any stranger. But it did. . . .*

I tried to sleep after Jeffrey was gone, but I couldn't. When I heard Mom come in downstairs a few minutes later I flicked my light back on.

"She's home," Jessica announced loudly. I heard

her running into the bathroom. I grabbed the book from my bedside table and pretended that I'd been reading. A moment later my twin barged into my room through the door that I'd unlocked as soon as Jeffrey left. "Mom's home!" she repeated.

"So?" I asked.

"Liz, don't you hope she had fun with Mr. Collins?" Jessica asked.

I made her wait while I turned a page in my book. "You know what my answer is, Jessica."

"Hmmm," she said, sitting on the edge of my bed. "I guess it's probably hopeless. Tonight was more like a date with Dad than a date with Mr. Collins."

I glared at her, but she just sat there in her Sweet Valley University nightshirt, innocently fiddling with the gold lavaliere that matched mine. "So who else do you think Mom would want to go out with?" she asked, nudging my blanket-covered legs. "Come on! Help me think, Liz!"

"Are you out of your mind?" I shouted, slamming down the book. "Doesn't it mean anything to you that Mom and Dad were happy being together tonight? Doesn't that matter to you at all?"

Jessica shook her head. "Sure, it was nice, Liz. But it doesn't change anything."

"But this could be the start of their getting back

together," I insisted, hoping it was true. "If you just leave them alone, they'll work it out!"

"I don't think that's going to happen," Jessica said. "I really don't."

We argued about it for a while longer, until both of us were genuinely angry with each other. Then Jessica stormed out of the room. A moment later the phone rang.

"Hello?" I snapped.

"This is Maria. Is that you, Liz?"

Maria apologized for calling so late, but something upsetting had happened, and she thought I'd want to know. I couldn't imagine anything more upsetting than any of the things that had happened to me over the past few hours. But as soon as she told me what she'd overhead at my dad's campaign office that night, Jeffrey, Todd, and even my parents' relationship flew out of my mind.

Maria had stopped by the campaign headquarters to pick up a book she'd forgotten that afternoon. While she was there, the phone rang, and when she picked up the receiver, she'd heard Mr. Knapp's voice on the extension. She hadn't even realized he was in the office. And he hadn't known she was on the line.

"Basically," Maria related, "Knapp said he framed my father because Dad wouldn't go along with some big scheme he wanted."

My stomach lurched. "Maria! I can't believe it. I mean, I *can* believe it. But—"

"And that's not all," Maria continued. "He was also saying that he's been working on *your* father and that he's going to make your father do certain things once he's elected mayor."

"What?" I gasped. "That can't be true! Dad would never let him."

"I know," Maria agreed. "I don't really understand it either. But maybe he's doing something to get your father elected, and if it came out, it would hurt his reputation instead of Knapp's."

"No way, Maria. I can't—"

"What I'm saying," she interrupted, "is that your father doesn't even realize it. That's the whole point. Don't you see?"

I wanted to go straight to my dad's apartment and tell him everything Maria had overheard. But she convinced me that he would never believe us unless we had evidence. We decided to get the evidence the following afternoon, no matter what we had to do.

Tuesday night

Dear Diary,

For once I have news that has nothing to do with Todd, Jeffrey, or my parents' possibly impending divorce. Between what Maria overheard on the phone the other

266

night and the details Terry Knapp was able
to fill in for us about his uncle's ambitions,
we thought we had a pretty good idea of
what Mr. Knapp was up to. But we still
needed evidence before we could go to my
father with what we knew. So, with the
help of Winston and Terry, Maria and I
came up with a plan. . . .

Maria and Terry huddled outside in the rain
Tuesday evening as I made a dash for the front
lobby of Mr. Knapp's office building. I distracted
the guard while the two of them crept in and
slipped inside the entrance to the stairs.

While Maria and Terry searched Mr. Knapp's
office, I paced around the front lobby, smiling at
the guard and pretending to watch out the glass
doors for my mother.

But the familiar figure I saw emerging from a
taxi out front was a man—Mr. Knapp! My heart
sank to my feet, a dead weight. *He must be on his
way to his office!* I realized.

The first order of business was to get out of
sight. Then I had to get to Maria and Terry before
Terry's uncle did. I asked the guard for directions
to the women's room, and I scurried up the stairs,
two at a time. I burst into room 415.

"Oh, Liz!" Maria gasped. "What—"

"He's coming!" I said, panting.

Terry went pale and shoved a filing cabinet drawer shut. "What?" he demanded. "Right now? We've got to go!"

I shook my head. "There's no time! We have to hide!"

We scrambled wildly for the closet and piled inside. I fought to control my breathing. Behind me, I could practically hear the pounding of my friends' hearts. Briefly—ridiculously—my mind replayed the image of Jeffrey scurrying into my bedroom closet. It was cut short as Mr. Knapp walked in and flipped on the overhead light.

Through the crack of the closet door, I had a narrow view of the office. Mr. Knapp pulled off his raincoat and shook it out. Behind me, I felt Terry's shoulder go stiff. And I realized what Terry was thinking: *Please don't let him hang up his coat!*

If Mr. Knapp opened the door and found us there . . .

But he didn't. He laid the coat across the back of a chair, pulled out his briefcase, and picked up the telephone.

"It's me," he said into the receiver after he'd punched in a number. "Yeah, that's all taken care of. We're in great shape. It's smooth sailing from here on." He paused to listen. "OK," he said, chuckling. "No, I won't be needing to make any anonymous bank deposits, like I did with our friend Santelli."

Maria gasped, and my heart nearly stopped. But Mr. Knapp went on talking. "Fine," he said. "That's right. Wakefield has a big speech coming up tomorrow night. That'll be the clincher." He waited for a minute, and I clenched my fists in anger. "OK," Mr. Knapp concluded. "I'll just make copies of the plans and bring them over so we can present them to the investors. . . . Right. Bye."

To make a long story short, Diary, it turns out that we were lucky Knapp showed up when he did. Maria and Terry never would have found the incriminating files in the drawers they were searching. But as I watched through the door, the rotten sneak pulled a large folder out from behind a file cabinet. He photocopied several sheets from it, returned the file to its hiding place, and sauntered out of the room with a smug, self-satisfied look on his face.

I'm not a violent person. But I wanted to punch him right in his big, smirking mouth.

Naturally, Maria and Terry and I ran for that secret file as soon as Mr. Knapp was gone. I pulled out a bunch of letters on stationery from the Knapp Development Corporation. There were pages of cost estimates and market analyses. And there was a sketch of a boardwalk with arcades and shops.

"That's our beach!" Maria cried in outrage, jabbing a finger at the drawing.

And I found a receipt for a teller's check for ten thousand dollars—the amount of money that Knapp had deposited into Maria's father's account.

We copied everything that looked important, and we sneaked back downstairs and out of the building.

When I brought the stuff to Dad at his apartment a little while later, he was shocked, hurt, and angry. "But I don't know what to do now," he said, as if he were talking to himself. "I just don't know what to do."

I nodded, but I couldn't find any words to say.

"I can't trust anybody anymore," he said, his voice full of pain. "I don't know who's involved in this. I don't know whom to trust."

Suddenly I knew that there was one person he could trust completely. "How about Mom?" I asked quietly.

"Alice," he said, closing his eyes. I think he forgot I was in the room.

I took a deep breath and stood up, feeling bolder and more hopeful. "Let's go home," I urged, as if I were the adult and my father the child. "You can talk to Mom about it—she'll be able to help."

We drove home through the rain, and we poured out the whole story to Mom. Dad talked about quitting the campaign, but Mom wouldn't hear of it. She suggested he go to his friend, Detective Cabrini, at the Sweet Valley police department. But Dad said he couldn't because the only evidence he had—he looked over at me—was inadmissible in court.

They talked things over, and Mom was great. She helped him explore every possibility, and she showed him that he wasn't responsible for Knapp's rotten—and illegal—behavior. And she helped him come up with a plan.

"Tomorrow night—at the big rally," my mother said slowly. "Maybe there's something you can do about Knapp then."

I wanted to hang around to hear the rest of the plan, but I was so happy to see my parents in the same room that I was sure I would cry if I stayed. Besides, from the way

271

*they were holding hands and staring intently
at each other as they talked things through,
I knew they'd forgotten I was there.*

*I felt as if a huge weight had been lifted
from my shoulders. I knew my parents
would stay up late into the night, working
out the details of the plan. And somehow I
was sure that their separation was over.
Now I'm up in my room, but they're still
downstairs, talking. And I'm positive that
it's only a matter of time now before my
dad moves back in!*

*P.S.: So far, Jeffrey has stayed silent.
Will it last?*

The front steps of City Hall were packed the
following evening, as the whole town gathered for
the political rally. Jessica and the other cheerleaders were whooping it up, complete with pom-poms
and red-and-white uniforms. Balloons, banners,
and flags blew in the breeze.

"Did Dad go to the police?" I whispered to Mom
as we waited for Dad and the other candidates to
be introduced.

"I think so, but I don't know what the outcome
was," she said. "I guess we'll know pretty soon."

When Dad stepped up to the microphone, the
crowd cheered. He talked about all the things we

all love about Sweet Valley, but then he warned that there were people who wanted to destroy those things. I watched Mr. Knapp's face twist into a scowl as Dad obviously veered from the speech they'd written together.

"Unless we are sharp enough to spot sharks among us," Dad said, "we'll be gobbled up like so many other towns in California."

The crowd had grown quiet, and I rose on tiptoe to see over everyone's heads.

Then Dad said that some people had been trying to exploit our town, and that one man had tried to stop it.

"He saw behind the false promises and the comfortable lies, and he refused to play the game!" Dad said. "He suffered for it, ladies and gentlemen. He suffered terribly." He paused for effect. "I'm talking about Peter Santelli!"

The crowd was surprised and puzzled. Dad went on to say how dirty politics could get, and to reveal that he himself had been used as well. Mr. Knapp tried to make a run for it. But Detective Cabrini intercepted him and took him down to the station.

"My friends!" Dad cried after the crowd had quieted down. "I want you to know that I will never give you reason to doubt my motives or my decisions—"

273

"Yeah!" yelled a supporter.

"—because I'm withdrawing from the race," Dad concluded.

I was stunned. So was the crowd. But one by one people began clapping, until a thunderous applause filled the air. I hoped that Mr. Knapp could hear it from the police station. Dad stepped down from the podium and made his way down the steps. And one person was shoving her way through the crowd to him. When my parents met in a fierce embrace, there were tears in my eyes.

> *Election night, late*
> *Dad convinced Mr. Santelli to get back into the race, and he threw his support to Maria's father. And guess what, Diary? Mr. Santelli won! But the members of the Wakefield family are the real winners tonight. Tomorrow Dad is coming home! Permanently.*
> *Hip, hip, hooray!*
> *Or as Jess might say, "Cool beans!"*

Part 4

Wednesday morning

Dear Diary,

Dad will be at home for good when I return from school this afternoon. And Todd's coming to our family celebration dinner tonight. I'm so happy that everything in my life is working out at last.

Except for Jeffrey. I wish I could take back what I did with him . . . and what I did to him. I don't know if he'll ever forgive me, or if I'll ever forgive myself. And I feel awful every time Todd tells me he loves me. Would he still love me if he knew my terrible secret? I feel like such a fraud.

Friday afternoon

There's a new junior at school—Claire Middleton, a transfer from Palisades High. She's in my history class, and I've run into her around town now and then. Enid and I would love to get to know her. Claire seems nice, and she sounds smart in class. But she's shy. I keep trying to talk to her after history, but so far I haven't had much luck. I hate seeing a new student spend so much time by herself. She must be lonely.

Wednesday, 3:20 P.M.

I finally found a way to convince myself that I can be a positive force in the world of romance—despite recent events with Todd, Jeffrey, and my folks. It's called Operation Pair-Up. I guess the seeds for the plan were planted last Friday night, at Patty Gilbert's party. Dana Larson was giving us another installment of the "I'm fed up with love" speech she's been repeating so often lately. . . .

"There's just no one out there for me!" Dana said, tossing her short blond hair. The glitter she'd sprayed over it shimmered when she moved, and a cloud of sparkles danced around her face like baby fireflies.

With her tall, slim figure, wild clothes, and exotic looks, Dana was so striking that I was surprised she didn't have to beat the guys off—especially since Dana was the closest thing our school had to a rock star, as the lead singer and songwriter for the Droids.

"Sure there is," I said. "There's someone for everybody!" *Two someones, in my case*, I added to myself, with a silent grim laugh.

"Well, I'm tired of looking for him," Dana replied. "It's not as if I haven't tried dating different guys. But between the musician types who are totally obsessed with themselves and the guys who have nothing to offer at all, I'm starting to wonder if it's worth the effort. If you ask me, love's completely overrated!"

A few minutes later Dana even came up with a spur-of-the-moment song about her disillusionment with love.

"I'm fed up with love," she sang, her husky alto sounding wonderful and professional, even with only an acoustic guitar she'd grabbed from Andy Jenkins for accompaniment. "Don't know what I was thinking of, letting romance fog my mind and waste my precious time. . . ."

The song was silly and sarcastic. And everyone was laughing—except for Aaron Dallas. He stood alone at the snack table, wearing his usual button-down shirt and khaki pants, and he looked utterly bored as he dragged a potato chip through a bowl of onion dip.

Todd wrapped an arm around my shoulders and pulled me over to our friend. "Hey, buddy," Todd said cheerfully.

To be honest, I'd felt a little uncomfortable around Aaron lately. I mean, he was Jeffrey's best friend. What if Jeffrey had told him about that night in my bedroom? I watched Aaron carefully for any signs of animosity toward me. But his grumpiness that night seemed to be more general than that.

"You know, she's absolutely right!" he said.

"Who's right?" I asked.

"Dana," he said, gesturing toward the singer. Dana still stood in the center of the room in her fishnet hose, black leather miniskirt, and fringed jacket, improvising the verses to her new song. "Love stinks," Aaron declared.

I caught Todd's bemused look. *Not another one!* he seemed to say.

"The world would be a much better place without it!" Aaron continued. "I'm so sick of seeing happy couples everywhere I turn! And I hate the way all of my friends have to check in with their girlfriends before they can do anything with me!"

He eyed Todd severely. "It really bugs me!"

An hour later Todd and I were sitting in his car at Miller's Point, discussing the party and Aaron's apparent depression. "Do you really think he's serious?" I asked. "I'll bet if the right girl came along, he'd change his mind fast. I bet even Dana 'Fed Up with Love' Larson could fall in love again."

Todd laughed. "Maybe we should get the two of them together! We'd be doing Sweet Valley High a favor, sparing everyone all that moaning and groaning!"

He'd been joking, but I latched onto the idea immediately. There was something appealing about the idea of matching up funky, hyper, creative Dana with conservative, practical, easygoing Aaron. "I think you're on to something!"

Todd looked horrified. "Liz, I was only kidding."

"No, it's perfect!" I exclaimed. "Aaron and Dana both think they hate happy couples. But they'll feel differently once they're part of one again."

Todd laughed and leaned forward to kiss me. "You're such a romantic," he said.

We talked about it for a few minutes longer, with Todd trying to discourage me. He tried to tell me that our two friends were entirely too different. But I became only more enthusiastic about the idea.

"Haven't you heard that opposites attract?" I asked. "Maybe if they had a little encouragement, Dana and Aaron could see beyond their differences and become friends."

Todd cocked his head. "It would be an interesting experiment," he admitted.

"Let's do it!" I said.

Todd was reluctant, but he finally gave in. "OK, OK!" he said. "I'll go along with you."

We turned Operation Pair-Up into a bet. If we could get Dana and Aaron together, Todd would owe me three wishes. If the plan failed, I owed *him* three wishes.

We started the very next day. We enlisted the help of a few of our friends to make sure that Dana overheard someone say that Aaron had a crush on her. Then we arranged to have Aaron hear that Dana had a crush on *him*. Within a few hours, it was clear that both of them were surprised but intrigued.

Tuesday night I invited Dana to the movies with me and Todd. And Todd invited Aaron. Things were awkward at first. But over a Guido's pizza afterward, Dana and Aaron warmed up to each other. Each seemed surprised by what they had in common—and impressed by what the other said. Unfortunately, Operation Pair-Up hit a major snag when the topic of love came up. And both reiterated their antirelationship vows.

I knew I had to kick the effort into high gear, so I did. The next day at school, I told Dana that Aaron couldn't stop talking about her. And I made Todd tell Aaron the same thing about Dana—and suggest that Aaron invite Dana to a concert the following weekend, double-dating with me and Todd.

> *Saturday night, late*
> *The outdoor concert was great. And I'm well on my way to earning my three wishes from Todd. By the end of the evening, Dana and Aaron had eyes for nobody but each other. Dana even agreed to go watch Aaron play soccer on Tuesday!*
> *You've already guessed the downside, Diary. In the interest of love, I had to agree to let Dana tag along to the game with me and Todd. Which means I have to go to a soccer game—a game in which Jeffrey also will be playing. . . .*

Dana generally hated sports, but her eyes were shining as she watched Aaron play soccer. I tried to watch Aaron too, but my eyes kept straying to Jeffrey's familiar figure. The only thing that kept me from giving myself away was that Dana was too intent on the game to pay much attention to me. And Todd, thank goodness, had arrived at the game late. I saw him search the crowds for us unsuccessfully, but I didn't stand up and wave. Finally I saw him take a seat next to Winston, Andy Jenkins, Ken Matthews, and some other guys. Ken's eyesight wasn't good enough yet for him to play football again, but he was still an active supporter of SVH sports.

I breathed a relieved sigh to see that Todd had given up on finding me. At least I wouldn't have to worry about him learning the truth—in case I couldn't keep my secret feelings for Jeffrey secret.

"No wonder he's got such a great body," Dana said with a whistle as Aaron swept the ball away from a Big Mesa player. Her eyes followed his every move.

"That's for sure," I breathed. But it wasn't Aaron's moves I was watching. Aaron may have been the team's top scorer, but his best friend, Jeffrey, was a close second. And when it came to best *legs*—well, Aaron couldn't compete. The sunlight glinted off my former boyfriend's blond head as he raced down the field to catch Aaron's pass with one outstretched foot. Every movement of his body was fluid—relaxed but perfectly controlled. He could have been a gymnast or a dancer.

I sighed, and Dana squeezed my hand. "I know what you mean," she said. "This game is incredibly suspenseful. I'm wound up tighter than a guitar string!"

By the time the whole gang gathered at the Dairi Burger for the victory celebration, I was sure that Operation Pair-Up had worked. Dana and Aaron kept sharing these heavy, lingering gazes. And I knew they were both getting close to publicly renouncing their pessimistic stands on romance.

Friday night
Our plan blew up in our faces tonight.
And it was all Todd's fault. Rather than
letting nature take its course, he left a silly
love letter in Dana's locker, supposedly from
Aaron. But Dana showed it to Aaron, and
he recognized Todd's handwriting. So Dana
figured out who was really behind her until-
then budding romance with Aaron!

Todd was at my house when Dana called. She yelled at me over the phone and then slammed the receiver down so hard it practically burst my eardrum.

I was nearly in tears as I turned to Todd. "Are you satisfied now?" I demanded. "Are you happy that you've ruined Dana and Aaron's chance for happiness? That's what you wanted, wasn't it?" Everything was clear to me. Todd had sabotaged Dana and Aaron's chances just to be sure he won that silly bet.

I got more and more angry with him, and he got angry with me for being angry. We both hollered a lot. And then Todd grabbed his jacket and stormed out the door. I slammed it behind him as hard as I could.

Monday, 4:30 P.M.

Dear Diary,

Todd still isn't speaking to me! Neither is Dana. At least Jessica is— though that wasn't the case a few days ago. She went spastic on me Friday night. She came home right after Todd left, and she started wailing about how her life was ruined and it was all my fault! She wouldn't say a word to me for the next twelve hours—and I had no idea what had set her off! But she apologized yesterday morning and shed some light on the subject. . . .

"See, I was kind of ticked off when you decided to get Dana together with Aaron," Jessica explained as we sat on the patio Sunday, waiting while Dad fixed brunch inside. It seemed that my sister had been entertaining her own ideas about Aaron Dallas at the time, and I had stepped on her toes—not to mention her ego. "I thought it would serve Dana right if the Droids were beaten in the Battle of the Bands," she said.

The Battle of the Bands was coming up the following weekend. It would pit the Droids against several other musical groups at school, including my friend Andy's new band, Baja Beat. Jessica and Lila—in order to win a trip to Los Angeles with the winning band—had volunteered their services as roadies to a group I'd never heard of. It was called Spontaneous Combustion.

"And it's not working out the way you thought?" I guessed.

Jessica groaned. "*I'm* working, but *it's* not! Liz, every muscle in my body aches. I have to shampoo my hair three times after every practice to get the smell of cigarette smoke out of it. And Lila never lifts a finger! I'm the one who has to jump every time Spy or Motor or Wheels wants something!"

I couldn't keep myself from laughing. "Spy, Motor, and Wheels?" I asked. "Jess," I continued after I caught my breath, "you're not really working for people named Motor and Wheels?"

"Yes, I am," she said. "And it's not funny!" A few minutes earlier she'd related a nightmare she'd had in which she accompanied the group on tour across the entire country. Now she said that her real life was just as bad. "Last night," she revealed,

"Wheels had the nerve to ask me if I wanted to be his *chick!*"

I was laughing so hard that I nearly fell out of my chair. "His . . . *chick?*" I choked out.

Jessica's lips twitched, and soon she was laughing, too. "I informed him that Jessica Wakefield wasn't anybody's *chick*. Then I poked him in his wimpy chest, hard, with one of his stupid drumsticks. I think he got the message!"

"Good for you!" I said, meaning it. "I only wish I was as successful in my attempts at communicating with people these days."

Tuesday night
I told Jessica yesterday that I've done a lousy job of communicating with people lately. She doesn't know the half of it!

Tonight I picked up the phone to call Jeffrey. But I chickened out and hung up as soon as I heard his voice on the other end of the line. I guess I'm glad now that I had the sense to leave it be. I just hope he can do the same. I'm still terrified that he's going to tell Todd about hiding in the closet while Todd and I kissed. And about sitting on the bed, kissing me, before Todd arrived.

If I've learned anything in the past few

weeks, it's that you can't fix a problem by creating another one! I should have realized the truth: that to feel better about my relationship with Todd, I needed to deal with it head-on. Why did I think being a matchmaker would ease my conscience? The other thing I've learned is not to meddle in other people's romances.

Thursday evening
The good news is that Todd is speaking to me again. The bad news is that he's only speaking to yell at me.

But the potentially disastrous news is that it almost happened: Jeffrey almost told Todd the truth about us!

I must have a guardian angel looking out for me, because at the last second Jeffrey changed his mind. . . .

Penny and I finished going over page proofs for the *Oracle* after school on Thursday. I was waiting for Jessica to come by after cheerleading practice so we could drive home together, so I waved as Penny left for the printer. Then I pulled out the diskette that contained the rough draft of my Yeats paper, planning to revise it until my sister showed up.

I always enjoyed being alone in the *Oracle* office in the late afternoon. It was peaceful and private. And I was surrounded by framed issues of the newspaper, the smell of newsprint, and favorite photographs from past editions as well as the computers, tape recorders, and reference books that helped me pretend I was already a part of the world of journalism. Besides, in a funny way, I felt at home in the *Oracle* office—as if I were working in a much more cluttered version of my own room.

I looked up from the computer screen when the door opened. "Jess—" I started to say.

But it was Todd who walked in, his hair still wet from his postbasketball shower. For a moment my heart jumped. Was he coming to apologize? But Todd froze as soon as he saw me, clearly surprised. He clenched his jaw.

"Uh, I didn't know you would be here," he said stiffly. "The coach asked me to drop off this schedule change for John Pfeifer."

I pointed to a box marked Sports Editor. "You can leave it there," I said.

He did, and then he headed to the door. When he reached it, he stopped, as if he were trying to make a decision.

"Todd?" I asked softly. "Was there anything else you needed?"

"You!" I wanted him to cry. *"I need you,*

Elizabeth!" Then I wanted him to take me in his arms and apologize for everything he'd done. That's when I would apologize for overreacting, and we would seal our reunion with a passionate kiss. . . .

It didn't happen exactly that way.

Todd took a deep breath. "I'm tired of us being mad at each other," he said in a voice that sounded more irritated than apologetic. "Can't we just make up and pretend that none of this ever happened?"

I nodded, my eyes shining. "I'm tired of it too," I said. "I've tried to talk to you so many times in the last few days, but you seemed to be avoiding me."

"I guess I was," he said with a shrug. "But if you want to apologize now—well, I'm willing to listen."

My eyebrows shot up to my forehead. "Wait a minute. You want *me* to apologize?"

"You said you've been trying to for days," he said.

"I said no such thing!" I protested, my voice rising. "I said I'd been trying to *talk* to you."

"Right," he said. "And I assume you meant you wanted to apologize for the whole ridiculous idea of setting up Dana and Aaron."

"First of all, remember whose idea it was in the first place—*yours!*" I reminded him. "Second, for a ridiculous idea, it happened to be working out just as I thought it would—Dana and Aaron really seemed to like each other!"

"Seemed to," he said. "But they were obviously too different for it to work out. You don't have to blame yourself, Liz. I mean, your intentions were good. You just wanted them to be happy. You can't really help it if your plan backfired."

"I don't blame myself!" I cried. "Dana and Aaron didn't break up because they're not compatible. They broke up because of that idiotic note you wrote!"

"Oh, so now it's *my* fault!" he yelled back. "Liz, that's just like you—always trying to protect your *perfect* reputation by blaming other people when things go wrong."

"Just a minute, there!" barked a third voice. We both turned to see Jeffrey standing in the doorway, his arms folded in front of him. "How dare you talk to Elizabeth that way!"

"Maybe you should just butt out, French," Todd warned. "What are you doing here, anyway? This isn't your battle."

"Todd!" I screamed, appalled that he would talk to Jeffrey like that.

"Believe me, I didn't drop by the office just to enjoy the sounds of you harassing one of the nicest, most sensitive people I know," Jeffrey said as he advanced toward Todd with eyes like ice. "I happen to work here, remember?"

"Well, do your work and get out," Todd said. "This is a private argument!"

"Stop it!" I yelled.

"Who do you think you are?" Jeffrey demanded of him. "You think that just because you're a big-time basketball player, you can go anywhere in this school and say anything you want!"

"I do not—" Todd began

Jeffrey cut him off. "First you break her heart by running off to New England. Then, as soon as she puts her life back together and finds a way to be happy again, you come waltzing back and expect her to welcome you with open arms!"

"No, Jeffrey!" I said, stunned. "You know it wasn't like that!"

"You're just a sore loser, French!" Todd yelled. "She chose me, and you can't stand that. You—"

I grabbed Todd's arm in an effort to get his attention, but he shrugged me off. "No, Liz," he said quietly. "This has been a long time coming."

"This isn't about being a sore loser," Jeffrey said, lowering his own voice as well. "All I wanted was for Elizabeth to be happy. And she was happy with you—at first. What I can't stand is to see you treating her this way!"

"Jeffrey, it's all right!" I said. "Todd and I were

just having a silly argument that got blown all out of proportion. I won't stand here and let you talk to him this way!"

Jeffrey was stunned speechless. He turned to me with that same look of hatred I'd seen just before he climbed out my bedroom window.

Todd took the opportunity to get another jab in. "I know what your problem is, French. You're jealous, pure and simple. Elizabeth loves me—not you. It's been me all along—only me—and you can't handle that!"

"She loves only you?" Jeffrey repeated. He laughed bitterly. "For your information, Wilkins—"

I gasped and grabbed the edge of a desk to steady myself. This was it. Jeffrey was about to tell Todd about that horrible, mixed-up Saturday night when they'd both climbed through my window. He would tell Todd of our stolen moments together and the secret kisses we had shared. Any chance I had of reconciling with Todd was dead. I felt as if I might as well be dead too. Tears began pouring from my eyes.

"Jeffrey!" I cried, not meaning to speak aloud. I gazed at him, pleading for him to keep my secret.

Jeffrey gazed back at me for a moment that seemed like an hour. He looked at Todd's face, which was no longer angry but sad and tired. Then he glanced at me again, and his green eyes softened. "For your information, Todd," he repeated, "Elizabeth does love you—more than anything. But she loves me too."

I held my breath.

"She loves me like a brother," he said, still speaking to Todd but looking at me. "And I love her too much to stand by while you hurt her again!"

He turned to face me, and I thanked him with my eyes. In his eyes, I saw that my secret was safe forever. If he hadn't blurted it out during a fight like the one we'd just come through, he would never tell. For a moment Jeffrey reached out and touched my shoulder. Then he spun around and strode out of the office. I sat down weakly.

"Are you OK?" Todd asked cautiously after Jeffrey was gone.

I nodded. "Just worn out."

"Is it true what he said?" Todd asked. "About you loving me more than anything?"

I looked up at him. "Would it make a difference at this point?"

"I don't know," he replied, shaking his head. He sat down, too, and looked at his hands. "I am still so angry with you, Elizabeth. I can't believe you would be so unfair to me over a little thing like that stupid note I wrote to Dana."

"I'm still angry with *you* too," I said quietly. "But maybe this has to do with a lot more than Dana and

Aaron. Ever since my parents' problems started, you and I have had trouble communicating."

He nodded an acknowledgment.

"So what do we do about it?" I asked. Then I voiced another question—one whose answer I feared: "Or do you even *want* to do anything about it?"

"I don't know Liz. I just don't know." He jumped up, suddenly agitated. "I need time to think!" he said, ramming his right fist against the palm of his left hand. "Maybe in a few days . . ."

"Maybe," I agreed. But there wasn't a trace of love in Todd's eyes—just confusion and hurt and pent-up anger. Without another word, he left the room.

Five minutes later I was still sitting in exactly the same position. Instead of the screen in front of me, I was still staring at the door that had swung shut behind Todd. Suddenly it opened. My sister bounded into the room, still in her cheerleader uniform.

She rolled her eyes. "Isn't that just like you, sitting in a cramped office on a beautiful day, writing. *Bo-ring!* I bet you haven't spoken with another human being in hours!"

"Actually, Jess," I said wearily, "I'd give anything for a little boredom right now."

> *Saturday evening*
> *Ah, Diary, life does have some rewards.*
> *Dana and Aaron are the happiest couple on*

earth! Dana was so embarrassed about the matchmaking Todd and I had done that she'd been avoiding Aaron ever since she found out what happened. Finally Todd told Aaron the whole story. He confronted Dana before the Battle of the Bands today, and they both admitted that they were crazy about each other! After that, Dana sang like a dream—newly inspired, no doubt. And the Droids beat all the other bands.

By the way, that includes Spontaneous Combustion, which spontaneously combusted—or at least caused a minor explosion. It was all due to Jessica's having plugged socket A into outlet B, or some such thing. The band's leader, a guy named Spy, fired her for being "one dumb chick." Jessica was not heartbroken.

Speaking of heartbroken, I'd give anything to have Todd hold me in his arms again and tell me that he still loves me. I know I still love him. But I've made so many mistakes that I doubt he'll ever forgive me. Maybe I'll join a convent.

Monday

I've demoted Dana and Aaron to second-happiest couple on earth. Can you

*guess who the first-happiest couple is? Yep,
that's right. Me and Todd! He had never
stopped loving me. But he was afraid I
didn't love him anymore.*

I found a typed note in my locker just before
lunch: *I love you, Liz, and I'm sorry. Meet me under
the clock after school so we can kiss and make up!*

My spirits soared the same way they had during
my surfing adventures—I felt buoyant, as if I were
riding a sparkling wave in perfect harmony with
sea and sky. Todd still loved me!

The rest of the afternoon passed in a blur. My
teachers probably thought I was nuts. But then
that last bell rang at three o'clock, and I raced
down the hall to the main lobby and pushed
through the front doors. Somebody was already
standing under the clock—Todd!

In a flash we were in each other's arms. Then
our lips met in a gentle kiss.

"I'm sorry, Elizabeth," Todd said.

"No, I'm sorry," I insisted. We both apologized
a few more times, and then we were once again
kissing with a passion I had feared was gone forever.

*I guess I was right the other day when I
said that the problems between me and*

Todd went much deeper than a messy attempt at matchmaking.

There were so many issues we'd never resolved. We never cleared the air about all those times I snubbed him because I was afraid about my parents' separation. I even went out of my way to find fault in him. I was so afraid of being close to somebody and then falling out of love, as my parents had. So I ran to Jeffrey for comfort, instead of Todd. I think I knew that I could never again have a long-term commitment to Jeffrey. Maybe that's why I went to him. He was safe—like all those guys I dated during that week when I was playing the field.

I think I've learned the lesson I tried to teach Dana and Aaron: You can't give up on love. When it comes right down to it, love is the only thing that counts. And no matter how upset or hopeless I've felt, I know now that it's Todd's love—along with my family's—that has kept me whole.

As we embraced under the clock in front of Sweet Valley High, Todd apologized for sending Dana the card that had caused her to break up with Aaron. "But now we're even," he added. "You sent your own card, and it's made everything right again!"

I tilted my head, confused. "You mean, *you* sent *me* a card to make everything right again."

"I didn't send you a card," Todd said, shaking his head. "You sent me a card."

"I didn't send you a card!" I exclaimed. We both reached into our pockets, and Todd pulled out a card that was identical to the one I'd found in my own locker.

Just then a car honked its horn. Aaron was at the wheel, with one arm wrapped around Dana's shoulders. They grinned and waved as they passed by. And suddenly we knew exactly who had written our identical notes.

"I think they just got even with us!" I surmised.

"And they returned the favor," Todd said. He tipped my chin up for another kiss. "It looks like we all get a happy ending."

A minute later I reminded him of our bet—the bet that I had now won.

"Let's see . . . ," I began, thinking about my three wishes. "A dozen roses would be nice, and someone to do my chores and carry my books for a week would be a real treat."

Todd laughed. "I deserve it," he admitted. "I was going to make you wash my car!"

"But after everything that's happened lately, there are other things I'd like more," I said. "Are you ready?"

"Your wish is my command."

"Then I wish you and I will never have such a pointless argument ever again."

"One," counted Todd.

"And I wish we'll always be together and as happy as we are right now."

"Two," he said, holding up two fingers.

"And I wish you'd give me the biggest, best kiss ever—right this very instant!"

The only unsolved riddle in my life right now is Jeffrey. I wish with all my heart that he would find someone to love— someone besides me.

Monday, a week later
I always thought that Sweet Valley was a sort of modern-day Eden. Was I ever wrong! Today a survey I wrote appeared in the Oracle. *My plan was to ask people what they'd like to change at school. I figured that people were basically as happy as I've always been here. I thought they'd ask for fun things—better snacks in the vending machines, longer lunches, and fewer tests.*

But there's a lot of real dissatisfaction out there. I started to realize it as soon as I

broached the idea for the survey, last week.
Penny immediately said she would elimi-
nate the exclusive sorority, PBA, because
it's elitist. I have to say that I agree. Today
at lunch I got an earful from a whole group
of people. . . .

"I'll tell you what I'd change," Manuel Lopez
said. "I'd change the way they teach history around
here. This whole area of California was settled by
the Spanish from Mexico centuries before white
Americans came over the Rockies. The Spanish
were the real discoverers of California."

His girlfriend, Sandra Bacon, looked surprised.
"I didn't realize that!"

Jade Wu put in a vote for what she said was a
"real issue": getting rid of boring cafeteria food and
installing pizza ovens.

"This is what I'd change," Dana piped up. "Pay
less attention to boys' sports. It's totally ridiculous
that the whole school focuses on these primitive
macho competitions."

Aaron's forehead wrinkled. "So when I play soccer, that's primitive macho competition? And here
I thought it was just soccer!"

"Boys' sports programs get more money than
girls' sports," Sandra said. "I read it in the school
budget outline when it was put up for a vote."

The conversation went on. And with every comment, I felt my heart sinking and my eyes opening. I never knew what was going on just below the surface of what seemed to be a happy, healthy environment.

Tuesday afternoon
Some terrible events have taken place in Sweet Valley lately. Penny's boyfriend, Neil Freemount, came into the newspaper office after school today, while Penny and I were working, and he told me some things I didn't know. . . .

"How's Andy today?" Penny asked Neil. I looked up, surprised at the tone of her voice. She hadn't spoken casually, but rather as if she and Neil both knew that his best friend, Andy Jenkins, had reason to be upset or in trouble.

"He's really mad," Neil said. He looked over at me and explained, "Charlie Cashman and his buddies have been pulling these racist stunts against Andy and Tracy lately."

I guess I should give a few details about all these people I'm mentioning, Diary.
Tracy Gilbert is Andy's girlfriend. She's a junior, but I don't know her very well—

301

*though her cousin Patty is a friend of mine.
I guess I've mentioned Andy before. In addition to being Neil's best friend, he's an
all-around good guy who also happens to
be a science whiz and a musician—he
plays French horn in the school band and
is the lead guitarist for that group Baja
Beat, which took second place in the Battle
of the Bands. Incidentally, Tracy and Andy
are African American.*

As for Charlie—well, does the term school
bully *mean anything to you? Basically, he's a
low-life creep who could take first place in
the National Obnoxiousness Tournament.*

Neil and Penny filled me in on what had been
going on. First Andy had found the inside of his
locker piled high with garbage from the cafeteria
trash cans—apple cores, pizza crusts, soda cans,
and other trash. On the inside of the door was a
note: *Go back to Africa, where you belong!*

Then Andy had won a prestigious summer
scholarship at the Monterey Bay Aquarium, and
Charlie and his friends insisted that he'd been
chosen only because of his race. The bullies had
tried to pick a fight with Neil and Andy in the
parking lot of the Dairi Burger the other day.
And they'd slashed the tires on Tracy's car.

302

"Has Andy reported any of this to Mr. Cooper?" I asked, referring to our principal—more commonly known as "Chrome Dome."

"No," Neil said, shaking his head. "That's what's so frustrating. He says he can handle it on his own. He says he's not asking for any help from anyone *white*. Period."

Penny and I were floored. "He said that?" Penny asked. She began nervously tapping a pencil on the desk.

"Yes," Neil said, raking a hand through his hair. "That's what I don't get. I mean, that's racism too, isn't it? Making generalizations about a race like that?"

"I don't know if it's exactly the same thing," I said slowly, trying to sort out the issues as I spoke. "It is true that white people have discriminated against blacks for hundreds of years. Maybe Andy had a good reason to feel angry and suspicious about the white establishment."

"That's true," Penny agreed.

Neil bit his lip. "Yeah, but he said that to *me!* I mean, we're supposed to be friends. How can he put me in that category with—"

"Just go easy on him," Penny advised him. I thought how lucky Neil was to have a girlfriend so smart and level-headed. "He needs support right now," she continued, "and a friend. Don't judge

303

him while he's upset. That's not fair."

"You're right," Neil said. "I do want to help him. But the question is, will he let me?"

Wednesday
I've already received a stack of written responses to the survey. Some were intriguing. All were enlightening. Olivia and I were going through some this afternoon at the Oracle *office. Two in particular made me sit up and take notice. . . .*

"Liz!" Olivia said, holding up one of the survey responses. "Listen to this one!" She took a deep breath and read aloud: "'It's not right that girls aren't considered good enough to play varsity football. If you've got the speed and the skill, there's no reason a girl couldn't be a quarterback.'"

I took the sheet of paper from her. "Wow!" I breathed. "A girl who wants to play football. That's fantastic! I wonder who she is."

Olivia shrugged. "I don't know. We've got some terrific athletes on the girls' teams. I wonder if there's any actual rule that says a girl can't play varsity football."

"Whoever she is, I bet she's a really interesting person," I said. "I'd like to get to know somebody like that."

"Maybe you already do know her," Olivia pointed out.

Now *that* was food for thought. I was about to reply, but another response sheet caught my eye. I gasped. "Oh, no!" I whispered, reading and then rereading the paragraph.

"Liz!" Olivia said, concerned. "You're suddenly as pale as a ghost. What is it?"

"Oh, Liv. This one confirms some awful things I've heard about what's been going on at school lately." I opened my mouth to read it aloud, but then I stopped. "I can't even bear to say the words out loud. Here, take it." I handed her the paper quickly, as if it might contaminate me.

Olivia's eyes grew round as she scanned the page. Then she slumped back in her chair, as stunned as I was. "Who would have thought there were people so horrible, right here at Sweet Valley High?" she asked.

Diary, I can hardly stand to copy down the words. But I think it may be important to keep a record of things like this. So here goes:

I think they should kick out anyone from this school who isn't a real American. Like blacks, Hispanics, and Asians. They always get advantages over us.

That is so awful, Diary. And it makes

me *sick to realize that people I know— maybe even people I call my friends—feel that way. I'd like to think it's just a few racist jerks like Charlie Cashman, who, according to Neil, comes from a whole family of racist jerks. But I have to consider the possibility that such sentiments are more widespread.*

Since my survey ran in the paper, I've discovered that Sweet Valley High is hiding a lot of dissatisfaction and disturbing feelings—like a deadly riptide beneath a sparkling ocean wave.

I find myself remembering a Yeats poem I wrote an English paper about a few weeks ago. In "The Second Coming," Yeats says, "the center cannot hold." Right now that's how I feel about Sweet Valley High. Wait, let me find a few more lines of that poem. Here it is:

From "The Second Coming," by William Butler Yeats

Things fall apart; the centre cannot hold; Mere anarchy is loosed upon the world, The blood-dimmed tide is loosed, and everywhere The ceremony of innocence is drowned.

My innocence is drowned, Diary. It's been shoved underwater, tumbled in the surf, dragged out to sea, and sunk to the bottom of the ocean. And I have this dreadful feeling that the worst is yet to come. (I know, nobody uses words like dreadful anymore. But if you think of it as "full of dread," then it's exactly what I mean.) My pretty little town—even my beloved school—isn't as safe and friendly as I thought. We're all sitting on a time bomb. When will it explode? And who will get hurt when it does?

Friday afternoon
Andy and Charlie got into a fight in the hallway after biology class today. Mr. Collins had to break it up. I feel guilty about my survey, but Mr. Collins reminded me that asking the question hadn't caused the underlying tensions at school. Something else would have brought them to the surface even if I'd never come up with the idea of surveying the students.

Besides, I remind myself, the first racist incident I know of was the garbage in Andy's locker. And that happened three days before the survey came out.

Things will get worse before they get better. There are so many bad feelings whirring around, like demons let loose from Pandora's box. Andy is still shutting out Neil. And that's making Neil angrier and angrier.

I sit in the cafeteria and listen to the swirl of conversation around me. People are complaining about racist attitudes, elitist organizations, and sexist policies. But it's more than just the school. I sense that the whole town is holding its breath, waiting.

> *Saturday noon*
>
> *I can't believe what happened last night. Andy was attacked! It happened in the back parking lot of the mall, the one that's usually almost empty. . . .*

Penny and Neil were coming out of the mall when they noticed a movement under a lamppost at the far end of the parking lot. A group of boys was rocking a car and shouting. My friends couldn't make out their words or faces, but it was clear that they were set on violence.

"Go back inside!" Neil said to Penny, pushing her toward the door. "Call the cops. It looks like those guys are going to pound someone pretty bad."

Penny hurried to the phone while Neil ran toward the shouting.

Neil has been too upset to say anything about the events of last night, but it seems pretty clear what happened. . . .

As Neil watched from a distance, the gang of boys dragged someone from the car and closed in like a pack of wolves. Then Neil reached that corner of the parking lot and recognized Andy's father's car. Somebody noticed Neil approaching, and the mob scattered. He would have gone after them—except that Andy was curled up on the ground, unconscious.

Monday afternoon
Everyone at school is talking about what a hero Neil was this weekend. It must have taken a lot of courage to walk right up to a mob like that. But I have a funny feeling about it. I can't believe that a whole gang would flee from a single teenager. When I asked, Neil didn't come right out and say that he didn't get close enough to recognize any of Andy's attackers. But that's what everyone has assumed, from what he did say. And Andy barely remem-

bers anything about the attack.

Personally, I'm sure it was Charlie and his thug friends. What I don't understand is why Neil would protect them.

Saturday

I'm lying next to the pool, watching Jessica swim. For the first time in weeks, I'm relaxed and at peace.

Not all the news is good. It turned out that Neil really did know who beat up Andy. It was Charlie and his friends—and somebody else I never suspected. Nobody did. Neil finally broke down and told Andy and Penny the truth at lunchtime one day this week. Penny later gave me the whole terrible story. . . .

"We have to talk," Neil said, his voice no louder than a whisper. "About Friday night . . ."

"What?" Andy asked.

Neil swallowed hard. "I was . . . I was there."

"I know you were there," Andy said. "You bailed me out. I'll never forget it."

"No!" Neil said painfully. "I was *there*."

Penny looked from one boy to the other, confused.

"I know," Andy repeated, his face growing puzzled.

310

Neil squeezed his eyes shut. "No," he said from between his clenched teeth. "I was there with the other guys. *I hit you too.*" He paused. "Don't you get it? I hit you too! I was so mad at you for thinking I was like Charlie that I *was* like him. I hit you!"

It took a lot of courage for Neil to tell Andy the truth. Now I'm not sure if Andy will be able to forgive him. Penny's having a lot of trouble with it too. She's trying to understand, but she isn't sure if they can salvage their relationship.

Sweet Valley High may have lost its innocence, but we've gained some wisdom. A few positive actions have come out of the whole mess. Jessica started a petition to show support for Andy, and a ton of people signed it. Some of us are working with the guidance counselor, Mrs. Green, to put together a race-relations course. I think we'll all be better people from now on. And isn't that what growing up and getting an education is all about?

Even Jessica, president of the elitist PBA sorority, seems to have learned a lesson from all of this. . . .

My sister lounged by the pool with me on Saturday morning. She was unusually quiet for

Jessica—meaning that she was pausing for breath between subjects.

"I've been thinking about what you and Penny said about Pi Beta Alpha being elitist," Jessica said. "Of course, my first thought was, 'Of course it's elitist! It's meant to be. Who would want to join a sorority that will let in just anyone?'"

I raised my eyebrows. "Does this mean you've reconsidered your position?"

"Well, not completely," Jessica said, dipping her foot in the clear, clean water. "We still have standards to uphold, after all. But maybe we should be a little more open-minded in our approach to recruiting."

This sounded too good to be true. I waited for the other shoe to drop.

"Of course, PBA will always be for the prettiest, most popular girls at school. But I'm thinking of expanding the definitions of pretty and popular— I'm thinking of inviting that new girl, Claire Middleton, to pledge. I mean, if she can cut it."

PBA was famous for setting up challenges that unsuspecting pledges had to complete before being considered worthy.

"Oh, really?" I said, surprised but pleased. "You know, Claire seems like a sweet girl, but she's so shy that I've had trouble drawing her out. Maybe being invited to join your sorority will make her feel like she belongs."

Jessica rolled her eyes. "I hate the way you always talk about PBA as *my* sorority. I know you never come to meetings, but technically you're a member too, Liz."

I shrugged. "Only because you wanted me to join," I said. "But tell me—how does inviting Claire to join qualify as expanding PBA's horizons? She seems nice—I guess for PBA, that's a strike against her. But what else? She's good-looking; she's got that gorgeous long dark hair. I suppose she's too new to be popular, but—"

"You know, Liz, it would be perfectly obvious to any *normal* person. Amy or Lila would have understood in an instant why Claire is . . . different."

"If Amy and Lila count as normal," I said with a laugh, "then I'm glad to be an aberration."

She frowned. "Come on, Liz. You've seen the way Claire dresses. Big, loose sweatshirts and baggy jeans—like a tomboy. I mean, it's positively gross! But with the influence of some of the best-dressed girls in school, I think she could be quite attractive."

"I'm sure she'll be thrilled about your concern," I said. But my sensitive twin didn't pick up on the sarcasm.

Friday evening
More excitement is on the way for
Sweet Valley High. And this time it's a lot

313

*more positive! Coach Schultz made a big
announcement at the pep rally today. . . .*

Everyone was buzzing with the latest rumor as
we crowded into the gym and found seats on the
bleachers.

"Have you heard the news?" Enid asked as
Todd and I shoved our way to her row.

"What news?" I asked. The gym was stuffy
from holding so many people, so I pulled off my
cardigan before I sat down. The football team
was lining up on one side, preparing to make a
grand entrance. Across from the players, Jessica
and the other cheerleaders were building a
human pyramid.

"Scott Trost," Enid said. "He flunked another
history test this week. Coach Schultz has been talking to Chrome Dome all day, but it doesn't look
like there's any way around it. Scott's on probation
for the rest of the term—meaning the rest of the
football season!"

Todd and Enid and I all stared at each other.
The rumors were true. Scott, who had been playing quarterback ever since Ken's accident, was off
the team for good.

We searched the crowd for Ken and saw him
sitting in the front row of the bleachers, looking
cheerful and relaxed as he talked with Terri

Adams. He seemed healthy and strong—as if he'd never been in the accident that had blinded him for all those terrible weeks.

"I wonder if Ken's heard the news about Scott yet," Enid said. "Now that he can see again, do you think . . ." Her voice trailed off, but I knew exactly what she was thinking.

"Ken wouldn't be ready for that kind of competition right now," I argued. "Besides, his vision still isn't back one hundred percent. Terri told me it could be months before it is."

Todd thought I was wrong—that Ken was more than ready to step in and lead our team back to victory. I didn't argue, because I didn't want to sound defeatist. But something told me that Ken wasn't physically ready to play football again, no matter how much he might want to.

It was the usual Sweet Valley High pep rally— full of people wearing red and white, all applauding and yelling "Go, Gladiators!" until they were hoarse. But the last announcement Coach Schultz made was anything but usual.

"We're going to go into tomorrow's game against the Palisades Pumas with our current lineup. But after tomorrow, due to some reorganization—"

The crowd erupted in a buzz of gossip about Scott's probation, and the coach had to raise his voice to be heard. "We will be holding tryouts on the playing field Monday after school for the position of quarterback!"

I think Todd is right. I think Ken will try out for quarterback, ready or not. But I think somebody else will try out too— Claire Middleton! No, she didn't actually tell me. But I interviewed her for the school paper today, and I couldn't miss the way her pale green eyes lit up when she talked about football. I bet she's the mystery girl who answered my survey by saying that there was no reason girls couldn't play football. And I hope that everyone at school remembers to be open-minded.

Saturday morning
Tryouts for quarterback have been going on all week. Ken and Claire are ahead of the competition. Ken's a stronger passer, but Claire runs like the wind, and she's small and agile enough to dodge other players like nobody else can do. Dave Pollock is still in the running as well, but the other two are clearly better players. Coach Schultz will have to pick two quarterbacks—first-string and second-string. Today there's an intrateam scrim-

mage. Monday morning the coach will an-
nounce his decision.

I'm worried about Ken. Terri thinks
that playing all week has been too much for
him. She suspects he's having blackouts
again—when his eyes fail him for just a
second or two. But he denies it. He says
he's fine.

At least he's being supportive of Claire.
The rest of the team—and much of the
school—is giving her a hard time. But Ken
respects her as a player. And he's im-
pressed with her determination and love
of the sport.

As for Claire, she was still a total mys-
tery to me until a few minutes ago. Steven's
home from school for the weekend, and he
just told me some very interesting news. . . .

"You know," Steven said as the two of us sat at the
kitchen table, eating bagels, "this may be a complete
coincidence, but there was a guy in my freshman
composition class named Middleton. He was a real
football hero too. I wonder . . . nah, there's no way.
They couldn't be related. Too much of a coincidence
for there to be that much football in one family."

"Maybe not," I said. "Do you know where he's
from?"

Steven shook his head. "It's a pretty horrible story, Liz. He was quarterback of our junior varsity team. They said he was destined for great things—supposedly he had offers from pro teams already, and he was only eighteen. Then he started having these terrible headaches. He was diagnosed with a brain tumor, and within a couple of months he was dead."

So that's it, Diary. I'm only speculating, but it all makes sense. Claire's older brother was her role model. He taught her to love football. And he was the one behind her intense desire to make the team. I hope she does, Diary. I really hope she does.

Saturday,
getting toward midnight
My sister can be such an insensitive, idiotic jerk sometimes! I can't believe what she and the other cheerleaders did to Claire at the scrimmage today. It turns out that Claire criticized cheerleading last week for being sexist and silly (both valid points, if you ask me). Jessica and her friends were determined to get their revenge. . . .

Claire was quarterbacking for the A team. On her first possession, she faked back and threw a beautiful spiral to Danny Porter, thirty yards up the field.

"Yeah, Claire!" I heard Dana holler in her distinctive alto. "Show the guys how to play ball!"

A few people in the crowd were echoing Dana's sentiments, but most were booing and catcalling. Few fans wanted to see Ken outplayed by a girl.

The coach called a time-out, and Claire pulled off her helmet. That's when the cheerleaders made their move. At Jessica's signal, they jumped to their feet, pom-poms twirling, and my sister led them in a new cheer. Most of it was pretty innocuous—even supportive. But the last line was completely uncalled-for: *"We know about Ted!"*

The effect on Claire was astonishing. Her face turned white, and two spots of color rose in her cheeks. Trembling, she grabbed her helmet and walked off the field.

"You don't have to have a fit about it," Jessica said to me when Steven and I confronted her as the game resumed with Dave Pollock taking Claire's position. "We were only trying to spice things up a little," Jessica said. "We didn't mean any harm."

"How can you say that?" I sputtered. "I mean, what was that last line supposed to mean? Don't you know who Ted is? Were you deliberately trying to taunt Claire about her brother?"

As it turned out, Jessica and the other cheer-leaders had no idea who Ted was. They'd heard about a guy's picture, signed "Ted," in Claire's locker, and they'd assumed it was a boyfriend.

When Steven filled them in on the truth about Ted, Jessica's hands flew to her face and she turned pale. "You mean . . . are you trying to tell us that we just did a cheer teasing Claire about her older brother? Her *dead* older brother?"

> *Saturday night,*
> *a week later*
> *One small touchdown for Claire Middleton, one giant leap for the women's movement! Tonight was the big football game against Big Mesa. After Claire ran out of the scrimmage last week, the coach said she didn't have what it takes. He named Ken as starting quarterback. But after he heard the full story about what happened, he told Claire to suit up and play second string. . . .*

The score was tied at halftime. Ken had been playing well, but as the game headed into the third quarter, he looked tired. He faltered on a pass, and Big Mesa intercepted it and ran the ball in for a touchdown. The rest of the third quarter, the

Gladiators couldn't do a thing. By the start of the fourth quarter, the score was 14–7, and Sweet Valley was behind.

Then disaster struck. Ken backed up to throw the ball. He paused for a split second, stumbled, and shook his head as if to clear it. He lofted the ball, but no Sweet Valley receivers were anywhere near it. Big Mesa intercepted it again.

On the sidelines, Ken told the coach he was having trouble with his eyes and recommended that he be pulled from the game.

"Middleton!" Coach Schultz barked. "You're in."

On her very first play, Claire ran even faster than she had in tryouts—faster than a human being should be able to run. And she made a touchdown! The crowd went crazy. And it was Jessica who was leading the pro-Claire cheers.

Claire was on fire. She called the plays, threw incredible passes, and ran with a speed and agility that confounded Big Mesa's defense. With less than a minute left to play, the score was tied, 14–14. And Claire came through, throwing a perfect pass for a final touchdown. We made the extra point just as the final buzzer sounded, and Sweet Valley High won the game—thanks to its new female quarterback!

Claire Middleton changed a lot of people's minds tonight about what a girl can and

*cannot do. I think she's exactly what our
school needed after that whole racist episode.
She's living proof of the power of busting
through the stereotypes that hold people back
and drag us all down. It's a lesson this school
is not likely to forget any time soon.*

> *Friday night, very late*
*Whoever said that love makes the world
go round was right! Todd and I had an incredible night together. In the last few weeks
we've been spending a lot of time talking
things through. We're determined to keep
our relationship strong and communication
lines open. And it seems to be working. I love
Todd so much, Diary, that it overwhelms me
at times. Tonight was one of those times. . . .*

Miller's Point was as romantic as always. There
were a few other cars around. In fact, I recognized
Aaron's—I hope he and Dana were having as great
a time as Todd and I were!

We parked near the trees, in our special, private spot. And the stars seemed to have been
hung there just for us. That's how magical the
night was. We held each other and snuggled and
kissed for a long, long time—until Todd was
breathless and my heart was pounding. Of

course, we wanted to stay there forever together. But we both had just enough self-possession left to realize it was time to go somewhere public, before we did something we might regret.

We stared at each other for a full minute, and I couldn't believe how attractive he looked in the moonlight, with his dark eyes so intense. He squeezed my hand and pulled me very close to him. I remained there for the entire fifteen-minute drive to the Dairi Burger.

In the parking lot, we turned to each other again. This time we burst out laughing. After all, it was pretty funny—the only way to keep our hands off each other was to stuff our mouths with food, in a bright room surrounded by dozens of our friends. Then we jumped out of the car and walked inside.

The best part of the night wasn't the kisses Todd and I shared at Miller's Point. Well, OK, maybe that was the best part. But a close second was what happened afterward, at the Dairi Burger.

Todd and I were greeted by yells from all parts of the room. We spotted Ken, Terri, Winston, and Maria in a booth and squeezed in beside them. It wasn't until after we were seated that I noticed that Todd and I were sitting in the same booth, and on the same sides, as we had been on the night when Jeffrey asked me to meet him at Miller's Point. I looked over to the corner booth where Jeffrey had been sitting, and I did a double take. Jeffrey was there again, in the exact same spot. But this time he was with a date!

From the back, I didn't recognize the girl. She was small and graceful, with beautiful red hair. And I hate to admit it (I do have my womanly pride, you know), but as Jeffrey gazed across the table at her, he was glowing in a way he never had done when he was with me.

The truth, Diary, is that Jeffrey and I meant everything to each other at a certain time in our lives. And it was difficult for both of us to admit that the time had passed. Now that we've both moved beyond it, we're both better than ever. At the restaurant tonight, Jeffrey looked up from his booth, caught my eye, and winked at me!

Finally, you'll forgive the cliché (I hope) if I say that tomorrow is the first day of the rest of my life. Let's just hope it's a sunny one. . . .

Epilogue

By the time I closed my diary, the sky outside my window was shot through with a peach-and-rose sunset. I walked to the window—the same window that Todd and Jeffrey had climbed through on that long-ago night. I gazed at the deepening sky—and at my own tearstained reflection, ghostlike in the glass.

"I've been such a hypocrite," I whispered. I'd judged Todd for kissing Michelle in his backyard. But how many times had I kissed Jeffrey behind Todd's back? I had no right to criticize him. And it was time for me to make it up to him.

I grabbed the telephone and punched in Todd's number.

"Oh, hello, Elizabeth," said Mrs. Wilkins. "I'm afraid Todd's not here. He left for the airport with Michelle more than two hours ago."

"The airport?" I asked, puzzled.

"She decided to go back to Vermont early," Todd's mother told me. "She said she had to face her family problems rather than run from them. But I don't know where Todd's gone off to. He should have been home more than an hour ago."

"Thanks, Mrs. Wilkins," I said. "If I see him, I'll tell him you're wondering."

Suddenly I knew exactly where Todd was.

Sure enough, when I pulled the Fiat into the parking area near "our" spot at Secca Lake, Todd's BMW was already there. A sense of déjà vu washed over me. This was exactly what had happened the night of Todd's long-ago coming-home party, but in reverse. That night I had been sitting on the wide, flat rock, staring out at the lake, and Todd had come to find me. This time it was Todd on the rock. I stopped for a moment, gazing at his huddled form against a breathtaking background of lavender and orange. The sun was sinking into the lake.

"Todd!"

He turned, and an ache shot through my heart. Tears were falling, unchecked, down Todd's face.

"Oh, Todd," I said, beginning to cry as well. "I'm so sorry!" I ran the last few yards, until I was holding him in my arms, both of us trembling with emotion. "I love you," I whispered, stroking his hair.

"I love you more than anything—and I'll never doubt your word again."

"I thought I had lost you," he whispered. "I didn't know what to do."

I smiled through my tears. "You can't get rid of me that easily, Wilkins. We have too much history."

Then he put his arm around me, and I leaned against his shoulder. Together we watched the sun slip into the lake, until the sky was a velvety black and the first glittering stars appeared.

Bantam Books in the Sweet Valley High series
Ask your bookseller for the books you have missed

#1	DOUBLE LOVE	#46	DECISIONS
#2	SECRETS	#47	TROUBLEMAKER
#3	PLAYING WITH FIRE	#48	SLAM BOOK FEVER
#4	POWER PLAY	#49	PLAYING FOR KEEPS
#5	ALL NIGHT LONG	#50	OUT OF REACH
#6	DANGEROUS LOVE	#51	AGAINST THE ODDS
#7	DEAR SISTER	#52	WHITE LIES
#8	HEARTBREAKER	#53	SECOND CHANCE
#9	RACING HEARTS	#54	TWO-BOY WEEKEND
#10	WRONG KIND OF GIRL	#55	PERFECT SHOT
#11	TOO GOOD TO BE TRUE	#56	LOST AT SEA
#12	WHEN LOVE DIES	#57	TEACHER CRUSH
#13	KIDNAPPED!	#58	BROKENHEARTED
#14	DECEPTIONS	#59	IN LOVE AGAIN
#15	PROMISES	#60	THAT FATAL NIGHT
#16	RAGS TO RICHES	#61	BOY TROUBLE
#17	LOVE LETTERS	#62	WHO'S WHO?
#18	HEAD OVER HEELS	#63	THE NEW ELIZABETH
#19	SHOWDOWN	#64	THE GHOST OF TRICIA
#20	CRASH LANDING!		MARTIN
#21	RUNAWAY	#65	TROUBLE AT HOME
#22	TOO MUCH IN LOVE	#66	WHO'S TO BLAME?
#23	SAY GOODBYE	#67	THE PARENT PLOT
#24	MEMORIES	#68	THE LOVE BET
#25	NOWHERE TO RUN	#69	FRIEND AGAINST FRIEND
#26	HOSTAGE	#70	MS. QUARTERBACK
#27	LOVESTRUCK	#71	STARRING JESSICA!
#28	ALONE IN THE CROWD	#72	ROCK STAR'S GIRL
#29	BITTER RIVALS	#73	REGINA'S LEGACY
#30	JEALOUS LIES	#74	THE PERFECT GIRL
#31	TAKING SIDES	#75	AMY'S TRUE LOVE
#32	THE NEW JESSICA	#76	MISS TEEN SWEET VALLEY
#33	STARTING OVER	#77	CHEATING TO WIN
#34	FORBIDDEN LOVE	#78	THE DATING GAME
#35	OUT OF CONTROL	#79	THE LONG-LOST BROTHER
#36	LAST CHANCE	#80	THE GIRL THEY BOTH LOVED
#37	RUMORS	#81	ROSA'S LIE
#38	LEAVING HOME	#82	KIDNAPPED BY THE CULT!
#39	SECRET ADMIRER	#83	STEVEN'S BRIDE
#40	ON THE EDGE	#84	THE STOLEN DIARY
#41	OUTCAST	#85	SOAP STAR
#42	CAUGHT IN THE MIDDLE	#86	JESSICA AGAINST BRUCE
#43	HARD CHOICES	#87	MY BEST FRIEND'S
#44	PRETENSES		BOYFRIEND
#45	FAMILY SECRETS	#88	LOVE LETTERS FOR SALE

#89   ELIZABETH BETRAYED
#90   DON'T GO HOME WITH JOHN
#91   IN LOVE WITH A PRINCE
#92   SHE'S NOT WHAT SHE SEEMS
#93   STEPSISTERS
#94   ARE WE IN LOVE?
#95   THE MORNING AFTER
#96   THE ARREST
#97   THE VERDICT
#98   THE WEDDING
#99   BEWARE THE BABY-SITTER
#100 THE EVIL TWIN (MAGNA)
#101 THE BOYFRIEND WAR
#102 ALMOST MARRIED
#103 OPERATION LOVE MATCH
#104 LOVE AND DEATH IN
         LONDON
#105 A DATE WITH A WEREWOLF
#106 BEWARE THE WOLFMAN
         (SUPER THRILLER)
#107 JESSICA'S SECRET LOVE
#108 LEFT AT THE ALTAR
#109 DOUBLE-CROSSED

#110 DEATH THREAT
#111 A DEADLY CHRISTMAS
         (SUPER THRILLER)
#112 JESSICA QUITS THE SQUAD
#113 THE POM-POM WARS
#114 "V" FOR VICTORY
#115 THE TREASURE OF DEATH
         VALLEY
#116 NIGHTMARE IN DEATH
         VALLEY
#117 JESSICA THE GENIUS
#118 COLLEGE WEEKEND
#119 JESSICA'S OLDER GUY
#120 IN LOVE WITH THE ENEMY
#121 THE HIGH SCHOOL WAR
#122 A KISS BEFORE DYING
#123 ELIZABETH'S RIVAL
#124 MEET ME AT MIDNIGHT
#125 CAMP KILLER

SUPER EDITIONS:
   PERFECT SUMMER
   SPECIAL CHRISTMAS
   SPRING BREAK
   MALIBU SUMMER
   WINTER CARNIVAL
   SPRING FEVER
   FALLING FOR LUCAS

SUPER THRILLERS:
   DOUBLE JEOPARDY
   ON THE RUN
   NO PLACE TO HIDE
   DEADLY SUMMER
   MURDER ON THE LINE
   BEWARE THE WOLFMAN
   A DEADLY CHRISTMAS
   MURDER IN PARADISE
   A STRANGER IN THE HOUSE
   A KILLER ON BOARD

SUPER STARS:
   LILA'S STORY
   BRUCE'S STORY
   ENID'S STORY
   OLIVIA'S STORY
   TODD'S STORY

MAGNA EDITIONS:
   THE WAKEFIELDS OF
      SWEET VALLEY
   THE WAKEFIELD LEGACY:
      THE UNTOLD STORY
   A NIGHT TO REMEMBER
   THE EVIL TWIN
   ELIZABETH'S SECRET DIARY
   JESSICA'S SECRET DIARY
   RETURN OF THE EVIL TWIN
   ELIZABETH'S SECRET DIARY
      VOLUME II
   JESSICA'S SECRET DIARY
      VOLUME II

SIGN UP FOR THE SWEET VALLEY HIGH® FAN CLUB!

Hey, girls! Get all the gossip on Sweet Valley High's® most popular teenagers when you join our fantastic Fan Club! As a member, you'll get all of this really cool stuff:

- Membership Card with your own personal Fan Club ID number
- A Sweet Valley High® Secret Treasure Box
- Sweet Valley High® Stationery
- Official Fan Club Pencil (for secret note writing!)
- Three Bookmarks
- A "Members Only" Door Hanger
- Two Skeins of J. & P. Coats® Embroidery Floss with flower barrette instruction leaflet
- Two editions of *The Oracle* newsletter
- Plus exclusive Sweet Valley High® product offers, special savings, contests, and much more!

Be the first to find out what Jessica & Elizabeth Wakefield are up to by joining the Sweet Valley High® Fan Club for the one-year membership fee of only $6.25 each for U.S. residents, $8.25 for Canadian residents (U.S. currency). Includes shipping & handling.

Send a check or money order (do not send cash) made payable to "Sweet Valley High® Fan Club" along with this form to:

SWEET VALLEY HIGH® FAN CLUB, BOX 3919-B, SCHAUMBURG, IL 60168-3919

NAME_____

(Please print clearly)

ADDRESS_____

CITY_____ STATE _____ ZIP_____

(Required)

AGE_____ BIRTHDAY_____ /_____ /_____

Offer good while supplies last. Allow 6-8 weeks after check clearance for delivery. Addresses without ZIP codes cannot be honored. Offer good in USA & Canada only. Void where prohibited by law.

LCI-1383-193